More Critical Praise for Don Lee

for *Yellow*

"[F]ew writers have mined the [genre of ethnic literature] as shrewdly or transcended its limits quite so stunningly as Don Lee . . . Elegant and engrossing . . . [A] rich and unusually complete portrait of contemporary Asian America." —*Los Angeles Times*

"Accomplished . . . Lee alternates between humor and pathos in delineating his characters' endeavors to find people who will give their lives meaning." —*Washington Post*

"Completely realized . . . poised . . . This is a collection for readers often left unsatisfied by the brevity of short stories . . . [F]inely crafted." —*Boston Sunday Globe*

"[A] frontal assault on matters of identity . . . [Lee] proves himself a worthy practitioner of realistic fiction in the vein of writers like Richard Yates and Andre Dubus . . . It's a tricky proposition to write about ethnicity and not crowd readers with right thinking. But Lee does it, and in the process proves that wondering about whether you're a real American is as American as a big bowl of kimchi." —*New York Times Book Review*

"Lee's close examination of the Asian American experience is at once amused, critical, and satirical. Race is one of the collection's motifs, but Lee never beats the reader over the head with it, and not once does he fall into the holier-than-thou trap."

—*Denver Post*

"[A] gem of atmospheric glimpses into the Asian American experience at the turn of the twenty-first century . . . Lee's stories interconnect and overlap, evoking a universe of their own . . . The Asian American experience, as these stories reveal, has grown ever more rich and complicated, making the notion of a collective community difficult to imagine, let alone render . . . Don Lee has captured this truth beautifully, wisely, and with winning economy."

—*Cleveland Plain Dealer*

"Heartfelt but witty, these short stories, written in an effortless style and with deft restraint, depict the fears, contradictions, and joys of Asian American lives." —*Boston Magazine*

"The common setting [of fictional Rosarita Bay] gives the accumulated stories a novelistic breadth with the electric snap of short stories . . . [P]owerful, well-crafted, and provocative."
—*Seattle Post-Intelligencer*

"[Lee] is a thoughtful craftsman, a distiller of image and incident, a tone poet . . . His carefully modulated stories present engaging characters who are believable and complicated, situations that are unusual without being quirky." —*LA Weekly*

for *Country of Origin*

"The central preoccupations of Don Lee's first novel feel like urgent issues for our times. The characters wrestle with slippery questions of race and identity, and the story unfolds in that liminal space where America interacts with another culture."
—*New York Times Book Review*

"[An] engrossing first novel . . . about origins and destinations that succeeds rather effectively in dramatizing all sorts of questions about where we have come from and where we are going . . . A nicely textured travelogue of Tokyo's underlife, all a swirl of action, a whirl of love and sex and race and politics, local and international."
—*Chicago Tribune*

"[An] elegant and haunting debut . . . [*Country of Origin*] hinges on a taut plot and then widens in concentric circles to become a novel of ideas." —*Entertainment Weekly*

"In this innovative first novel set on the eve of Japan's economic boom, Lee, a Korean American who grew up in Tokyo and Seoul, tells a poignant story of prejudice, betrayal, and the search for identity."
—*Newsweek International*

"A lesser writer might lose control of such a story, turning it into pulp or, worse, some kind of half-baked noir. But Lee is a polished and extremely diligent writer, his focus first and foremost on his characters . . . Lee demonstrates an intimate knowledge of how cultural labels can be both slipshod and stubborn."

—Seattle Times

for *Wrack and Ruin*

"Masterly . . . Lee has outdone himself here. His prose moves and sparkles. He gives his characters a depth and thoroughness not commonly achieved by practitioners of the comic novel, a label that seems almost a disservice to a book as thoughtful as this one."

—Washington Post

"Playful and lighthearted, *Wrack and Ruin* has an accidental elegance that is unself-conscious and refreshing."

—New York Times Book Review

"[A] highly appealing novel that swerves ever so gracefully from rollicking humor to poignant moments of reflection."

—Booklist

"The trick to reading Don Lee's wonderfully silly second novel is to take nothing seriously, even when you should . . . This novel thrives on unlikely unions, unseemly humor, and happy endings while maintaining a constant examination of family and identity."

—Publishers Weekly

"Entertaining . . . a darn good story."   —*San Francisco Chronicle*

for *The Collective*

"A fine prose stylist meditates on idealism and pragmatism in his novel of ambitious, young Asian American artists . . . Here, he credibly addresses the political and social concerns of a specific demographic, while also rendering a work that will feel relatable to nearly everyone who reads it."

—Time Out New York

"Lively and suspenseful, this novel masterfully probes the high-stakes contest between integrity and belonging. Lee's sympathy for his deeply human characters will captivate any reader."

—MSP Star Tribune

"[A] must-read for everyone interested in the discussion of racial identity and its place in our supposedly postracial world."

—BookBrowse

"A hilarious and winning story . . . this book's plangent, and also celebratory undercurrent, flows on, whispering to the reader that the other collective it speaks of—friendship in youth—is equally unstable, and prone to collapse. The best parts of this keenly felt novel will remind you why."

—Boston Globe

"Lee comes with an agenda—an important one—about ethnicity and art, but he also delivers a heartbreaking, sexy, and frequently funny story about fractured friendships." —Entertainment Weekly

for *Lonesome Lies Before Us*

"Like a great album—Parsons's *Grievous Angel,* let's say—*Lonesome Lies Before Us* is both a collection of brilliantly realized moments and a work that transcends the sum of its parts. There are no minor observations in this novel, no scenes that don't matter. In the end, the depth of feeling attained by the exceptionally sensitive Lee lingers, inspiring more spins through his songlike prose. A novel more full of life, musical and other, is hard to imagine."

—Chicago Tribune

"If *Lonesome Lies Before Us* isn't the best American novel of the year, it's one of the most *American* American novels. It's intensely concerned with the civic institutions that shape everyday lives, and with who's affected when they disappear. That's too much weight for the average country song to bear, but Lee's novel carries it just fine." —Washington Post

"Mr. Lee plucks familiar chords with a sure hand, glancing on themes of grief, jealousy, and second chances . . . But what really stamps this book on the heart is Yadin's vulnerable spiritual journey from loneliness toward something like grace."

—Wall Street Journal

THE
PARTITION

Stories

DON LEE

BROOKLYN, NEW YORK

Published by Akashic Books
©2022 Don Lee

ISBN: 978-1-63614-031-5
Library of Congress Control Number: 2021945694
First printing

The following stories, in different form, first appeared in the following magazines: "Late in the Day" in the *Southern Review*, "The Partition" in *VQR*, "Confidants" in the *Georgia Review*, "Years Later" and "UFOs" in the *Kenyon Review*, "The Sanno" in the *Sewanee Review*, and "Reenactments" in *One Story*.

Akashic Books
Brooklyn, New York
Instagram: AkashicBooks
Twitter: AkashicBooks
Facebook: AkashicBooks
E-mail: info@akashicbooks.com
Website: www.akashicbooks.com

Also by Don Lee

For Jane, Margot, and Rose

CONTENTS

LATE IN THE DAY

• • • • • • • • • •

HE MISTOOK HER FOR COURTNEY AT FIRST—same drape of hair, broad mouth, body that was at once diminutive and excessive. She entered the lobby as people milled about for the reception, and he was surprised and too grateful she had decided to make the trip from LA after all. But the woman, upon closer inspection, didn't really resemble Courtney at all, only at certain angles. Her name was Sonia Chen, a friend of one of the film festival organizers, an editor or something or other at a local poetry foundation or journal—Peter didn't quite catch the particulars when they were introduced.

"First time in Chicago?" she asked. "When'd you get in?"

He had left LAX at six in the morning and arrived at noon, Central Time, dead time, wandering around the city, staring up at the Gothic skyscrapers in a jet-lagged miasma, unable to nap when he was finally allowed to check into his hotel room. He was still a bit punchy, slow on the repartee.

"What's up with the baseball cap?" she said, teasing. He had on black jeans, boots, a black tee and suit jacket, topped by a faded blue cap with a well-worn bill. She scrutinized the logo—an electricians' local. "Is that a Hollywood director thing, or a political thing, or a bald thing?"

"A little of all three," he said.

"People should embrace their shortcomings," she told Peter.

A gray-haired gentleman approached and shook his hand. "I'm really looking forward to the film," he said, and turned to Sonia. "And of course seeing you in it. It's great you're here. I heard you were a no-show."

Sonia leaned toward Peter as the man left them. "What the fuck," she said.

"He thinks you're Courtney Lu, the female lead." So it wasn't just him, wasn't merely a matter of wishful thinking and obsession.

"Yeah?" She looked at Courtney in the poster of *Late in the Day* on the wall. "I don't see it. You?"

"No."

"Although she's got tits. They real?"

"I believe they are."

"As in you know, or you surmise?"

"They look pretty natural. We shot a few nude scenes."

"But you haven't had the opportunity for a close, hands-on examination of the mammaries in question?"

"No."

"I thought directors always had affairs with their actresses."

"Some do. I didn't."

They separated to go into the screening, and Peter sat in the back row, as was his custom. He had seen *Late in the Day* so many times now, he no longer watched it, no longer cringed at what they could have done better, simply gauged the audience's reactions, sometimes daydreaming or, as had happened a few times, nodding off.

Six months ago, *Late in the Day* had premiered at the 2010 Honolulu Asian American Film Festival, and the response had been overwhelmingly positive in the beginning—hailed a breakthrough for APA cinema, a bravura anti-ethnic ethnic film, all of the cast members and the majority of the crew Asian Americans, yet with nothing self-consciously Asian about it. No accents, no generational conflicts, no culture clashes, no references to immigration or identity or assimilation, no geishas or comfort women or green-grocers, no one using chopsticks even. It was simply a contemporary love triangle in Silver Lake, and although the characters were Asian American, they did not once talk about being Asian American, which was extraordinarily refreshing, everyone said. In the beginning. But then there were some whispered qualifications, followed by grumbled qualms, followed by outright condemnations. The point of contention was that one of the actors, Darren Lin, wasn't full-blooded Asian. He was a hapa haole, half white and half Asian, and he happened to get all the punani in the film, while the Asian dude only got to yearn after the girl and was, as always, left out in the sallow cold.

The screening ended, and there was applause—respect-ful, verging on animated, but not thunderous, certainly no standing-O. Then the part Peter hated the most, the Q&A. The festival host apologized for Courtney Lu's absence, explaining she'd had a scheduling conflict, and started Peter off with a softball, asking how he financed the film. He launched into the familiar story about borrowing money from his family and friends and bankrolling the rest with

credit cards, shooting the whole thing in eight days with
a budget of forty thousand dollars. It sounded like a success story, but it wasn't. After Honolulu, he had thought
he might get invites to bigger festivals—Toronto, Venice,
Sundance—and land a distribution deal, at the very least
for cable, but hopefully for DVD and video-on-demand
and maybe even theatrical as well. Yet none of that was
forthcoming. The anti-ethnic ethnic angle didn't go over
very well with the money people—they wanted martial
arts, human trafficking, gangs; they wanted geishas and
comfort women. And now Peter was relegated to ped-
dling the film on this circuit of small Asian American film
festivals, from San Francisco, San Diego, and Vancouver to
Boston, New York, and Chicago, trying to generate press
and reviews and word of mouth. His last realistic chance
for distribution was at South by Southwest in Austin next
week.

The host opened up the floor for questions, and there
were a few from film students about what equipment he
had used and how he had transferred the digital to thirty-
five mil. Then a man—the same gray-haired guy who'd
confused Sonia for Courtney in the lobby—stood and said,
"I understand there's been some controversy attached to
this movie."

Peter glanced about. "Controversy?" he said. "Really?"
He got a laugh.

"How do you feel about it?"

Like slitting my wrists, Peter thought. Like committing
mass murder. Like quitting the film business. "I think every
filmmaker's responsibility is to provoke emotion," he said.
"So the fact that this film has produced strong emotions

can only be regarded as a positive thing." A tactful, san-
guine, limp-dick answer if ever there was one.

He expected the man to needle him further, launch
into some sort of a diatribe. Peter had gotten grilled, evis-
cerated, on an excruciatingly personal level, at other festivals, leading to awkward confrontations and flop sweats—
thus the baseball cap. But the man didn't push tonight,
and neither did any of the other questioners. A largesse of
Midwestern nice?

At the postscreening reception back in the lobby, he
waited for burblings of what was not broached, but no one
went beyond polite compliments and congratulations with
him, and it wound down quickly enough, time finally for
dinner.

"Korean barbecue all right?" Tim, the festival host,
asked. "Now, if I can figure out how we'll all get there."

"I can give him a ride," Sonia said.

"You don't mind?" Peter asked.

Her car—a twenty-year-old Land Cruiser—was filled
with books, clothes, and a gaggle of exercise equipment:
running shoes, bike shoes, helmet, gloves, a pump, swim
goggles, sunglasses, a bicycle under a gray tarp in the cargo
area. "Sorry," she said, tossing things from the passenger
seat to the back. "I try to do my training during my lunch
hour."

It didn't smell very good inside the car. "Training for
what?"

"Oh, triathlons."

"Like, the Ironman?"

"No, no, nothing that hardcore. Sprint distance—
half-mile swims, fifteen to twenty on the bike, 10K runs.

I'm weakest in the swim. The hardest part is finding a decent pool nearby. Sometimes I sneak into hotels if I'm working downtown."

"How'd you get into it—triathlons?"

"A while back I found out I had lupus. The doctors were giving me steroids and antimalarials, and I felt really awful and weak all the time. The conventional advice then was to rest and not exert yourself, but I've always been a runner, and I decided to push myself and keep running, and the more mileage I put in, the better I felt. It sort of grew from there. Now I do a circuit of five, six races a year around the country."

He didn't know much about lupus. He was fairly certain, however, that it was a chronic condition, and that there was no cure.

"You don't look sick at all," he told her.

"I've been in remission for years."

"You mind if I ask, what's the long-term prognosis for lupus?"

"You mean is it fatal?"

He hadn't intended to be indelicate. "Well, yes."

"These days, rarely," Sonia said. "A lot of people—the vast majority—have completely normal life spans. A lot's changed since I was first diagnosed."

Her equanimity aside, the disclosure made Peter view Sonia differently, though he couldn't articulate exactly how.

They drove away from the city, the buildings becoming squatter, less gentrified. "Where we going?" he asked.

"Albany Park."

"Koreatown, I assume?"

She nodded.

"I get taken to a lot of Koreatowns and Chinatowns."

"You've had it pretty rough, promoting this film, haven't you?"

After Darren Lin, the detractors and blowhards on the internet forums had turned on the other hapa associated with the film—Peter himself. What kind of name is Mueller anyway? they'd asked. Doesn't sound like an Asian name to me. WTF, you seen his photo? He looks completely Anglo. They started calling him a "white hapa," one that might be half Asian by blood, but passed for white, and therefore could never understand what Asian people had to go through day to day. When they learned his father had met his mother in Guam, they claimed the sexual stereotypes in his film were a product of his own upbringing. Typical rice king, they called Peter's father—another white guy with a thing for Asian women. Fucking GIs. Never mind that he hadn't been a serviceman but a civilian contractor, as had been Peter's mother, a second-generation Korean American, both of them instructors in University of Maryland's overseas program. Peter, they said, was clearly emulating the racist master/submissive-slave system under which he was raised, and, just like his father had exploited his mother, he was now trying to exploit the Asian American community to boost his film career.

"What'd you think of the film?" he asked Sonia. "Honestly."

"Honestly? I liked everything up until the last part, that plot twist with—what was her name, the girl Courtney Lu played?"

"Lianne."

"It kind of ruined it for me, I have to say. It made her

one-dimensional suddenly, just this evil slut. Doing that seemed unnecessary. If I didn't know better, I'd say it was personal, almost vindictive. You sure the film doesn't have any autobiographical aspects?"

"I'm sure."

"You really weren't involved with Courtney Lu?"

"No."

"Did you want to be?"

He tugged on his seat belt. "All right, maybe I did."

She laughed. "It disappoints me sometimes, how transparent people are."

He and Courtney had traveled in the same circles in Echo Park and Silver Lake for years—overlapping, but never linking. He had written the part specifically for her, with the hazy notion that in falling in love with the hapa in the film, she might fall in love with him. She did fall in love with the hapa. With Darren Lin. An eight-day shoot, and it was evident halfway through that they were sleeping together.

Peter changed the ending to the film overnight, a sloppy, illogical rewrite that no one on the cast and crew had liked, and in retrospect they'd been right. It had been a mistake. The film would have been much better served with the original anti-ending ending so typical of indie movies. A quiet moment. Nothing resolved. The characters staring off into the distance, smiling almost imperceptibly as the camera slowly swept up and out to a view of Silver Lake.

The restaurant was in the middle of a strip mall. Inside, there was the din of exhaust fans as meat sizzled over live coals on each table. Tim had reserved the tatami room in back, and they sat cross-legged on pillows after removing their shoes. Big bottles of OB beer and soju had already been opened, and waitresses laid out banchan—little side dishes of pickled vegetables, kimchi, scallion pancakes, and potato salad—as everyone settled in, almost twenty of them in all. It was eleven thirty, and Peter was famished, picking away at the banchan hoggishly.

There were toasts. His glass of soju kept getting refilled, and the main courses started to come, bulgogi and kalbi, which they arranged over the charcoal with tongs. It wasn't long before they were all a little drunk and raucous.

"Dude, loved the little cameo by Alan Kwan," the fellow across the table said, referring to an actor whom Peter had brought out of retirement for a brief scene. "*Days of Scorn*'s always been a favorite."

"That movie was terrible, man," his friend said.

"Yeah, but it's one of those movies that's so bad, it's good, know what I mean?"

"That Courtney Lu is hot," the friend said. "You didn't use a body double, did you?"

"No, that was all her," Peter told him.

"Nice. Wish she could've made it tonight."

"What's she working on next?" the fellow across the table asked.

"I don't know," Peter said. It had been over a year since they'd wrapped, and he and Courtney didn't really talk anymore. The entire cast had appeared at the premiere in Hawai'i, but their attendance at the other festivals had been sporadic. He didn't know if Courtney was still with Darren or not. It felt indecorous to ask. "She was up for a big-budget action thriller, last I heard."

"Aw, man, that kind of sucks," the fellow said. "Good for her career, maybe, but I hate to see her sell out. What's the part?"

"Sex slave?" his friend said.

"Kung fu dragon lady?"

"Picture bride?" they uttered at the same time, and laughed.

"Lies," someone said.

Peter glanced diagonally across the table. It was the gray-haired gentleman, sloshed now, face red.

"Your movie's all lies," he said. "There's not one single thing in it that's true. You think it's revolutionary? Bullshit. Bullshit!"

Hoping for rescue, Peter turned to Tim and Sonia, who were sitting at the other end.

"It's the same old shit," the man said. "You make the Asian girl a whore, the Asian boy a weenie."

"Aigoo chamna," a woman muttered.

"A wimp!"

"Hey, Frank?" Tim said.

"What would you know," Frank told Peter. "Stupid white boy."

People groaned.

"All right, Frank, enough," Tim said. "Pour Peter some more soju there. Salud!"

Everyone stumbled out of the restaurant near two a.m., shouting out goodbyes, arguing over who was sober enough to drive. "You okay?" Peter asked Sonia.

"Tip-top. Hop in."

As they pulled out of the parking lot, he said, "That was fun."

"Oh, come on. You going to let one little comment get to you?"

"Who was that guy?"

According to Tim, the man was with the Chicago Chinese American Chamber of Commerce, one of the festival sponsors.

"I don't think I'll be sending a thank-you card."

"You are way too soft, you know. You need to let shit like that go."

He was exhausted and frayed and a bit inebriated. As a kid he had looked more Asian than white, and even after his physiognomy had changed with puberty, he'd always identified himself as Asian—not mixed, not half, not both. He didn't know what to think or feel anymore. All he wanted now was to sleep. He pictured the bed in his hotel room, the plush sheets and duvet, the thick feather mattress pad.

They reentered the city, winding through streets and across bridges, skyscrapers looming. "Fancy," Sonia said as they approached his hotel on the Magnificent Mile.

"Tim's sister works in the marketing department. She got me a suite, gratis."

She stopped short of the hotel's entrance on Michigan Avenue, where uniformed doormen awaited, put the car in park, and twisted toward him. He thanked her for the ride and began telling her what a pleasure it was to meet her, when she interrupted. "I've never seen the rooms before," she said. "You mind if I come up for a look?"

He was surprised. Well, that was easy, he thought. He wavered, though, tired, almost beyond concupiscence. Yet wasn't this what, in the back of his mind, he had been hoping for all night, from the moment he'd spied her coming into the reception? Sonia was beautiful—almost as beautiful as Courtney. And, really, wasn't this one of the few supposed benefits of touring, a perk he had yet to sample, recompense for the grind of the road and the anxiety of the screenings? How could he even think of turning her down? What was the matter with him? He was a man, wasn't he, a healthy, single mongrel dog with a normal libido?

They went up to his room, and he gave her a tour of the suite: the living room and bedroom, appointed in russet and gold, the two bathrooms with their Italian marble, the view of the city lights. He was still trying to make up his mind, presumptuous as it seemed. A one-night stand wasn't necessarily what he wanted or needed right now. On the other hand, he told himself, there wouldn't be anything terribly wrong with it. It'd be a release; surely it wouldn't be unpleasant. And her mere presence here was flattering.

Sonia removed his baseball cap. She smelled of Korean barbecue. She kissed him, and he wanted to feel something, but all he was able to do was summon an image of Courtney lying on her stomach in bed, naked beneath a twisted sheet. It wasn't even a real image. It was a staged still shot from the movie.

Sonia took his hand and led him into the bedroom. He was crashing, barely able to stay awake, not much good, deadweight. "Open your eyes," she said, her hair sliding down to his face as she lay atop him. "Look at me."

Somehow they managed to carry through, and she went to the bathroom, returned in one of the thick terry-cloth robes. "You know this was originally an athletic club for members of the Masonic order?" she said. "It was crazy opulent. It had an indoor golf course with water hazards! Shooting range, running track, basketball court, boxing arena, the whole kit and caboodle. Women were only allowed in the ballroom, of course, and they had to go through the back entrance. On the roof there's this chimney thingy. They were planning to dock dirigibles to the building. Can you imagine? Like, the *Hindenburg*! But they never got around to it. The place opened in 1929, right before the stock market crash, and they had to shut it down after four years. Oh, the follies of men with dreams of grandeur."

He couldn't help it—he yawned.

"Am I losing you?"

"I'm sorry. I usually have more energy than this."

"You know, the pool's open twenty-four hours."

"The pool?"

"You seen it? I do laps there occasionally."

"No, I haven't gone down."

"Let's take a dip. It'll wake you up."

"Now? It's—" He glanced at the clock and groaned. "It's past three."

"No one will be there. It's something to behold. Johnny Weissmuller—you know, Tarzan—and Esther Williams used to train there. You see, some cinematic historical reference for you."

"You want to skinny-dip, don't you?"

"Men are such prudes."

"I don't have swim trunks."

"You can wear those black boxer briefs."

"What about you?"

"I happen to have a suit in my bag."

"Of course you do," he said. "Do we really have to?"

"Come on, it'll be romantic."

"Wouldn't it be just as romantic to fall asleep together, here, like this? I'm really comfortable right now." Why did women, he asked himself, have such strange notions, always insisting on spontaneity, romance, and communication?

She dragged him down to the fourteenth floor in a matching terry-cloth robe, and, as advertised, the pool was spectacular, huge—junior Olympic size. There was a coffered ceiling, yellow stucco walls with blue Spanish majolica tiles, marble columns, wrought-iron lanterns, and a terra-cotta fountain of Neptune, framed by palm trees. Sonia dove in and stroked quickly and efficiently to the other end, flip-turned, and came back to him just as he was easing into the water.

"Isn't it glorious?" she said.

The water was warmer than he'd imagined. The lights overhead had been dimmed in favor of those below, making the place feel cozy and tropical. "Can we go back to the room now?"

"Swim with me." She floated on her back, languidly scissor-kicking.

Laboring, he breaststroked after Sonia while she effortlessly glided ahead, utterly happy. "Let me ask you," he said, "did finding out you have lupus, I don't know—" He inadvertently swallowed some water and coughed. "Did it make you appreciate things more, realize what's important, what's not?"

"No, the opposite. It made me more"—she searched for the word—"indiscriminate."

"What does that mean?"

"It means I'll spend the night with practically anyone, so don't flatter yourself, hotshot."

"Thanks."

"So if I'm the whore," she said, "you're the . . . weenie?"

"It was a serious question." He was broke, deep in debt. If nothing happened at South by Southwest next week, his film, and maybe his career, would be dead, no small thanks to the people he had thought he could count on—*his* people. He would have to go back to his job at the film processing lab. He wanted Sonia to tell him something to take away from all of this, something illuminating, something wise.

"Profundity doesn't come like that," she said.

"How does it come, then?"

"Beats me. You're the artiste, the auteur. You tell me."

"You're no help whatsoever. Slow down."

She waited for him to catch up. "When we were fucking," she said, smiling slyly, "were you thinking about Courtney Lu?"

"No."

"Maybe your problem's not a hapa/Asian thing," she said. "Maybe you just don't know anything about women."

"Are you mad at me?"

"Just a general observation, not an attack. Did you ever tell Courtney how you feel about her?"

"It was more complicated than that."

"Was it?" she said. "That one scene in your movie, where she said to the Asian guy, 'Just tell me love is possible. That's all I want to know,' and then he can't bring himself to respond, the stupid fuck. That was a true moment. That

was honest. That's all anyone wants. To know someone will
love them, take care of them, never leave them."

He looked at her face, glimmers of light refracting off
the water, and he knew it was just fatigue, or the sappiness
of the situation—it was damn romantic here—but he felt a
tug of real affection for Sonia. "Where is it you're an editor
again? A women's magazine?"

"Mock me if you want. I'm trying to enlighten you.
You might make better movies."

"Or really corny, sentimental ones."

She splashed him.

"Is it that simple?" he asked.

"Could be."

It was an appealing thought, that it could be so simple,
that all the squabbles and complexities of art and race, of
finding one's place within the sticky warrens of this fac-
tious life, could be trumped by the elemental drama of
people trying to say they love each other. "Where's your
next triathlon?" he asked Sonia.

"San Diego."

"When?"

"Next month."

"Drive up to LA and see me."

She laughed. "No, you'll be on to your next starlet by
then."

"Come visit."

She hooked her arms around his neck and spun him
around with her, an aquatic pas de deux. "Kiss me," she
said. "Kiss me like you'll never see me again."

He kissed her, tasting chlorine, holding tight, knees
bumping as they treaded water. He wanted it to be mean-

ingful, he wanted it to be true, to let everything else fall away and pretend for a second that this was all that mattered, that it was genuine and clear and unassailable. He kissed her.

She didn't come to visit. They traded a few emails, but the exchange quickly flagged, Sonia's responses adopting an oddly perfunctory tone, and whatever promise there had been between them in Chicago leaked away into improbability.

Two years went by. *Late in the Day* never picked up distribution and was relegated to being sold as a curio—in the form of a self-produced DVD—on online indie film sites, bought mainly by new devotees of Courtney Lu interested in seeing her early work, in which, of course, she happened to be naked. Her small part as an explosives/marital arts expert in the big-budget action thriller led to a role on yet another forensics crime drama on TV, which aired as a midseason replacement and was an unexpected hit. Peter occasionally ran into her in Echo Park, and she never had time to stop and talk.

He had to declare bankruptcy, and there was a long ordeal with lawyers and appearances in court and settlements with creditors, but finally he was able to surface from the muck and move on. He worked at the film processing lab, lived at his parents' house in Silver Lake, and, on the side, directed—all without pay—an underground music video, a PSA for public-access television, and then a YouTube political ad for a hapa senatorial candidate, who briefly led in the polls but narrowly lost the election in the end. During the campaign, he met a once-semifamous novelist, Judy Wang, a childhood friend of his mother's, it turned out. She sent him an old story of hers, "Upon the Shore," and asked if he might care to adapt it into a short film. He wasn't terribly passionate about the project. Her books were too precious and saccharine for his tastes—standard Chinese American immigrant weepies, with lots of folklore allusions and tributes to the old country, characters gazing wistfully out to sea—and this story was not any different. Yet he wrote a script because he had nothing else to do. She found financing for it, largely from her anesthesiologist husband and his cronies, and they shot a thirty-minute short in San Francisco's Chinatown. Almost immediately, through Judy's remarkable lobbying efforts, it was picked up by PBS's independent filmmakers series, with funding to produce an accompanying thirty-minute documentary, a retrospective on Judy, which was exactly what she had been scheming for all along—a way to revive her waning literary career. Feeling a little manipulated, Peter nonetheless admired the woman's guile.

Upon the Shore had its premiere at the 2013 Honolulu Asian American Film Festival—not given nearly as prestigious of a slot or location as the last time around with *Late in the Day,* five p.m. on a Wednesday at the Asian Art Museum in Chinatown. There was a decent crowd, though, the small screening room filled out by Judy's friends, mostly ABCs, American-born Chinese, affluent enough to fly to Honolulu from the Bay Area for this relatively inconsequential event.

Judy positioned herself as the featured panelist during the Q&A afterward, Peter a mere sidebar, accoutrement to her spectacular red silk cheongsam with its princess collar, her huge hammered-gold earrings and matching necklace, her elaborately braided and pinned hair. The film's cast of mother and daughter were also onstage, and they, too, were consigned to the background. Judy did all the talking.

In a way, Peter was relieved not to be the center of attention. Watching the film earlier, he had been embarrassed anew by its schmaltziness. If Judy was a hack, he had become one, too.

"These stories come to me out of a deep sense of history and tradition which is ingrained in my blood," Judy told the audience. "I try to represent what's in my heart, what's in everyone's heart, what it really means to be Chinese. There's an emotional, psychic lineage that ties us all together, that can't be broken by the expanse of oceans or generations. There's an old Chinese proverb: 'To forget one's ancestors is to be a brook without a source, a tree without root.' Even if a particular story of mine is set in contemporary America, I feel those ancient voices speaking to me. They inform me, they sing and whisper to me."

The audience—saps, all of them—murmured in appreciation. Peter could not believe that this was what his life had come to, that he still had to finish the documentary about Judy, that, for at least three more months, possibly much, much longer, he had to continue to be associated with her.

Near the end of the Q&A, someone raised a hand in back, stood, and was given the mic. "This is a question for Peter Mueller," she said. "I was wondering, could you tell us what it is that speaks to you?"

An awful question, one that he had no desire or idea how to answer. "Sorry?" he said, stalling. "Could you elaborate?" She looked familiar, this woman.

"What is it that inspires you? What compels you? Why do you make films? What are you trying to say? What were you hoping to accomplish with this film in particular?"

Jesus, he thought. The woman was smirking, enjoying this. Everyone waited, including Judy, who stared at him, openly curious how he would acquit himself. "Honesty," he said. "That's all a filmmaker, any artist, can ask of himself. To be honest. I'm always looking for that true moment"— and here he realized the woman, smiling broadly now, was Sonia Chen—"and I think it's the, uh, accretion of those true moments that will, hopefully, elevate a film into art, that will allow you to make the emotional connection you want."

The audience nodded, satisfied, not noticing that he had evaded saying anything at all about *Upon the Shore*.

He met Sonia in the lobby. He didn't know what to do, what was appropriate. Kiss on the mouth, the cheek, a hug, a handshake? They reached for each other, leaned forward, redirected their heads at the last second, puckered the lacuna, and end up embracing, arms trapped awkwardly between their chests.

"It's so good to see you," he said. But she didn't look good. She had lost a lot of weight, too much, appearing anorexic now, and a rash splashed across her cheeks and the bridge of her nose, big patches of discoloration, pinkish and splotched like birthmarks.

"Where's your ball cap? Did you get plugs?" she asked, same sense of humor, rising onto her toes for an inspection. She was wearing a hat herself this time—a white bucket with a floppy rim—and blocky eyeglasses, along with a tight-necked long-sleeved blouse and long pants, unusual for the ninety-degree heat outside, as if in an absurdly mis-guided attempt at disguise.

"What are you doing here?" he asked.

"Oh, I moved back home a while ago." Home, where she grew up and where her mother still resided, she ex-plained, was in Kaimuki, near Kahala.

Peter wasn't aware she had been born and raised in Oʻahu, and he realized how little he knew about her, how little he had asked. "How have you been doing?"

"Can't you tell by my rosy cheeks?" Then she shook her head. "Not well," she said. "You?"

"Okay," he told her.

"Are you free? You want to get a drink or something?"

"I have this thing, this dinner, I need to go to," he said.

"What about tomorrow? How long you in town for?"

"I'm flying out first thing in the morning." He couldn't afford more than two nights in a hotel. The festival was only giving him a small per diem, and even the money for the flight he had to borrow from his parents. "Listen, why don't you come to this thing with me?" he said.

"You sure it'd be okay?"

"Why not?"

"I don't know. How many people are going?"

"Too many. I think it'll be more like a banquet."

That was precisely how the dinner was fashioned, they learned—almost as a wedding banquet. Judy had rented out an upstairs room of the Golden Chau Chow restau-rant, and it had been set up with six round tables, each with ten seats. The upstairs, at least, was a respite from the chaos downstairs—with its overly bright decor of dragon mu-rals, lanterns, mirrored walls, and chandeliers—waiters and waitresses nimbly sidestepping one another as they rushed past the bubbling aquariums, balancing enormous trays of food.

Judy was momentarily perturbed. "You didn't tell me you were bringing a friend," she said, staring at Sonia's skeletal frame and the patches on her face as if they might be communicable. She didn't hide her annoyance at having to move a guest from the head table to make room for Sonia.

"And what do you do, Sonia?" Judy asked when they were settled. "Are you in film as well?"

"No. I used to work as a fundraiser for a poetry foundation in Chicago. Nowadays, I'm not doing much of anything, really. I volunteer once in a while at a literacy center."

"That sounds . . . fulfilling," Judy said.

"She competes in triathlons," Peter said, and everyone at the table looked at him with an incredulity that bordered on fury, in particular Judy's husband, the anesthesiologist. His name was Frederick Morgenthal, sixtyish, elegant pinstriped suit, carefully styled white hair, tall and slender like Judy. For all her fealty to tradition, she had married a rice king.

Peter was amused by their reaction—he was glad now that he had brought Sonia.

She whispered to him, "I've been too sick to train anymore."

"The lupus?"

"Complications therein. They don't really know what's going on. I had a flare. The usual joint pain, dizziness, nausea, fever. They changed my meds, but it got worse. This rash, and my eyes and hair started to go." Unabashedly, she lifted the bucket hat to show him her thinning hair, and the others at the table blanched. "They think it might be nephrotic, renal, you know, but it doesn't make sense—I should be gaining weight, not losing it. I'm on cytotoxins now."

The first course arrived, a platter of cold appetizers that included pickled jellyfish and roast suckling pig with crispy skin, arranged by color—white, brown, green, and pink. According to the menu at each place setting, there would be eight courses in all, excluding the rice and dessert, which was customary for banquets, the word for eight, *baat,* sounding like the word for prosperity, *faat.* Next would be honey-glazed walnut shrimp, fried stuffed crab claw, shark's fin soup, braised abalone and sea cucumber, baked lobster with ginger and scallions, stewed duck with scallops and black mushroom, and steamed whole sea bass.

Sonia hardly partook, restricting herself to white rice and tea.

Judy motioned to her with her chopsticks, seemingly enraged. "Eat, eat!"

"I'm sorry. I have no appetite these days," Sonia said, pushing along the lazy Susan.

"How's the documentary going?" Judy's husband asked Peter.

"Good. It's coming along nicely." He was done with the most odious part—the interviews with Judy and the other principals—and was now gathering archival photos and clips.

"You know, I noticed one scene today, a boom mic dropped into the frame," Morgenthal said. "Did you spot that?"

"What scene was that?"

"At the graveyard."

"You sure it wasn't a tree branch?"

"No, it wasn't a tree branch," Morgenthal said indignantly. "I had a few other thoughts. I'll send you some notes."

"I look forward to them," Peter said, and Morgenthal glared at him for a second longer, measuring the degree of Peter's sarcasm, before cracking open a crab claw.

"I'm sorry to have to tell you this," Sonia said, "but I think it was a boom mic, not a branch."

"I know," Peter said. "I'm just fucking with him, he's been such a pain in the ass."

"I guess you won't want my notes, then," she said, and the old Sonia, the vibrant woman he met in Chicago, momentarily peeked out from beneath the hat and eyeglasses.

Just before the shark's fin soup, Judy got up to make a toast, thanking her husband and the other financial supporters, the cast and crew, her friends, her family, her agent, her assistant, her editor, her attorney, her accountant, the restaurant staff—somewhere in there Peter got thrown in with her personal trainer.

"This woman is the bitch goddess from hell, isn't she?" Sonia said.

"You're seeing just a fraction of what I've had to endure."

"How have you not strangled yourself?"

"It's been a heroic effort."

Alix Li, who had a supporting role in *Upon the Shore,* said to Peter, "You want a shot? Let's do a shot." She grabbed a bottle of baijiu, and they each quaffed down a shot.

"What about you?" Alix asked Sonia.

"I don't drink anymore."

"I wish I had your kind of discipline. Me, I'm susceptible to every possible vice. It's what makes me so bewitching." She poured another round of shots. "Gotta do a second. Odd numbers are unlucky in China, you know. Or so I've been told. Na zdravje!"

In a short flashback in *Upon the Shore,* Alix had assumed the role of the mother as a young woman—a picture bride languishing in a Chinatown laundry, steaming shirts—and Alix, having grown up in Connecticut, never quite mastered the accent required for the character's lines, trenchant as they were: "Why they no pay me, three month already."

Judy continued her speech, more hokey, quasi-Eastern-ancestral-familial-mysticism crap, relating a story about a ghost and a peasant on the banks of the Heavenly River. This was what Peter had always hated about her books, that they perpetuated every stereotype ever invented about Asians. Contrary to *Late in the Day,* there would be no controversy about *Upon the Shore,* no one would question Peter's right to do the story or argue over his motivations, even though he wasn't the least bit Chinese, because the film was safe, and innocuous, and completely irrelevant. It was a trifle, a self-Orientalizing ornament. Judy had always wanted one of her novels to be adapted into a feature, but there had never been any takers. She had turned to Peter in an act of mutual desperation. He had become a coolie for hire, available for New Years, weddings, and funerals.

"Do you want to get out of here?" Peter asked Sonia. "Let's get out of here."

"Can you leave?"

Judy, who was greeting each table with her husband, decidedly thought he could not. "It'd be rude. It'd be very disrespectful to my guests," she said.

"I'm sorry," Peter said. "My friend's not feeling well." Sonia herself had offered this subterfuge, and they scampered out of the room with the giddiness of truants.

"God, that was excruciating," he said.

"You didn't want to hear more parables about Zhuangzi and the Happy Fish?"

Outside the restaurant, they ran into Alix, who had stepped out for a cigarette. "You two behave now," she said.

On the street, they discussed where they might go. "Someplace for coffee?" Peter said. "Maybe somewhere on the water?"

"Where's your hotel?" Sonia asked abruptly.

"My . . . hotel?" he said. She seemed too frail for a conjugal reunion.

"No, you idiot," she said, laughing, "that's the furthest thing from my mind. I am not looking for a mercy fuck. Are you in Waikiki somewhere?"

"Yeah, a fleabag off Kuhio."

"Let's go to Ala Moana. It's on the way. It's a nice night for a walk."

They retrieved her car—a new Camry—and drove east, past the Ward Center, where the festival headliner, *Every Road Has a Wanderer,* would be showing on Saturday, closing night. It was a postapocalyptic, shaolin-warrior, time-traveler epic, the third feature by Dalton Lee, a ponytailed Korean American wunderkind who had won the Audience Award at Sundance straight out of the gate with his first film. Peter had heard that Darren Lin was in the new one, playing a cross-dressing warlord prince with tele-kinetic powers.

Sonia turned down the air-conditioning and put on some music—soft alt-folk-rock.

"This is a lot cleaner than your last car," he said.

"It's my mother's."

"How is it living with your mother?"

"You have a mean streak, don't you?"

"No, I can empathize. I'm sort of in the same situation right now."

"You're living at home? What's your excuse?"

"Suicidal tendencies?"

At Ala Moana Beach, they parked in the lot, and, rather than to the sand, they strolled onto a grassy peninsula with large shade trees, encircled by a walkway.

"This is the only time I can come to the beach—at night," Sonia said. "Ridiculous, isn't it? I'm in Hawai'i, and I have to avoid the sun. I can't tell you how much I miss Chicago."

"You don't miss the winters."

"I do. Even the winters I miss. I feel like by coming here, I've been sent out to pasture. I feel like I've come here to die."

Apprehensively, Peter asked, "Is there a chance of that?"

"Sure, there's a statistical chance, but I've had flares before, and I've always recovered. Don't worry. I'll be all right. I know you must be shocked to see me like this, but I saw your name on the festival schedule, and I really wanted to see you."

"I'm glad you did."

They continued walking, and Sonia hooked her arm inside his. "Isn't it lovely out?" she said.

It was a gorgeous evening, seventy-five degrees now, not too humid, light trade winds, gibbous moon, long rippling clouds stretching from the mountains.

"This was going to be a hotel resort complex," Sonia said, "but the developers hit a snag and it got turned into a park. We used to come here for picnics when I was a kid. One of my uncles had a specialty, hamachi collar. Ever had it? Yellowtail? It's the cheek, the meatiest part. It's got an incredible amount of flavor. He'd grill it with sea salt, shoyu, and lemon. Unbelievably good."

"Do you still have a lot of family here?"

"Some, but most are on the Mainland now. I've always felt people here have an unspoken inferiority complex. If you stay, it's like you're a bit of a loser, someone who can't make it in the real world."

The perfect place for someone like him, he thought. It was so far removed from everything, from all of his problems, and for a second he entertained the idea of moving to Honolulu, where nearly everyone was just like him, a hapa, and starting a new life, one that might include taking care of Sonia and abandoning filmmaking for good.

"You don't have to tell me what you thought," Peter said.

"Of what?"

"The film. I already know."

"Do you?"

"It's a piece of shit. I'd say I sold out, but there's no hope for any kind of payout, so it's even worse, the extent I've compromised myself."

"It's not that bad."

"The thing is, I kind of thought of it as a throwaway, that no one would actually see it. Now it's going to be on PBS and be part of my— What do you call it?"

"Oeuvre?"

"I'm accountable for it now."

"Being on PBS is nothing to sneeze at."

"I'm ashamed of it. It's so fucking trite."

"Don't beat yourself up. You did the best you could with the material you had. You'll make other films."

"The jury's very much out on that." The irony was, though, *Upon the Shore* probably would get him further work, projects that would follow the predictable ethnic angle, and at this point, he would take whatever was offered to him—gladly. He had known this all along, but hadn't been willing to admit it to himself. "You really didn't think it was that bad?" he asked Sonia.

She smiled tiredly. "At what point can I stop being kind?"

Despite his own deprecations, he was hurt. Yet what had he expected, asking her so directly? If anything, he had admired Sonia for her candor. "I blame it all on you," he told her.

"Me? How am I to blame?"

"I listened to you, and now I'm making really sentimental movies."

"I think I was misinterpreted."

They passed a swimming area at the tip of the peninsula, protected by high breakwaters built with lava boulders, and they saw a teenage couple wading into the water, the girl shrieking about its frigidity.

"Did you ever get back together with Courtney Lu?" Sonia asked.

"No."

"No other starlets?"

"Starlets are only interested if you have a measure of power."

"How the mighty have fallen."

"Never very mighty," he said.

"That didn't seem to deter Alix Li, though."

He turned to her. "Hm?"

"Didn't you sleep with her?"

"How did you know?"

She laughed. "Plain as day, plain as day."

"It was a mistake."

"She doesn't seem too torn up about it. She's attractive. Maybe you should give it another whirl."

"No, I've learned my lesson. What about you?"

"You mean have I been dating anyone? Does that really require an answer?" She steered them around a puddle on the walkway, then said, "All right, I will admit I did go out with Tim for a while."

"Tim? Tim Na?"

"It was more like a fling."

"Tim *Na*?" The festival host in Chicago.

"Why's that so surprising?"

"I don't know." It wasn't that he had expected her to be celibate during their time apart, carrying a torch for him. He should not have felt betrayed. He had had no such compunctions when he was having sex with Alix Li on the set after-hours. Yet, with no justification, he could not help feeling as though a tacit agreement had been broken—a reel of images spliced, a jump cut introduced, violating continuity.

"Tim's a nice guy," Sonia said.

"I don't see the two of you together."

"Well, we're not. I didn't treat him very well."

They looped around to the other side of the peninsula, and Sonia said, "Let's sit." They settled onto a wooden bench near a milo tree. Across the channel from them was the Ala Wai Yacht Harbor, the twin towers of the Prince Hotel, the Ilikai, the Hilton Hawaiian, and, farther east, the high-rises in Waikiki against the backdrop of Diamond Head. Night lights reflected on the water. Another fatally romantic scene.

"I've thought of you," he told her.

"Oh?"

"I wish we could have seen each other again."

"I don't recall you trying to arrange that."

"You didn't seem very encouraging about it."

"Maybe you should have tried harder," Sonia said.

"Maybe I should have."

She took off her hat, scratched her scalp, and played out her hair with her fingers. "It's all right. It was just one night. It wasn't that memorable, hotshot."

"Thanks."

She laughed again. "You know, you asked me that night what's important and what's not."

"I remember that."

"When you figure it out, tell me. Because I'd really like to know."

He put his arm around her and brought her close, her bones feeling avian underneath her flesh. They sat for a long time on the bench, looking across the water. It was comforting, and romantic, but counterfeit, he knew, a false moment—liminal, potent with possibility, lying there would be a chance for something more—and he thought maybe this was what truth was, a collection of falsehoods with which you chose to define yourself, and for which you were grateful. Moments like these, sitting on a park bench with a relative stranger, memorialized until they became larger and more meaningful than they deserved. Like that moment in Chicago, when they'd kissed in the pool, and their heads began to dip beneath the surface, and still they didn't let go.

COMMIS

• • • • • • • • • •

WHEN THE CALL CAME FROM MY BROTHER, I wasn't the least bit surprised. The only wonder was that they'd lasted this long, into the dog days of August. But now, my parents had decided to close their restaurant for good, my brother told me, and they wanted me—their fugitive daughter—to come home to Missouri to help them shut it down.

I didn't have much going on to excuse me. Like most people in the food-service industry that Covid year, I'd been furloughed in March 2020 and then laid off. I'd been living off unemployment, collecting more money, actually, than I had as a commis cook at BoYo, the fine-dining iza-kaya in Old City, thanks to the extra six hundred dollars a week the government was doling out. The first month of the shutdown, I had lazed around my apartment in South Philly as if on vacation, thinking BoYo would reopen at any moment. After running out of shows to stream and grow-ing bored with baking focaccia, my two roommates—both prep cooks at other restaurants—and I began incubating artisanal products for possible side hustles. We molded can-dles and soaps, fermented vinegar and kombucha, infused edibles, pickled beets and okra, assembled bentos to sell in the corner bodega, and macerated citrus, nuts, seeds, and herbs for Italian liqueurs—limoncello, nocino, amaro.

Then George Floyd was murdered, and our summer became all about activism, marching up and down the parkway between City Hall and the Museum of Art, repeatedly taking a knee, getting teargassed and pinned on I-676, followed by volunteering for neighborhood cleanups, meals on wheels, food banks, and cookouts for the homeless. As the election neared, we turned to canvassing and making calls and writing postcards and going out to rural PA to register voters.

But when the federal subsidy program expired at the end of July, we had to shift to more mundane concerns, like how to pay the rent. We started looking for kitchen jobs. There was nothing. The only places that were hiring were grocery stores, pharmacies, warehouses, and delivery services. I kept getting rejected. I was turned down for four different positions at Target, including cart attendant. Everyone was looking, which made finding an entry-level job as a stocker or picker ridiculously competitive, companies asking for relevant experience.

The only experience I had was at my parents' Chinese restaurant and at BoYo, the latter acquired through pluck more than luck. After I graduated high school in May 2018, I'd immediately fled to Olney, a Korean American neighborhood in North Philly, where a cousin lived (I had told my parents I'd only be there for a short visit). On my second night in town, I set off to get a job at BoYo. I'd already tried calling and emailing and sending in my résumé, to no avail. I needed another tactic to get in the door. So I dressed up, put on makeup, and went there pretending to be a customer.

The restaurant was a square box, sleek and elegant, with wide plank oak flooring, black wainscotting, brick walls painted gray, and exposed ceiling joists. It was very dark in there, with just one narrow picture window facing the street, but up-lighting and recessed mini-spots gave it a warm glow. A tiny bar fronted the room, behind which were eight two-tops of natural walnut that could be arranged in different configurations, flanked by six booths along the walls. Everything was dominated by the open kitchen in back, built around a custom Jade range, which was crowned by a massive steel hood. It was the most beautiful restaurant I'd ever stepped foot in. (I admit that up to then the fanciest place I'd eaten in had been an Olive Garden, but I wasn't a complete hick. I had a TV. I had the internet. I had books. I knew about food.)

The chef's counter, which I'd reserved weeks before, was on two adjacent sides of the kitchen—sadly, away from the hot line, but I could still see a lot of the action from my chair. And there in front of me was Bosse Park, or Bo, himself, examining tickets that were coming out of the receipt machine and consulting with his sous chef. I hadn't been sure he would be working service that night, although I had heard he rarely took days off. Like his staff, he was wearing a short-sleeve white shirt, black pants, and a gray apron. No toques or tunics here. He was shorter than I'd expected, but otherwise he looked like his pictures—midthirties, solid-bodied, with a broad, pleasant face and neatly combed, thick hair.

I ordered small plates of the raw diver scallops, steamed egg custard, smoked eel croquets, broiled baby eggplant, and dry-aged duck breast. I was blowing a big chunk of my savings on the meal, but I didn't care. I hadn't eaten anything all day so I could devour these dishes.

As I was finishing my last morsels, Bo walked past me, and he nodded subtly. "Excuse me, chef," I said, startling him. He winced, actually. He was, by reputation, quiet and reserved, shy. He didn't usually talk to his diners.

"Yes? How may I help you?" he asked, betraying the slightest trace of a Scandinavian accent. He was, like me, Korean by blood, but he came from another world. His father had been a South Korean diplomat, and Bo had been born in Stockholm, then raised in Hong Kong, Tokyo, Paris, Oslo, and Copenhagen.

"I'd like to work here," I told him.

"As a server?"

"Cook."

"I'm very sorry. There are no positions available."

"I'll do anything. I'll clean toilets to start. For free. I want to stage with you."

"I'm so sorry. There are no openings. Would you care to look at the dessert menu?"

The next day, I waited for him outside the back service entrance. "I'm sorry," he told me again. "We really don't have anything."

Three hours later, his sous chef passed by me at the door. Inside, she told Bo, "Hey, that girl's still there."

He came out once more. "Maybe I can refer you to some other restaurants," he said.

"There are no other restaurants I want to work for, no other chefs," I said. "There's only this restaurant, and you. I've studied everything about you. I won't take no for an answer. I'll stay here all night."

This wasn't that outlandish of a ploy. I knew he preferred to hire people who were raw and moldable, rather than culinary-school graduates or restaurant veterans, and that he admired persistence. He himself had done exactly the same thing to get his first job at Noma—posing as a customer, then camping out at the back door.

"Have you ever worked in a professional kitchen before?" he asked me.

For an entire week, he had me clean the toilets, and the floors, and the mats, and the prep tables, and the pots and pans. Then he let me clean mushrooms and greens. Then pick apart herbs, juice corn, and seed cumquats. Then chop onions and dice beets. Midsummer, he put me on the payroll.

Twenty-two months I worked at BoYo. As a commis, I unpacked deliveries, labeled and rotated stock, cleaned stations, prepped ingredients, and measured out portions. But my other duties changed from night to night, getting assigned to different chefs de partie, going from the fry station to the sauté to the grill. I was learning so much. Toward the end, I was being allowed to line-cook and plate. I was working twelve, thirteen hours a day, six days a week, beat to shit after every shift, but I loved it—loved being able to take ordinary, plain ingredients and make something beautiful out of them.

Now, I didn't know when or how BoYo would ever reopen. There wasn't space on the sidewalk in front of the restaurant for outdoor dining, and 25 percent occupancy inside was a joke. While other businesses were pivoting to delivery and takeout, Bo had said in an email to his staff that trying to modify the menu to-go wasn't workable. With expenses for ingredients, overhead, taxes, delivery fees, and a skeleton crew, we'd have to sell chicken wings for forty dollars to break even.

I was afraid Bo would soon be closing his restaurant permanently, as my parents were closing theirs, along with thousands of other restaurants across the country. I was afraid I'd never work as a commis again.

I got home a week before the final day of service. I didn't know how long I'd have to stay. I was hoping no more than two weeks. But there was a lot to do—vendors to contact, services to cancel, equipment to return or sell, all the financial, tax, permit, and insurance issues to take care of, and then we'd have to break things down and move everything out and do a deep cleaning of the entire place.

For now, I was in the kitchen with my mom and dad, in the weeds. Word about the closure had gotten around, and all of a sudden, for no reason we could figure (it wasn't like we were the only Chinese restaurant in town, and we'd never been the most popular), the phone would not stop ringing with orders.

"Where were all these fuckers when we needed them?" my brother, Victor, said.

Opposed to many Asian businesses that year, the restaurant hadn't been spray-painted with threats or slurs, the windows hadn't been smashed, there hadn't been any rants or boycotts, just some prank calls ("Can I have a side of corona with that?"). But beginning in late January, business had started to drop off, then plummeted with the "kung flu," "Chinese virus" bullshit, until one day there were just three orders. Things never fully rebounded after that, although my brother, the de facto manager of Asia Palace, had done his best to keep them afloat.

He erected plexiglass barriers, put out sterilized pens and bottles of hand sanitizer, and taped up fliers touting the restaurant's safety, health, and hygiene procedures. He'd always resisted signing up with delivery apps, objecting to the commissions—the restaurant mainly takeout, anyway— but now he hired a few drivers, high-school boys willing to work as tipped employees for half the state's minimum wage. This location, Asia Palace's third, was a freestanding former Dairy Queen on 50 Highway on the edge of Warrensburg, and it had a drive-up window we'd never used. Victor pried off the plywood covering and recruited a couple of high-school girls to staff the window so customers could call ahead for cashless, contactless pickup. He made sure all the high-school kids were white. He also planted American flags and an election sign for Fuckface outside the restaurant ("Purely a marketing decision," he said to mollify me).

Tonight, the kitchen was as hot as I remembered, feeling twenty degrees warmer than it was outside, even with air-conditioning. My dad was at the wok station, my mom was wrapping dumplings, and I was at the Fryolator, dipping egg rolls and General Tso's chicken into the oil, while my brother continually walked in, ripping sheets off his check pad and shouting out phone orders. He'd laid off all the high-school kids weeks ago.

At one point my mom ran out of scallions for the crab rangoons, and I chopped several bunches of stalks for her. My dad stared at me intently. "What?" I asked him. He didn't answer and went back to tossing beef and broccoli.

There were no unique dishes at Asia Palace, nothing that varied from the standard American Chinese fare that could be found in any one of the forty thousand mom-and-pop Chinese restaurants in the US—more than the number of McDonald's, Burger Kings, KFCs, Pizza Huts, Domino's, Taco Bells, and Wendy's combined. Over the years, I'd suggested refinements, more adventurous dishes, and my dad always told me, "Customers don't want fancy. They want familiar. Americans like sweet and fried." Although he was Korean, he had never put any Korean food on the menu. "Too foreign for Missouri," he said. So it was solely the classics: orange chicken, egg foo yung, sweet and sour pork, fried rice, lo mein, Mongolian beef, egg drop soup, kung pao chicken.

We closed the doors at nine and cleaned the kitchen for an hour before heading back to the house, which was in a subdivision called Northfield. The rambler, built in 1978, was the only home I'd ever known, and it was showing its age, badly in need of a reno, especially inside. It had four bedrooms and two baths, fourteen hundred square feet. The most unusual aspect of the property was a wide breezeway between the garage and the rest of the house, letting passersby see right through to the backyard. Because the roofline above it was unbroken, it looked like someone had knocked down the front and back walls in an impulsive fit. There was never much of a breeze through there, but Victor and I had taken to sitting on the concrete patio at the end of the passageway and drinking beers after service.

As usual, our parents had already gone straight to sleep.

"Have they talked about what they're going to do after?" I asked Victor.

"No. When have they ever talked?"

He told me about watching the Super Bowl in February with our dad, who normally didn't follow football (or any other sport), but the Kansas City Chiefs had been playing and he'd felt obligated. At one point during the game, our dad had said to Victor, "You know, I regret I never went to any of your sporting events." Victor had been on the track team in high school, despite not being much of an athlete. He'd run the steeplechase, a discipline no one else had wanted to enter. Yet he managed to make the podium a couple of times and took pride in that. Our parents, though, were always working during his meets and were never able to attend a single one. Asia Palace was open every day except Sundays, Thanksgiving, and Christmas.

"And you know what I thought when he said that?" Victor said to me on the patio. "I thought, Yeah, that would've been nice, but it would've been nicer if just for fucking once we'd had a real conversation."

Maybe it was an Asian thing, having taciturn parents who barely spoke to their children except to berate or command, which had only made me more insolent and moodier as a teenager. (At least I knew that during this trip back home, our parents would not be bringing up the subject of my former lover, Cory Ellis—the reason for my exile to Philadelphia. They never willingly broached uncomfortable topics.) Unlike most other Asian parents, however, ours hadn't pushed us about school or extracurricular activities—too exhausted to do anything other than go to work, church, and sleep. I'd been shocked by how much they'd aged in the two years I'd been away. They slumped now with geriatric defeat. They weren't even in their late fifties yet.

Victor looked older, too, beefier, sporting a new goatee and mullet. We were twins, but had never resembled each other. We wouldn't look alike for many years, until we became middle-aged, when both of us would get kind of fat.

He pulled another Bud Light from the cooler. We hated Bud Light, but there was a stack of extra cases of it in the restaurant stockroom.

"What about you?" I asked him. "What're you thinking of doing after they close?"

"The fuck knows."

Victor had always lived with our parents. As far as I knew, he'd never had a girlfriend (or boyfriend?). I was certain he was a virgin.

"You could go back to UCM," I told him.

In contrast to me, he had been a decent student. After I'd left for Philly, he'd enrolled as a business major at the University of Central Missouri in Warrensburg, but dropped out before the end of his first semester. He'd been unable to keep up with his classes, overwhelmed with everything he needed to do at the restaurant—a situation he blamed, I'm sure, on me.

"What good would a degree do me?" he asked. "I don't need a degree for the jobs waiting for me out there."

"It might get you out of Warrensburg. You could get a job eventually in KC or St. Louis. Maybe Chicago."

Our aunt Aeyoung, my father's sister, lived in Albany Park in Chicago, which had once been a thriving Kore-

atown. The only vacations my brother and I ever took had
been to visit her. Victor had loved Chicago.

"Like you got out?" he said to me. "The way things are
going for you in Philly, you might have to come back, you
know. Live at home again."

"No fucking way. That'll never happen," I said.

"Yeah? I wouldn't be so sure, Penny."

Our parents had worked in food services at Osan Air Base,
about forty miles south of Seoul, and had befriended the
operations manager, Mike Weiss, who was a fellow Meth-
odist. In 1993, Uncle Mike, as we came to call him, was
transferred to Whiteman Air Force Base, home of the B-2
Stealth Bomber, eleven miles east of Warrensburg. He
sponsored our parents' immigration to Missouri and, several years later, before Victor and I were born, got them a
small business loan to open Asia Palace.

I started working at the restaurant when I was seven. I
folded menus and assembled takeout bags. I'd snap open
a paper bag, put a piece of cut-up cardboard on the
bottom, and insert the paper bag inside a plastic happy-
face bag—repeating this fifty times a batch. I worked the
counter and took phone orders and waited on tables. I
made rice and wrapped wontons. I peeled prawns and potatoes and washed dishes, using a foot stool to reach over
the sink. When I was ten, my dad started letting me fry
chicken wings. Oftentimes, the smells and the heat and
the aches from standing for so long made me wobble near
collapse.

Gradually my dad let me cook more. One Saturday
when I was fifteen, he had to be hospitalized with a burst

appendix, a rarity at his age, and the entire day I did the bulk of the cooking without a hitch, without recipes (since there were none), just going by what I'd watched. Thereafter, he made me his sous chef, and he also put me in charge of the Sunday dinners that we ate at home.

I became a devotee of cooking shows, competition shows, shows about chefs. I began following David Chang, Roy Choi, Danny Bowien, Eddie Huang, Kristen Kish, Ed Lee, Joanne Chang, Niki Nakayama, and Peter Serpico—Asian American chefs who were trying to redefine the notion of what Asian and American cuisine meant. But the chef who intrigued me most was Bosse Park, who had gone from Noma to Bouley to Lespinasse before opening BoYo and winning a James Beard Award for Rising Star Chef of the Year. Besides his culinary skills, his manner attracted me—his humility, his introversion.

People routinely referred to his restaurant as an izakaya, but Bo thought of it as an atelier—a workshop, a place to experiment. Yes, he admitted in interviews, his childhood years in Tokyo had had a profound influence upon him, inspiring him to present Japanese flavors in a new way. Yet he made no claims to authenticity, not identifying, for example, his raw diver scallops as hotategai, or his broiled baby eggplant as nasu dengaku, or his steamed egg custard as chawanmushi. He didn't want to be limited by labels. He was a Korean man cooking nominally Japanese food in America with French techniques and Scandinavian sensibilities. He knew it'd be impossible to satisfy all the expectations of what he should produce and how, and he wasn't interested in trying. He just wanted to be true to himself. He didn't care about trying to reconcile his disparate parts (he despised the term fusion). He could live with his contradictions. They were, he said, what made him whole. I loved this about him—his refusal to be codified.

I yearned for that type of freedom in Warrensburg. As a child, I'd always been mortified when classmates came to the restaurant, which was dingy and sad, no decor save for the golden fortune cat in the corner with its waving paw. At school, I was told I had a stinky smell. Kids would sing a rhyme, "Chinese, Japanese, dirty knees, look at these," and pull their eyes slanty. They'd call the restaurant and mimic an Asian accent and say, "Can I order dog?"

Then, beginning when I was fifteen, sixteen, something new started happening. Besides having to deal with drunk college kids, stoners, and tweakers at the counter, I had to contend with older men, white men. They would ask me out on dates. They would ask me if massages were available. They would ask me if I liked big men.

I first met Cory Ellis, though, not at Asia Palace, but at a barbecue at Uncle Mike's house. Cory was a ground crew specialist at the airfield, and he and Uncle Mike belonged to a mentoring group for enlisted airmen at Whiteman. I was seventeen at the time, he was twenty-three.

We small-talked for almost an hour. He was funny, kind of a wiseass, very good-looking. I reveled in the attention. I had been miserable and bored in high school. I had no friends. I'd hooked up with a classmate once and thought he'd be my boyfriend, but he told people I was a chink ho and joked I had a sideways coin slot for a vagina.

"So," Cory said, "what do you do at Asia Palace?"

"Everything. I cook. I clean. I work the counter. Sometimes I give rubdowns with happy endings."

He canted his head, calibrating what I might be doing. I smiled, and then he smiled.

"I might have to stop by, then," he said.

He lived off-base in Knob Noster, but he started making the drive to Warrensburg once or twice a week to the restaurant, becoming a regular and one of our few eat-in customers. He usually ordered the #55 Pepper Steak with Onion and the #80 Bean Curd Home Style, as well as another set of dishes to go: the #4 Boneless Spare Ribs, the #46 Shrimp with Lobster Sauce, and the #26 Vegetable Chow Mein—a couple of dinners to heat up in the microwave on ensuing nights, he said.

If I wasn't working front of the house, he'd peek into the kitchen door and say, "Hi, Mrs. Chung. Hi, Mr. Chung. Hey, Penelope. How are you all?" After a month of this, I wrote down my phone number on his credit card receipt, and, following some prolonged sessions of late-night texts, we met at a Super 8 motel in Sweet Springs, more than twenty-five miles away, where we were fairly certain no one we knew would see us.

The final night, instead of cleaning after we closed, we had a party. My brother and I got our dad a little drunk, then Victor booted up a karaoke app on his phone and connected it to a speaker, and my parents, who were members of the church choir and had nice voices, did duets of some of their favorite songs: "Living on a Prayer," "I Wanna Dance with Somebody," "Total Eclipse of the Heart." As I watched them sing, it occurred to me that they must have been around Victor's and my age when the songs were originally released—before they'd gotten married, before they'd decided to move to America, before they'd committed to opening a business together.

"You ever wish you'd never come here?" I asked my dad.

We were standing outside the restaurant, watching cars percuss past us on 50 Highway. I'd seen him go out, light a cigarette, and I'd joined him. I hadn't known he'd started smoking again.

"You can never know about life," he told me. "You can never guess what if."

This was the most I'd ever heard him wax philosophical. I had thought he'd just grunt and that would be the end of the conversation. I supposed that, even for him, the occasion gave rise to reflection.

"Are you and Mom going to be okay?" I asked.

"Yes," he said.

As it would turn out, the next few years wouldn't be easy for them. They would work at the Dollar Tree distribution center and the Frito-Lay warehouse, and then my mother would be an egg packer at Rose Acre Farms and my father would be a machine operator at Stald Aluminum, until they finally made up with Uncle Mike and he was able to get them jobs—good jobs with good benefits—at the deli bakery on Whiteman, where they would finish out their working lives.

"Victor, though, I worry about," my dad told me. "He bought a shotgun, you know."

"What?"

"It's under the counter. All year he doesn't go anywhere. He doesn't go to Walmart. He doesn't go to Bi-Lo. He just stays home. He doesn't say anything, but he's scared."

I had been scared, too. As a woman, particularly an Asian woman, I always had my guard up when I walked alone on the street, especially at night, prepared to be harassed or attacked. But this had been different. Beginning in March, I had not felt safe anywhere in public, in a constant state of anxiety, vague unease sometimes oscillating to terror. By the end of the summer, however, the feeling had started to dissipate, and I was surprised my brother was still so wary. (I didn't foresee that the hate would persist and escalate.)

Victor would be all right. He'd get a job at the T-Mobile store in Warrensburg, then after seven months would abruptly leave for Albany Park, where he'd help my aunt run her shoe store, and then they'd both move to Niles, the newer K-town northwest of Chicago, and eventually he'd manage a very successful high-end Korean sauna. He'd also get married and have a daughter.

"Don't you worry about me?" I asked my dad.

"No," he said. "The way you flip the pan, your knife skills, they're amazing. You're already a very good cook, and I think you'll become even better."

"I've missed being in a kitchen."

"Maybe soon you'll be able to go back to your restaurant."

"I have my doubts."

In October, though, Bo would reconfigure BoYo into a virtual kitchen with an entirely new menu—his take on Korean comfort food dishes like bibimbap, bulgogi sliders, shrimp pancakes, kimchi fried rice, and fried chicken wings. He'd call the venture BoYoGo, and it'd be takeout and delivery only. He'd hire me back then, and in time we'd return to in-restaurant dining with a full staff.

"I would say sorry I can't leave Asia Palace to you," my dad said, "but I know you never want it."

"A nice thought, though," I said.

And maybe here my dad and I might have hugged, but of course we didn't. He did, however, grunt audibly.

Cory was married. He confessed this to me in the motel, before anything happened. That was why he always ordered the three additional dishes to go from Asia Palace. When he got home, he would pretend he hadn't eaten dinner already at the restaurant, had only gone there for takeout, and he would share the second meal with his wife. I don't think I would have flirted with him if I'd known, I wouldn't have ended up sitting on the bed with him in the Super 8. Yet I went ahead with it. I thought it'd be a one-night stand. I didn't think we'd see each other for more than a year, and that I'd fall in love with him.

Before I left Philly to come back to Warrensburg, I had tried to reach him. I texted and then emailed, asking to meet, telling him that there were some things I thought I should say to him. He never responded.

I assumed he was still at Whiteman. I drove out to his house in Knob Noster, but, watching from down the block, discovered another family was living there. I didn't know how to find his current whereabouts. I couldn't exactly ask Uncle Mike or my parents, and Victor wouldn't have known. It turned out to be very easy. I signed up for one of those background-check websites for a five-day free trial. He was now working as a ramp agent for Southwest Airlines at Lambert Airport in St. Louis. His wife, or presumably his ex-wife, was now a nurse's aide in Seattle.

I texted him again: *I know you're in STL. I'd like to come talk. Ok?*

The next day, he replied, *Ok.*

I went to St. Louis on Sunday, when my parents would be going to church service and brunch. I got there just before the appointed time, one thirty, parking in front of his apartment, which was on Jefferson Avenue in a neighborhood called McKinley Heights. He lived on the second floor of a brick building that housed a barbershop and a Nicaraguan restaurant. I waited. He had said he'd be coming off the early morning shift and he'd meet me outside, but he was more than an hour late, and I thought he'd changed his mind. Finally, though, he rolled up in his truck and opened the door and slid out. He was wearing a pair of wraparound sunglasses, hiking boots, a grimy gray T-shirt, and black cargo shorts that came down past his knees. He was deeply tanned, but otherwise looked the same, down to his hair, still a military butch cut with a fade.

"I thought you were standing me up," I said.

"Overtime."

I had hoped we could go somewhere for coffee, maybe sit in a park, or he'd invite me into his apartment so we could talk privately and civilly, but apparently that was not going to happen. He stayed where he was, leaning against his truck. It appeared we were going to do this on the sidewalk.

"What do you want?" he asked.

"I want to say I'm sorry," I told him. "I don't know why I did what I did. I think about it almost every day."

"Here's something you might not be contemplating. No one gives a shit. It doesn't change anything, it doesn't change what you did."

In April of my senior year, Cory had broken it off with me. He stopped coming to Asia Palace, but one day, I saw a takeout order for the #4 Boneless Spare Ribs, the #46 Shrimp with Lobster Sauce, and the #26 Vegetable Chow Mein. The ticket said "Amanda" would be picking up the order. Cory's wife. I'd met her once—just before Cory dumped me. Uncle Mike had gotten her to join the church that spring, although Cory steadfastly refused to go. I never went, either, except on Christmas and Easter, which was when I was introduced to her, during the egg hunt. "You know, your English is really excellent," she had said to me. "You don't sound Asian at all!"

I slipped a note to Amanda inside her takeout bag. I made sure she would see it, writing in big letters with a Sharpie on a cut-up piece of cardboard (on both sides), *Your husband is a cheater,* putting the note on top of the food. What I hadn't expected was that, rather than confronting Cory, she'd drive right back to the restaurant and make a scene. "Who wrote this? Who's Cory seeing? You? Tell me!" And then it'd all come out, in front of my parents and Victor, and everyone at the church would hear about it, and somehow they'd decide that I was the transgressor, that I'd ruined this promising young couple's lives, and there'd be a rift between my parents and Uncle Mike, who'd thought of Cory as a son, that wouldn't be repaired for years.

"You have a right to be angry," I told Cory on the sidewalk. He'd quit the Air Force. He'd loved the Air Force, guiding B-2 Spirits loaded with bombs on the tarmac with his orange wands, saluting safe flight to the pilots.

"Do I?" he responded. "You'll allow me that? You'd give me that right?"

"I didn't mean it like that."

He pushed himself off his truck. "Don't text me again." He began to walk toward his apartment door.

"You weren't completely innocent, you know."

He laughed. "Oh, I see, you weren't really looking for forgiveness. You're looking to offload some blame."

He was, admittedly, on to something. I had convinced myself that I'd wanted to see him to apologize, but I now recognized that hadn't really been my objective. "Was it because I was underage, or Asian, or both?" I asked him.

"You always have to make everything about race, don't you?"

A woman passed us on the sidewalk and gave Cory a wide berth.

"You weren't underage," he told me.

Legally, this was true. The age of consent was seventeen in Missouri. Yet why was I the one who'd mostly been held at fault? How the fuck had that happened? Because I'd made the first overture? Because I hadn't been able to keep my mouth shut? Would it have been different if I hadn't been Asian—*dirty knees, such a tease, what's your fee*—and had been blond, freckled, and Christian, like Amanda? I had been a kid. A stupid, immature, lonely kid who hadn't known a thing about the world, much less about love. No one had forced Cory to go to Asia Palace, no one had made him book a room at the Super 8.

"Maybe technically you weren't a pedophile," I said to Cory, "but for sure you were a creep."

"We're done here," he said.

It was a week of hell. We had to empty the fryers of oil,

disassemble the griddle and stove, and degrease and scrub every surface in the kitchen, including the range hood, walls, ceiling, floor, and walk-in. Then we had to return the leased equipment and try to sell the equipment we owned. In the end, we hired an auctioneer to do a complete liquidation, relinquishing everything from the flattop with the refrigerated base, the ice machine, and the three-bay sink, to the hotel pans, colanders, knives, spatulas, rice cookers, and mop bucket, all for pennies on the dollar. We donated dry goods, like rice and cornstarch and white pepper, and sealed containers of condiments, like soy sauce and oyster sauce and chili oil, to a food rescue. But there was a lot of stuff no one wanted, even for free, not even other Chinese restaurants in the area, who said they already had a surplus: takeout boxes with wire handles, disposable chopsticks, egg roll glassine bags, thousands of packets of duck sauce and fortune cookies. We put them in the dumpster, along with the building signs. Finally the owner came by for the exit viewing. After doing a walk-through, he promised to return the security deposit within twenty-one days and took the keys.

We headed home and showered and napped. I checked in for my flight back to Philly the next morning, and then went into the kitchen. I'd volunteered to make dinner, and my mother insisted on helping me, despite my protests. She was not well. Her legs, covered with varicose veins, were always hurting. She constantly wore knee-high compression socks. I had her sit on a stool, and she trimmed some green beans for me.

I was making a duck and prawn paella, with sides of fried pimientos and a salad. At BoYo, we had taken turns cooking what were called family meals—dinners for the entire restaurant staff that we'd eat communally before the doors opened. Nothing really fancy, but it had to be good. Most of my early meals—hanger steak with béarnaise sauce, tandoori chicken, pollock with capers and brown butter—were duly appreciated, but the real hits had been some of the more adventurous Chinese dishes I used to suggest to my dad: Sichuan pepper quail, Cantonese crispy pork belly, clay-pot tofu and oysters.

That wouldn't have flown in the Chung household. We'd had an unspoken agreement. When we were at Asia Palace, we never had proper meals; we'd simply pick extras off dishes made for orders. On off-nights, the last thing we wanted to eat was Chinese food, or really any kind of Asian food. So for our Sunday dinners, I'd made a lot of Italian and Mexican and Indian and sometimes straight American food, pot roast with mashed potatoes becoming a family favorite.

I cubed duck breasts, then chopped artichoke hearts. As I was roasting red peppers, holding them with tongs over the burner, I realized my mom was crying.

"Oh, Mom," I said.

"It's fine. I'll be fine," she said, continuing to dice a tomato.

"You should let yourself grieve," I told her. "A restaurant has a body and soul. It's like losing a child."

Not looking up from the cutting board, she said, "When you went to Philadelphia, I thought I lost you forever, Penny."

"I embarrassed you," I said. "I made you ashamed."

"No. Only for a short time."

"Am I a selfish person? Do you think I'm a bad person?"

At last she looked at me. "You're a good person, Penny."

"If I hadn't left, maybe the restaurant would have survived."

"I don't think so."

She took the rice I had portioned out in a big bowl and walked over to the sink and began to wash and rinse it—de rigueur when making most types of rice, except when it came to bomba rice for paella, which needed to retain its outer coating of starch. I didn't have the heart to tell her.

"I'm sorry for all those years I was such a brat," I said to her. "I resented you and Dad. I didn't know. I had no clue."

She kept washing and rinsing the rice.

"Maybe I should stay," I said. "Maybe I should cancel my flight."

"Why?"

"To take care of you."

The water was finally running clear off the rice, and she gave me the bowl. "There's nothing for you here. Go live your life."

Even when BoYo resumed full operation, BoYoGo wouldn't be dismantled. It'd be too successful. Bo would set up a separate ghost kitchen at another location for the delivery service, and then he would decide to open a new fine-dining restaurant with Korean-influenced dishes called BoYoKo, and he'd make me its chef de cuisine. I look back at that period and marvel at my energy and passion, my ambition. It wouldn't last forever. Eventually, the grind would get to me, and I'd quit the restaurant business and become a food writer.

I fried the duck until it was browned, then added the vegetables with some garlic until they were tender. I poured in chicken stock and let it bubble for half an hour. Then I stirred in the rice and saffron, brought it to a boil, and simmered it, undisturbed, for twenty minutes. I tasted the rice. Even rinsed, it wasn't awful. I scattered prawns and peas on top of the rice, covered the skillet, and allowed them to steam. After five minutes, I turned off the heat, flipped the prawns, draped a kitchen towel over the skillet, and let it rest.

I brought everything out to the dining table. My dad and mom bowed their heads for a silent prayer, and then I handed out serving spoons to my parents and brother. "Jal meoggo," I said to them. It was one of few Korean phrases I knew. Eat well.

THE PARTITION

· · · · · · · · · ·

MAINLY, SHE WANTED TO BE LEFT ALONE. She didn't want a husband or a wife or a partner or a lover, she didn't want a companion or a pet or friends, she didn't want to be closer to her parents or siblings or relatives. She enjoyed her solitude, relished it. She had plenty to occupy herself—her work, her house and garden, her hobbies. She was not at all lonely. She was thoroughly happy, being alone.

This perplexed people. It seemed, even, to offend some people. They thought she had to be lying, dissembling some sort of psychological problem or prior trauma. They couldn't abide that anyone would actually choose to be alone.

There were many things about her that threw people off. First was her ethnicity, which people frequently believed was synonymous with race. Was she Chinese? Japanese? (She was Korean.) Subsequent was her nationality. Was she a North Korean or South Korean citizen, then? Or an immigrant? Did she have a green card? (She was a naturalized US citizen.) Then there was the question of her name, Ingrid Kissler. Was this an Americanization of her Korean name, something she had made up? Or had she once been married? (She'd been adopted by a white couple from Chanhassen, Minnesota, at the age of two, from an orphanage in Seoul.)

Most confounding to people was her sexual orientation and gender identity. They rarely asked Ingrid about such things directly, but everyone wondered: Was she gay? Bi? Trans? Nonbinary? Her appearance baffled them. She could have been pretty in a conventional way if she wanted, but it was obviously something she did not want. She wore no makeup or nail polish or jewelry, and she kept her hair short, styled—or antistyled—in a nondescript shaggy bowl cut that looked self-inflicted. She donned the same outfit every day: Dickies industrial shirts and pants and Vans skateboarding shoes, varying only the colors of the matching sets of work wear: navy blue, charcoal gray, or black. She was small, five four, and slight, only a hundred and five pounds. She didn't have any real curves, just the slightest widening of the hips when viewed from certain angles, and she was so flat-chested, people sometimes assumed she was chest-binding. Her features were delicate, her skin pearly. She looked very much like a prepubescent twelve-year-old boy.

Five years ago, in 2010, when Ingrid began teaching at Libbey College in Ojai, California, she had been the subject of much curiosity, speculation, and gossip. For a change, however, the attention hadn't been ferried by an undercurrent of intolerance. Quite the opposite. Everyone at Libbey was extravagantly politically correct, and they would have welcomed whatever designation she might have elected. The last thing anyone wanted to do was intrude upon her privacy, yet her colleagues, students, and administrators really needed to know how to *refer* to Ingrid: they, them, theirs? ze, hir/zir, hirs/zirs? Everyone was petrified they might make a mistake and insult her. The hesitations and stuttering got to such an awkward point, she started amending her email signature with *Pronouns: she/her/hers*—at the time, not a common practice.

For years, Ingrid had found people's continual need to *classify* her—label her with a clear, fixable identity—frustrating and exasperating. Indeed, it had often enraged her, epitomizing the racism and heteropatriarchy she had faced her entire life. The irony was that she wasn't trying to make a political statement with her androgynous appearance. Nor was she trying to be hip, though that was how she began to be regarded. Sometime in her midtwenties, she had simply stopped caring what she looked like. The work wear was practical and inexpensive—she didn't have to think about how to costume herself every morning. Her skin was good enough to go without makeup. Barbershops were five times cheaper than salons, and took a fifth of the time. She supposed that, technically, she was gender nonconforming or gender expansive, but she didn't utilize any of those terms for herself.

Her sexual orientation was a fuzzier matter. She had dated both men and women, but had been celibate for quite a while now. Yet she didn't think of herself as ace, asexual. She still had lots of sex—by herself. She just preferred not being in a relationship, not having to negotiate and compromise when it came to every decision, not having to placate and apologize and cajole when feelings were the slightest bit grazed, not having to bear with anyone else's mess or occupation of her space when all she wanted to do was unwind in roomy, solitary silence.

In Ojai, with her job at Libbey College, she had found
a place and means to do just that. The town was in Ventura
County, in a lush valley surrounded by mountains and rolling hills. Everything about it suggested rustic charm, the
pace unhurried, tranquil, the vibe artsy and eco-conscious.
It had a quaint main street lined with galleries, boutiques,
and restaurants, without a single chain store in sight (prohibited within city limits). The valley was studded with organic farms, citrus and olive groves, and vineyards. Flowers
were omnipresent, and the faint scent of sage and lavender
wafted around every corner. Occasionally, the conditions
at sunset were just right to produce the Pink Moment—
the sky and walls of the Topatopa Mountains flaming up in
a dusky-rose hue for a few glorious minutes.

There were only eight thousand residents in Ojai, a
mixture of hippies, boho-chic designers, entrepreneurs, re-
tirees, and, recently, a handful of celebrities. For decades,
the town had also been a destination for spiritual seek-
ers and wellness devotees looking to get blissed out on
the supposed electromagnetic vortex in the area, a force
field generated by plate tectonics, which had positioned
the valley to run east-to-west rather than north-to-south.
A number of high-end spas had sprouted up to accommo-
date tourists, offering amenities such as detox body wraps,
chakra cleanses, and energy readings for dogs.

There was something magical about this place, everyone said. A sacred spot with amazing healing powers.

When Ingrid first arrived in Ojai, she had thought all
this talk was hooey. Almost immediately, though, she fell in
love with the valley, with its beauty and temperate Med-
iterranean climate. The town was on the doorstep to Los

Padres National Forest and a mere twenty-five minutes from the Pacific Ocean. She could indulge in all manner of solo sports: hiking, biking, running, kayaking, stand-up paddleboarding. Maybe the place was a bit too New Agey for her taste, and maybe it was getting a bit too trendy, but after all the backwaters and hicksvilles and shit towns she'd had to live in, Ojai felt like a little utopia to her—idyllic, calming, luminous in its own secluded world.

Libbey College was just as inviting. Ingrid had found her niche teaching at the liberal arts school, which was tiny, barely fourteen hundred students. Her appointment was in the Department of Asian Studies, but she also taught courses in Comparative Literature, Cultural Criticism, and Women's, Gender, and Sexuality Studies. She felt grateful to be there, particularly after several torpid years as an itinerant visiting assistant professor, or VAP, at a succession of crap universities in rural Missouri, Pennsylvania, and Louisiana, teaching required general education courses to redneck dunderheads. Once, a student who had been sitting in the back of Ingrid's class told her that when she'd asked everyone to look at their assigned handouts, nearly all the students had propped up random sheets of paper, pretending to study them. The students at Libbey could not have been more different. They were fully occupied by their studies, *into* them. They did all their assignments and then some, looking up secondary and tertiary sources without prompting. They actually went to see their professors during office hours. They wrote beautiful papers that were—rather than a chore—a delight to grade. Ingrid loved the students at Libbey, loved everything about teaching there.

Most everyone was happy at the college, in no small part because it had money. An oil baron had begun making large donations to the school in the 1920s, and its endowment had grown to over a billion dollars, making it one of the richest small colleges in the country. Consequently, Ingrid was being paid ridiculously well as an assistant professor. She had, in addition, a research fund, a travel fund, and a conference fund. Furthermore, there was a unique home purchase assistance program for tenure-track faculty: after three years of service, they could get a loan of up to $75,000 to help them buy a house in Ojai—where the prices, like everywhere else in California, were astronomical—and, upon receiving tenure, the loan would be forgiven in its *entirety.*

Such largesse was a lifesaver for Ingrid, who had been buried in credit-card debt and student loans. Her credit score had been abominable, but slowly she'd become more solvent, until finally last year she had been able to purchase a house in Ojai for $423,000—previously an unimaginable amount. Even at that price, the two-bedroom bungalow was a fixer-upper, in sore need of updating, yet it had vaulted ceilings, a wood-burning fireplace, and a wall of glass windows that faced a profusion of trees: coast live oaks, black walnut, and Western sycamores. On the side of the house was a yard with enough room and sun for an organic vegetable garden.

She had at last found somewhere she could call home. She wanted to stay in this house in this town teaching at this college forever, and it was now all within reach. Three months ago, at the start of the fall semester, she had submitted her tenure application, and it had won the enthusiastic approval of her department chairs, her colleagues, and the Reappointment, Promotions, and Tenure Committee. All that was left was the provost's endorsement, and Ingrid had been told it was a sure thing. Already, she was thinking about what she might do once her tenure became official: buy a new stove, get her bathtub reglazed, perhaps order a Pinarello road bike.

But then, in mid-December, just after finals week, Darlene Li, the chair of the Department of Asian Studies, called Ingrid and said, "Can you come in? There's a problem."

The provost, Rich Parnell, was all of a sudden uncertain he could recommend Ingrid for tenure.

"I don't understand," she said to Darlene and Rich in his office.

She had done everything right. Her students adored her. Each year she'd been at Libbey, she had received a certificate of teaching excellence for having among the highest ratings, college-wide, in her class evaluations. She had gone to every meeting for her department and every session of the faculty senate and every reception, party, convocation, and graduation, and had served on the Affirmative Action, Policy and Governance, and Resources and Planning committees. She had had two essays published in journals, and presented papers at three Asian Studies conferences. For her major research project, she had translated a novel, *The Partition,* by a South Korean writer named Yoo Sun-mi, into English, and it had been released by a university press this past August. It'd received little notice from the media or in academia, just one (very positive) review in *World Literature Today,* and had sold only about a hundred and fifty copies thus far, almost all to libraries, but none of this was uncommon or shameful for an academic book. The point was, *The Partition* had been peer-reviewed and published by a reputable press. Perhaps at a top university, a translation might not have had as much cachet as a scholarly monograph, but at Libbey, where the demands for research were less rigorous, teaching taking precedence, it more than sufficed. And all the external reviewers who had evaluated Ingrid's dossier, she'd heard, had been effusive in their praise.

Except for one, Darlene and Rich now told her.

"He just sent his letter in—two months past the deadline," Darlene said. "It was a complete surprise. We'd assumed he wasn't going to respond. He hadn't answered any of our emails since initially saying he'd do it."

They were sitting around a conference table beside a window with a view of the main quad. Rich was wearing, per usual, a pressed button-down blue shirt and blue jeans. He was physically very imposing—tall, muscular, a former Ivy League crew member—and the jeans were an attempt to appear more approachable, less of a snob.

"Who is this reviewer?" Ingrid asked. "What'd he say in his letter?"

Per procedural rules, his name had to remain confidential, Rich said, but he was a professor of literature and linguistics at a major university in Seoul, and a translator himself. The professor had done a quantitative analysis of Ingrid's translation of *The Partition,* and had discovered gross errors in the book. It was clear, he said in his letter, that Ingrid's Korean was inadequate to the task. She had mixed up simple words, confusing, for example, "arm" for "foot." She had misinterpreted idioms and colloquialisms, substituting, for example, the phrase for "the kid who works part-time" with "the babysitter." She had misidentified the subjects of sentences, attributing, for example, actions or dialogue to the wrong characters.

Only about 37 percent of her translation of the original was accurate, the professor said. There were 18.3 percent of straightforward mistranslations, and 6.1 percent had been omitted. Egregious as these blunders were, far more troubling was the remaining 38.6 percent, which included infidelities so extreme, they were tantamount to wholesale fabrications. This wasn't, he said, simply a matter of embellishing lines with adjectives and adverbs, slipping in rogue clauses, or changing the syntax, all of which Ingrid had done. Taken together, these distortions had altered the *style* of the novel. Whereas the original lines were understated and deliberately plain, Ingrid's sentences were baroque in comparison, bloated with lyrical flourishes and metaphors, which was particularly outrageous because the novel was in first-person. As a result, the *voice* of the narrator was entirely different. It was akin to transforming Hemingway into Proust. Evidently Ingrid had been so challenged by the Korean in *The Partition,* she had resorted to blindly making things up and throwing them into the book. Her translation, the professor concluded, was flagrantly and staggeringly incompetent. In all his years in the field, he had never seen such a horrific miscarriage of translation.

Rich and Darlene waited for a response from Ingrid, who was, of course, mortified by the accusations. She knew that a single lukewarm review letter, never mind such a harshly negative one, could sink her tenure application.

"Well," she said after a moment, "this sort of quantitative approach to analyzing a translation—to be frank, it's a little preposterous. It's impossible to translate a text literally from one language to another, especially a novel, a creative work of art. Pure transliteration would make it gibberish, unreadable. These numbers and percentiles, they're not relevant metrics."

"The mistakes he cites, though," Rich said, "the confusion over simple words and phrases—could he be right? 18.3 percent of those kinds of mistakes? That seems like a remarkably high number of obvious errors."

"I doubt very much I committed that many."

"You're not a native speaker?" Rich said. "I thought you were."

"No, I only started learning Korean when I was twenty-two," she admitted. After graduating from Purdue with her bachelor's degree, she had taken an intensive summer class in Korean, then had gone to Seoul through the Fulbright's English Teaching Assistantship program, working as a teacher's aide at Daebang Elementary School and staying with a Korean family for a year. Thereafter, throughout her studies for her master's at Johns Hopkins and her PhD at the University of Minnesota, she'd enrolled in Korean classes.

"The peer-review process at the press—did the reviewers know Korean?"

"I don't know. I don't think so."

"But they gushed over the translation," Darlene said. "So did all the other external reviewers." She read from notes on a legal pad. "'Mesmerizing and darkly funny,' 'astonishing,' 'daring,' 'a work of sheer artistry.' That review in *World Literature Today:* 'This is an enthralling novel, nihilistic yet spellbinding, hypnotically strange yet thoroughly compelling.'"

"Yes," Rich said, "but none of those evaluators were able to read the novel in the original Korean and compare it to the English version, were they? That's the central issue here—the fidelity of the translation."

"Actually," Ingrid said, "many translators believe that in order to recreate the experience or essence of the source text, technical fidelity needs to be sacrificed, that it's often the *in*fidelities, rather than the fidelities, that contribute most to a successful translation."

Rich looked at her blankly.

"There are so many subtle things that go into translating a novel," she continued. "The implicit meanings between the lines, the socioeconomic implication of certain kinds of diction, the need to relate cultural contexts to a foreign audience. Translation has always been, by necessity, a *creative* art. Ultimately there can be no such thing as a definitive translation of any work. It's not something that can be done, or measured, empirically."

Judging by his dour expression, Rich didn't seem the least bit swayed, perhaps now was more ill-disposed toward her. He was an economist by training, Ingrid recalled—a bean counter. He only understood numbers and percentiles.

"Did the Korean publisher vet your translation?"

"I don't think they even asked to see it. Apparently they don't speak English very well." The original edition of *The Partition* had been issued in 2004, eleven years ago, by a small indie press in Paju, a husband-and-wife team. The novel had flopped in Korea, getting horrible reviews, which had called the book (and author) bleak, perverse, morbid, and amoral. *The Partition* was about a woman in her midthirties who works in a convenience store and lives with her husband and in-laws. One night, she kills her husband, mother-in-law, and father-in-law by lacing their dinners with arsenic. She then buys a circular saw and chops up their bodies and keeps the parts in a freezer that she conceals behind an embroidered silk-screen partition. Thereafter, she begins inviting homeless men and women to the house and cooks them lavish meals made with her husband and in-laws' body parts before having group BDSM with her guests.

Ingrid had happened upon a copy of *The Partition* in a used bookstore while in Korea and had kept the novel for years, move after move—one of the few good things to come out of her time in Seoul. It hadn't been a great book, but it'd fascinated Ingrid because it was surreal, anarchic, and from the point of view of a woman—so different from most of the Korean literature she'd read, which had been very traditional and male-oriented. Once at Libbey, Ingrid had translated twenty-five pages of the novel and had sent a proposal to Aquinas University Press in Colorado. An editor there, Deborah Smythe, had responded positively and contacted the husband-and-wife publisher, who gave the English translation rights for the book to the press for a pittance, not thinking they were worth anything.

"Didn't the author or her agent have to approve the translation?" Rich asked.

"The agent didn't seem to care. Too small-fry, I guess."

"What about the author? Did she read it?" Rich said. "It'd be helpful if *someone* over there could affirm this translation."

"She's a recluse," Ingrid told him. "The agent said she doesn't know English and she wouldn't want to be bothered with it, regardless. She has a reputation for being very eccentric and difficult to work with."

Since *The Partition,* which had been Yoo Sun-mi's second novel (and the only book of hers to be translated abroad), she had gone on to publish three more books with three more indie presses in Korea. None of them did very well. She'd never risen to any sort of stardom. She had, at best, an underground cult following, yet her fans seemed to be more interested in her hermitic lifestyle than her writing. She never did any interviews or appearances. Her background—where she grew up, what her parents did— was a mystery. No one knew where she currently lived in Korea or, really, what she looked like. The only photograph of her was a blurry silhouette on her first novel. There were rumors that Yoo Sun-mi was a pseudonym, and that she might in fact be a man.

"I'm sorry," Rich said to Ingrid. "I don't see how I can support your application, then."

"Because of one letter from a random professor in Korea?"

"He's translated Hemingway into Korean. Bellow and Roth as well."

All misogynists, Ingrid fumed, as was, apparently, this Korean professor. The provost as well.

Being denied tenure at a college or university was equivalent to being fired. They'd give her a contract for one more terminal year of teaching, and then she'd have to leave Libbey. Since her home assistance loan wouldn't be forgiven, she'd have to forfeit her house. She'd have to move somewhere else and begin anew, only it would be extremely difficult to begin anew since anyone looking at her CV would see that she'd been passed over for tenure at Libbey, which would likely preclude her from getting another tenure-track job.

"You'll have until the end of March if you wish to appeal," Rich told her. "Whatever the case, Ingrid, I think it'd be prudent to start making contingency plans."

She would have to go back to being a VAP, or maybe worse—work as an adjunct instructor teaching ESL or comp at a community college, on a semester-to-semester contract, with no benefits. She couldn't imagine anything more humiliating. For all intents and purposes, her academic career was over.

Three months later, in early March, she woke up in the wee hours of the morning and drove from Ojai to Santa Barbara to catch a six a.m. flight to Phoenix, then took another flight to El Paso, where she rented a car and drove two hours east on I-10 and then another hour southeast down an empty two-lane highway past vast ranchlands mixed with creosote flats, yucca, and cholla, before finally—after twelve total hours—arriving in Colima, Texas, a godforsaken hicksville town with just eighteen hundred residents in the middle of nowhere in the high desert, where she was supposed to meet, of all people, Yoo Sun-mi.

All winter, Ingrid had assumed everything was lost for her at Libbey. She hadn't even planned to file an appeal at first, thinking it pointless, and only agreed to do so at the urging of her colleagues and students, who were outraged that the provost had blocked her tenure application. He'd ambushed her, they said. He had been plotting all along to undermine her, because he was uncomfortable with her gender expression and sexual orientation—maybe her race and national origin, too. To them, it was a clear case of discrimination. They told her if her appeal failed, she should file a complaint with the EEOC.

Her students created a change.org petition addressed to Libbey's board of trustees, and her colleagues composed a letter to the president, demanding a fair and equitable appeals process for Ingrid. Darlene solicited additional evaluations from two Asian American professors in Translation Studies for her, and Ingrid began to draft a disquisition on translation theory. Citing scholars such as Even-Zohar, Toury, Bassnett, Snell-Hornby, Lefevere, et al., she discussed the issues of equivalence, fidelity, domestication and foreignization, and functionality, and tried to present the argument that translations of literature should not be slavish reproductions of the source text; rather, that shifts could and should be imposed based on the translated text's cultural specifications.

Still, she felt that none of these efforts would ultimately have any effect. The provost had not violated any procedures or infringed on her academic freedom, and he had plenary authority to award or deny tenure for whatever reason he saw fit. And—although she shared this with no one—deep down Ingrid knew that her translation of *The Partition* was flawed.

She had wanted to be a writer in her youth. She'd majored in Creative Writing at Purdue and was accepted into the graduate writing program at Hopkins. Yet her gap year in Seoul changed her. Once in Baltimore, she couldn't produce any new fiction. For workshops, she simply re-hashed old short stories, some of which she'd written in high school. She realized she was a fraud. She had talent at the sentence level, but was bereft of an imagination. She quit, waitressed for a while, then transferred to the PhD program in Comparative Literature in Minnesota.

Years later, she began thinking about doing a liter-ary translation, mainly because she was running across so many bad translations in her scholarship, especially of novels by Asian authors. The problem with translation, she thought, was that, in general, translators were not trained as creative writers. The majority were academics, and their translations were filled with clichés, wooden dialogue, and clunky syntax, the prose absent of any music. She thought she had the literary chops to become a superior translator, and embarked on *The Partition* as her first project. She dis-covered that translating the novel allowed her to tap into a part of herself she had been heretofore unable to access—a connection to Korea, to inspiration, to those ontological questions she'd always been asking: Who am I? Why am I here? But all along, she knew her aptitude in Korean was probably insufficient to convey the book properly. Thus, she wasn't feeling particularly passionate about her appeal.

Then she received a call from Deborah Smythe, her editor at Aquinas University Press. Word about the ten-ure debacle must have somehow gotten to Aquinas, and Ingrid assumed Deborah was now going to tell her that they would be pulling *The Partition* from distribution and disavowing its publication. But no. Deborah said Yoo Sun-mi's literary agent, Kim Gu-yong, urgently needed to talk to her.

Why? Ingrid wondered. They'd gotten wind of her translation's so-called infidelities all the way over in Korea?

She calculated the time difference between Ojai and Seoul and called the literary agent at nine p.m. California time, two p.m. Seoul time.

"Please call me Joseph," the agent said in Korean. "I gave myself the nickname after my favorite author, Joseph Conrad. Do you enjoy Conrad's work?"

"Not particularly," she said.

"Oh!" He chuckled awkwardly. "I see. Yes, anyway, are you free next week? Yes? I hope so? Yoo Sun-mi wishes to see you."

"Where? In *Korea*?" Ingrid asked.

"United States."

"She's here?"

"She's temporarily in Texas. She received news about *The Partition* and wants to speak to you about it. Not on the phone. In person."

So they had heard of the controversy, after all.

"Your college calendar states that next week is your spring vacation," Joseph said. "Will you meet with Yoo Sun-mi?"

She could have refused, but for some reason she felt she had to go. She looked up how to get to Colima. The literary agent had suggested she arrange for a two-night stay. When she'd asked why—she thought she'd only need to be there for an hour at most, just enough time for Yoo Sun-mi to give her an earful—he had said, "Perhaps you would like to do a bit of sightseeing while you are there?" She ignored him. She found a cheap casita on Airbnb, reserved it for one night, and booked her flights accordingly.

Now, as she entered Colima, she saw that the casita was on an isolated street next to a defunct ice factory. No one was there to greet her. The key was in a lockbox. "Casita" was Spanish for "little house," and it was indeed little, a single square space that contained a bed, a couch, a café table with two chairs, and a kitchenette. The only other room was a bathroom the size of a closet. Everything was old and musty and depressingly dark.

Exhausted, she tried to take a nap on the double bed, which concaved underneath her weight, but she couldn't sleep, so she took a quick shower and got back in her rental car to tour the town. It didn't take long. Colima appeared to occupy less than two square miles, with hardly any trees or grass, just dirt and sand, and its main street was dotted with run-down or vacant storefronts. Nothing seemed open for business. No one was on the sidewalks, and there were only a few cars (mostly pickups) trundling through the central intersection, which had a four-way blinking light—the closest thing to a stoplight in the entire town. Spread out on the bisecting highway was a Dairy Queen, a supermarket called Pueblo, a gas station called Stripes, and a Dollar General, the parking lot for each virtually empty. The town's vacancy was made eerier by the weather—cloudy, with a strange fog walling off the outskirts. What in the world was Yoo Sun-mi doing in Colima, Texas?

The literary agent hadn't relayed Sun-mi's contact information ("She is extremely private," he'd told her), had only said Ingrid should meet her at the restaurant in the Hotel El Viejo for dinner at eight p.m. When Ingrid got there, she found the restaurant was closed. "Pretty much everything in town's closed on Mondays," the woman at the front desk of the hotel said. "Sundays, Tuesdays, Wednesdays, too, actually."

Ingrid waited for Sun-mi in the courtyard that led to the restaurant entrance, sitting at a wrought-iron patio table beside a flowing tiered fountain, but the temperature dropped precipitously and she became cold. She moved inside to the hotel lobby, which was decorated with leather chairs, a terra-cotta tile floor, and horned bison and bull heads mounted on the walls. She waited, and kept waiting, until nine. She phoned the literary agent in Seoul again.

"Oh! I will call Yoo Sun-mi right away and remind her," he said.

She never appeared. Ingrid finally left the hotel at ten. What was that all about? she thought as she got in her car. Did Sun-mi summon her all the way to Colima just to stand her up, as a way of humiliating her? Had this been a bizarre prank? Was she even in the country—much less in this town—at all?

Starving, Ingrid looked for someplace open where she could get something to eat. She had to settle for Stripes, the gas station, which had some hot food—almost all of it nonvegetarian, however. Fried chicken, hot dogs, hamburgers, pizzas, tacos, and enchiladas. She got an order of potato-and-egg tacos—two for two dollars—and some chips and a gallon jug of water and took it back to the casita. She ate the food at the café table and then went to bed and promptly fell into a deep sleep.

She was awoken by rapping on the door.

"Aigoo chamna, mianhamnida!" the woman in the doorway—could *this* really be Yoo Sun-mi, this pretty, chic woman?—said, apologizing, and launched into a story in rapid-fire Korean that Ingrid could barely follow about losing track of time and the spotty cell phone service in town and not getting her literary agent's voice mail about the missed dinner appointment until after the fact and a pool tournament in which she could not miss a shot and the deceptive influence of Mexican candy.

"Gwenchana, gwenchana. Mannaseo bangapseumnida," Ingrid told her groggily, bowing, saying it was all right, it was an honor to meet her.

Sun-mi walked past her into the casita and chattered on in Korean about how hungry Ingrid must be after such a long trip and she wished she could take her out for these delicious cheeseburgers she'd discovered and she was sorry Ingrid had to stay in such sad accommodations; and Ingrid, realizing Sun-mi had been drinking, said not to worry, she had eaten some tacos and anyway she was a vegetarian and the casita was perfectly adequate and what time was it, by the way; and Sun-mi said only a little past midnight, why didn't Ingrid get dressed and they could at least go out for a nightcap; and Ingrid asked if anything was still open, especially since it was a Monday, and said in any event she didn't mean to be rude, but she was very, very tired, couldn't they meet for breakfast instead, her flight wouldn't be leaving from El Paso until three forty-five tomorrow afternoon so she would have most of the morning free; and Sun-mi asked why she was leaving then, hadn't her literary agency specified two nights; and Ingrid said she was very busy with school and her research and couldn't stay any longer; then Sun-mi said, in very good English with just a slight accent, "But I want to talk to you. I think it is important we talk. Don't you?"

"You know English," Ingrid said.

"Yes, I do," Sun-mi said. "Better than you know Korean, I hear."

Ingrid changed clothes in the bathroom, and they got into Sun-mi's car, a new Prius. Given Sun-mi's intoxicated state, Ingrid was nervous about her driving, but she proved to be quite capable on the road, smoothly swinging away from the casita onto the highway and heading west out of town.

"Where are we going?" Ingrid asked.

"I know a place that's still open. Are you lesbian?"

"What?"

"Lesbian?"

"No."

"Are you married? How old are you?"

"I'm thirty-seven. I've never been married."

"Why not? Don't you want children?"

Ingrid was used to such bluntness from her year living in Seoul. Koreans were notorious for their forthright questions. "No, I don't."

"Why do you wear those clothes? You look like a janitor. You should wear makeup, do something for your hair. You cut it yourself, I think? Not a good idea."

Ingrid chose to stop answering.

"You're too skinny. You need to eat more. You should wear padded bra."

Ingrid was ruminating about Yoo Sun-mi's own appearance—so different from what she had expected. She was slender and a couple of inches taller than Ingrid, with medium-sized breasts. She was dressed in a vest, snap shirt, jeans, and cowboy boots, but it was obvious she hadn't ob-

tained the outfit at a local saddlery or feed and supply store.
The Western wear was fitted, fashionably cut with good
material. She had had everything custom-tailored for her
in Korea prior to coming to Texas, it appeared. Just as carefully fabricated were her hair, which was long and wavy
and colored auburn, and her face, which was perfectly
proportioned, her skin radiant with layers of meticulously
applied makeup, even at this hour. She was very attractive,
her age indeterminate—anywhere between thirty-five and
forty-five. It was clear to Ingrid that Sun-mi had had multiple cosmetic surgeries. This wasn't unusual in South Korea, which had the highest rate of procedures per capita in
the world, the most popular being double-eyelid surgery,
nose jobs, glutathione injections, which slowed pigmenta-
tion in the skin to make it whiter, and bone contouring to
create a smaller oval-shaped face, like Sun-mi's. She looked
like a well-heeled housewife who was trying to pass as
a K-drama actress—polished and wholly synthetic. Ingrid
had imagined that the author of *The Partition* would be
drab, maybe a little ugly and awkward, and full of anger
and self-loathing. She had never imagined that Yoo Sun-mi
would be, instead, so bourgeois.

"What are you doing in Colima?"

"There's a foundation that gives residencies to international writers to go here—a writing retreat. They provide
a house, car, stipend, airplane ticket. They have two houses.
Another writer was supposed to come at the same time,
but the person cancel at last minute. I am here four weeks
now. It is a special place. I cannot explain. We are up very
high, nearly 1,600 meters. It is like an island, desert all
around, mountains on horizon, everything so far away. It's

beautiful, so empty. And the sky—endless blue. The light is so bright. I am writing like never before. I am almost finished with a new book. I am born again. It is because of your translation. Without it, the foundation never hears of me."

"You read my translation?" Ingrid said. The more Sun-mi spoke, the more mistakes she was making—small inconsistencies and errors that Ingrid's students in Seoul used to make, dropping articles, mixing tenses, not getting subjects and verbs to agree—but her English was certainly fluent enough to judge Ingrid's translation.

"This, we have to discuss," Sun-mi told her, and then said no more.

They drove farther down the highway, which was black-dark with no streetlights, no other cars coming or going. After about fifteen minutes, Sun-mi suddenly braked to a stop. "Sorry. Very hard to see the marker," she said.

She backed up, and Ingrid saw a small cairn on the side of the highway, the rocks painted white. Sun-mi turned toward a steel gate and rolled down the driver's-side window. A keypad was mounted on a post, and after she punched in six digits, the gate swung open automatically. She drove across a cattle guard onto a road of packed dirt.

"Where are you taking me?" Ingrid asked.

"Somewhere fun," Sun-mi said.

Ingrid didn't know why Sun-mi was dragging this out and being so mysterious. She fully expected now to be lambasted by Sun-mi for her sloppy translation. This was the reason, she realized, that she had agreed to come to Colima—she felt she deserved to be punished.

"Wait, how did you know where I was staying?" Ingrid asked. "How'd you get the address to the casita?"

"You gave it to Gu-yong."

Joseph, the literary agent? She didn't recall giving him any details. "No, I don't think so."

"Yes, I think so."

Nothing was in view, just the dirt road before them in the headlights, scrub and cacti in the periphery. They drove for at least half a mile, bouncing through ruts, and then there was another cairn painted white, and Sun-mi made a right. Soon, they came upon three vehicles—a jeep, a beat-up pickup truck, and a shiny, bright orange Corvette—parked at the base of a small hill, on top of which was a lone building.

"Come," Sun-mi said, using the flashlight on her enormous mobile phone to illuminate the path. "Watch for rattlesnakes."

"What?" Ingrid replied.

The building was a shotgun structure made of crumbling adobe, the windows boarded up with plywood. There was not a leak of light anywhere. Another keypad was affixed beside the front door, and Sun-mi tapped in another set of six digits. She shoved open the door and said, "You first."

Ingrid couldn't see anything beyond the door. The place looked abandoned. What were they doing there? For a second, she had the crazy thought that Sun-mi intended to reenact the crimes in *The Partition*—knock Ingrid unconscious from behind, kill her, chop her up with a saw, then store her body parts in a freezer for later consumption.

Sun-mi closed the front door, which seemed to trigger some sort of electronic mechanism. A red bulb overhead began to glow, unveiling a bare foyer, and then an inner door softly popped ajar. Sun-mi pushed it open, revealing the most sumptuous bar Ingrid had ever seen.

"Hey, Sunny," a young, hip-looking couple said.

"How you doing, Sunny?" the bartender said.

A middle-aged couple sitting at a table nodded toward them.

The room was long, windowless, dimly lit, and cozy, with a tin pressed ceiling, black flocked-velvet wallpaper, a dark hardwood floor, and brass chandeliers. There was a small bar with a gleaming copper top, and a row of button-tufted leather booths.

"Your usual, Sunny?" the bartender asked as Sun-mi and Ingrid settled onto two stools at the bar.

"Yes, Adam. For my friend, too."

The bartender had a handlebar mustache, bow tie, suspenders, and pin-striped slacks—an appropriate ensemble for what Ingrid gathered to be a replica of a Prohibition-era speakeasy.

As Adam prepared their drinks, Sun-mi said to Ingrid, "This is a members-only club, very secret. I paid a $1,000 initial fee. Colima looks like a nothing cowboy town, but many lawyers from Houston are buying ranches now, young artist people from New York are moving here. Very interesting. Maybe I will buy a house here. Maybe I will move to Colima."

"You're serious?"

"Not to live all the time. Some of the time. But maybe so. Many things are changing for me."

Adam served them their cocktails—Sazeracs, they turned out to be, made with cognac, rye, absinthe, sugar, and bitters. Ingrid took a tentative sip of hers. She'd never had one before. Usually, she limited herself to half a glass of cabernet twice a week. The Sazerac was sweet, spicy, and medicinal all at the same time.

"How'd you learn English?" she asked Sun-mi.

"Oh, many years ago I go to prep school in New England."

"Did you go to college in the US as well?"

"No, I go to Busan Women's College."

"To study literature?"

"Aerobic dance."

She thought Sun-mi was kidding at first. "That was your *major*?" How in the world did this frivolous woman produce *The Partition*? Flaubert had once said that writers should be regular and orderly in their lives so they can be violent and original in their work, but trying to apply this to Sun-mi was, to say the least, a stretch. Ingrid couldn't envision the woman next to her writing anything remotely subversive.

"After I graduate," she said, "sometimes I took literature classes at Sogang University. One professor I had is named Oh Hyung-jun. He became my friend. Recently a college asked Professor Oh to look into an American professor's file. Your file."

The external reviewer in Korea who'd given Ingrid such a damning evaluation? He was Sun-mi's mentor and friend? "He told you about my translation," Ingrid said, appalled by the professor's conflict of interest, his breach of confidentiality.

"Yes. When the publisher in Paju sold the translation permission, Gu-yong asked me if I wanted to see the book before publication. I said to him I don't care, it doesn't matter to me. But then Professor Oh told me about the translation, and I read it."

"And?"

"I wrote the novel so long ago, I couldn't truly remember it, so first I had to read it again, then I read your translation. In some ways it is wrong, in some ways it is good, in many ways it is different. Surprising, how much different. Why did you want to translate my book? Did you love it?"

"It was very vivid and visceral," Ingrid said, equivocating. "It was unlike anything I'd ever read."

"Professor Oh tells me you are in trouble," Sun-mi said. "You will lose your job, maybe, because of him?"

"It looks like I might."

"Professor Oh is sometimes a hard man, an unfair man. If I say to your college I accept your translation, I approve it, then things will be better for you?"

"You would do that for me?" Ingrid asked.

"I don't know," Sun-mi told her. "First I wish to know more of you, learn of you. I wish to see if I admire you. One meeting is not enough for me to tell. Will you stay an extra day in Colima so I can decide?"

She couldn't say no, of course, even though she wasn't sure if Sun-mi's endorsement of the translation, assuming she would eventually grant it, would be material enough to secure tenure for her from the provost.

The next morning, she paid a $200 fee to change her airline ticket and made a reservation to stay at the casita an extra night.

At around one thirty in the afternoon (it was supposed

to have been noon), Sun-mi picked her up from the casita and drove her into what passed for downtown Colima. Next to the post office was a gigantic shade pavilion, and underneath it was a food truck called The Fat Whale.

Unlike yesterday, there were people out today—an odd mix of ranchers, municipal workers, cowboys, and hipsters—all gathered under the pavilion, sitting at an array of picnic tables and eating their lunches from brown paper bags, Tupperware containers, Igloo coolers, and The Fat Whale's biodegradable takeout boxes.

Sun-mi ordered a sardine sandwich and a Scotch egg from the food truck, and Ingrid got a falafel hummus wrap. They sat down at a table with their meals, splitting a plate of crispy fried Brussels sprouts and drinking bottles of Topo Chico mineral water.

"My brain is in a little cloud from writing this morning," Sun-mi said. She was wearing a straw cowboy hat and a cream-colored linen jumpsuit today, her makeup as impeccable as it had been the previous night.

"What's your new novel about?"

"It is wild—even for me. That is all I will say. I have superstition about discussing a book before finishing."

"How about a couple of general questions, then?"

"Okay."

"What got you started writing fiction in the first place?" Ingrid asked. "What drives you to do it?"

"These are very difficult questions." Sun-mi chewed her food and pondered for a minute. "I began in high school, but never thought it was something serious for me or for anyone to do. But I kept doing it. I could not stop. For me, to write is to ask what is life, what is love, what is death. It is to study the mystery of being human, to try to understand what makes us desire, obsess, hate, lie, kill, sacrifice, dream, hope, sing. It is to know the many dilemmas of our human heart."

"Is it easy for you? Writing?" Ingrid asked.

Sun-mi laughed. "Easy? It is impossible! Every day I want to quit! Every day I think I am a failure! It is exhausting. It is harder than anything. But I like it because it is hard. It is a challenge, and it is satisfying when I struggle but then find the way to tell the story."

This was the difference between them, Ingrid reflected. As an aspiring writer, she had never been able to persevere through the struggle. She'd lacked the courage and the will.

Sun-mi got up from the table and fetched dessert from the food truck—sweet potato bread pudding with dates and pecans. "Will you have a bite?" she asked. "No? Not surprising you're so skinny."

Sun-mi, despite her prodigious appetite, was even thinner than Ingrid had thought last night. In Korea, designer clothes often came in only one size—small—and diet pills were popular among women.

"Now I ask some questions," Sun-mi said. "Do you have a boyfriend? Or girlfriend? You said yesterday you're not lesbian, but maybe you're bisexual?"

"I'm not seeing anyone right now, boy or girl or other," Ingrid said, irked by the resumption of this line of questioning.

"Why not?"

"I like being alone."

"Why? Were you raped one time? Or maybe you have mental problems?"

"That's ridiculously presumptuous," Ingrid told her.

"No, I don't think so."

"Yes, I think so."

"Your last name is Kissler. Were you adopted?"

Ingrid nodded.

"Have you been to Korea?"

She told Sun-mi about her year in Seoul as a Fulbright ETA.

"In Korea," Sun-mi said, "did you feel Korean or American?"

"Neither, to tell you the truth."

The trip had been a disappointment. She had hoped it'd be a homecoming of some kind, but she came away from it more confused than ever. She'd had a miserable time growing up in the suburbs of Minneapolis, where, in order to be popular, it seemed girls were supposed to be perky, pretty, and Caucasian. On occasion her adoptive parents took her to Korean Culture Days to meet other Korean adoptees and their families, but at the time, Ingrid had wanted to be white, not Korean. She got into grunge, dyed her hair pink, dressed in thrift-store clothes, and inked her arms with tattoos of a mandala, a waveform vector, and the words *Going Nowhere*. At Purdue, she was the bass player for a punk band, although she didn't know how to play bass, and began dabbling in ecstasy and coke until she had a breakdown of sorts. She cleaned up and made the decision to go to Korea after graduation, propelled by an amorphous idea that she might repatriate to her country of origin. But once there, she found herself being shunned as a gyopo, an ethnic Korean who, after residing overseas, had lost touch with her roots. Ingrid's mere presence—her body language, the way she walked—seemed to offend people. Before changing her hair color back to black and wearing more conservative clothes that covered her arms, she was routinely accosted by strangers and called a chang-nyeo, a whore. She was chastised for not being able to speak Korean well enough, for not being a real Korean, for being too American. She felt denigrated as an adoptee, someone who had been unwanted, illegitimate, abandoned, who had no lineage or family history she could claim as her own.

"Did you try to find your parents in Korea?" Sun-mi asked her.

"I guess that was entirely predictable, wasn't it?" she said. In recent years, there were so many Korean adoptees returning to the country in search of their birth parents, it had become a trope. "I tried, but I didn't have any luck."

"I am sorry for you. It is very sad to be an adoptee."

They finished eating, and Sun-mi asked Ingrid to accompany her on a drive. Instead of taking the highway again, Sun-mi turned south down a side street, which within a minute opened up as a country road that unfurled across a rolling terrain of grassland. Opposed to yesterday, it was clear out today, the sun angled high above them. Sun-mi sped up, and soon they were flying down the narrow two-lane blacktop. "I love this road," she said. "So much space. Nowhere in the world is like this except in America. The vibrations are very positive here."

She sounded like an Ojai spiritual acolyte, yet Ingrid began to appreciate the vista—the wide-open blue sky, the flat expanse of desert sprawling out from Colima, the mountains far away in the distance. The starkness of the land was both forbidding and seductive. There was indeed something special about the quality of light here, its sharp vivacity.

"Are you close to your adoption family?" Sun-mi asked her.

"No, not really." They had been kind to her, they had tried hard. But she'd never felt much in common with them. Her adoptive father had worked for Dupont, developing GMO corn for the ethanol industry. Her adoptive mother had been a VP in human resources for Target. Her older adoptive brother was a chemist now for Syngenta, and her younger adoptive sister was a logistics manager for Delta Air Lines. They all still lived in the Twin Cities area. She saw them every year at Christmas for four days, and that was it.

"Family is important," Sun-mi said. "Real family. Heritage. I think these white people, they were wrong to adopt you. I think the adoption of babies from a foreign country is kidnapping. It is a crime. You had no choice. They stole you away from where you belong. You should never have been taken from Korea. No wonder you cannot decide if you are a boy or a girl. No wonder you are alone. You are divided. It is like han. You know han and jeong?"

"Of course."

Han was purportedly a state of mind central to the Korean psyche, a collective sense of sorrow and incompleteness, largely in the wake of historical injustices, i.e., Japanese colonialism, the Korean War that divided the country in two, the democracy movements. It supposedly manifested itself as sadness, yearning, angst, bitterness, hatred, regret, and grief, and provoked a determination to endure in order to mete out revenge. *Jeong* was both han's opposite and its complement, a deep fondness and kinship among Koreans, a loyalty and attachment born out of shared hardships. In Korea, however, these concepts—especially han—had come to be regarded as imperial-era gaslighting, and Ingrid was surprised that Sun-mi was bringing them up.

"You are between," Sun-mi said. "You have han but not jeong. You are blocked."

She slowed down abruptly. Ahead of them, a white Border Patrol truck was parked off the road near a culvert. Colima was just sixty miles from the Mexican border. On Ingrid's way to the town, there had been an immigration checkpoint on I-10 outside of El Paso, and when she'd gotten off the interstate, she had spotted a tethered surveillance blimp from the highway.

"Here is also divided," Sun-mi said. "Here is also han. Colima has 70 percent Mexican people, but white people keep very separate. We are the only two Asian people in the area, maybe for many, many kilometers."

Staring out at the desert, Ingrid thought about Ojai, which, for all its liberal pretensions, was overwhelmingly Anglo—just 16 percent Latino, a remarkably low number for California, less than 2 percent Asian American, hardly any African Americans. She questioned why she felt so comfortable there.

They fell into silence, Ingrid lulled into a theta daydream by the drive. After a while—she wasn't sure how long—the pavement on the country road ended, changing to dirt and rocks, and Sun-mi turned the car around to go back to town. When they reached the spot where the Border Patrol truck had been parked, it was no longer there.

"Watch for snake," Sun-mi said.

"What?"

There was a huge snake on the blacktop in front of them, at least six feet long and bright pink. Sun-mi drifted toward the middle of the road—whether to kill the snake or avoid it by slotting it between the wheels, Ingrid didn't know. When they passed over the snake, she swiveled around and peered through the back window. Sun-mi had crushed it, the snake's head and tail obliterated by the tires in equal measure.

"Oops," Sun-mi said.

At around eight that night (it was supposed to have been seven), Sun-mi took Ingrid to a bar called Difuntos. Embedded in the dirt of the parking lot beside the bar were hundreds of squashed bottle caps, and an old, desiccated, bullet-riddled Pontiac station wagon sat on cinder blocks next to a fence. Difuntos had once been a funeral parlor, Sun-mi told her—hence, its name, "deceased" in Spanish. Like everywhere else in Colima, most everyone knew her here, greeting her as "Sunny" as they entered.

The interior space was large, with high ceilings, a long bar, and a stage for music, all of it a bit ramshackle and kitschy, the walls adorned with photos of Vincent Price as Dracula, *Kinky Friedman for Governor* posters, and painted sugar skulls for Día de los Muertos. Spread about were taxidermy of owls and bats.

"This bar is so funny," Sun-mi said to Ingrid. "Let's do a shot."

"No, I don't think so."

"Yes, I think so."

It was called a Paleta shot, named after the Mexican candy, a watermelon lollipop dusted with chili powder that was popular in Juárez, the female bartender told them. She blended tequila, mango and strawberry juice, lime, and hot sauce, and lined the rims of the shot glasses with Tajín, a Mexican spice.

They did the shots. "You like it?" Sun-mi asked.

"This might be the worse drink I've ever had."

"Two more," Sun-mi said to the bartender.

The dinner menu was limited, other than the cheeseburger so beloved by Sun-mi. She ordered one rare with everything, along with a Frito pie (chili served in a bag of Fritos, topped with cheddar cheese and onions) and a plate of fried pickle chips with queso.

"You have a very good appetite," Ingrid said.

"I just throw up later," Sun-mi told her.

Ingrid stared at her, nonplussed.

"Joking," Sun-mi said.

Ingrid opted for a plate of vegan red beans and rice.

After putting in their orders, Sun-mi bought two $2 cans of Lone Star beer for them and took Ingrid to the back of the bar, which led to an open-air arcade of pool tables, a shuffleboard, a couple of vintage video games, darts, and foosball. Beyond the arcade was a patio of crushed gravel with metal tables and mismatched metal chairs. There was a firepit and Christmas lights. Gram Parsons was playing from a jukebox. About half a dozen people were out there, the same number as inside the bar, all of them Anglos.

"Cigarette?" Sun-mi asked, pulling out a pack of Marlboro Reds.

Ingrid was surprised smoking was allowed, even on the

patio. Smoking was prohibited pretty much everywhere in public in Ojai. "Okay." She hadn't had a cigarette since graduate school, and she quickly got buzzed.

"Maybe you're starting to relax," Sun-mi said.

They smoked and drank until they were called over the PA system to pick up their orders, then they brought the food outside and ate. "So delicious," Sun-mi said. "I eat this cheeseburger four nights in a row after I write."

In spite of herself, Ingrid was beginning to like Sun-mi, although she still didn't know why she had asked Ingrid to extend her stay, what she wanted from her, who she really was.

"Is Yoo Sun-mi a pseudonym?" she asked.

"My real name is Baek Yoo-jin. You know the Baek name, the Baek family?"

"Not really. Isn't it a common name?"

"The Baek family is the Tendu Group."

Tendu was a chaebol, a family-controlled conglomerate in South Korea. It'd begun as a manufacturer of chewing gum, then had expanded to operate the largest chain of convenience stores in the country, as well as a dozen hotels worldwide.

"My husband, Dong-joo, is an executive for Tendu. He thinks my books are sick. He says if people knew I am the author of these books, it would be very bad for business, what would his family say, so we must keep it secret."

It was obvious now why Yoo Sun-mi was such a recluse, why she never did any publicity or let herself be photographed, why she hadn't initially cared about reading Ingrid's translation.

"Korean society still is very conforming, very strict,"

she said. "Dong-joo, first he feels shame I cannot have children. Then he hates my books, tells me to stop writing."

"But you wouldn't."

"No," Sun-mi said. "He said I cannot come to Colima, but I come anyway. I am so happy here. Everything becomes clear to me here, in this beautiful place, in the beautiful house the foundation gives to me. You must see the house."

When they finished their dinners, she drove Ingrid a few blocks north of town, up a hill into a residential neighborhood with well-tended houses. The foundation home was a boxy ell with an exterior of burnished stucco and vertical windows. Inside, it was a showcase of modern minimalist design: polished concrete floors, birch plywood built-ins, bright white walls, recessed lighting, and shelter-porn designer furniture and appliances.

"I asked the foundation if I can buy this house, but they said no," Sun-mi told Ingrid. "Come outside—this is the best thing."

She led Ingrid through a sliding-glass door to a pebble garden pocked with plumes of feather grass, lit up with accent lights and enclosed by a tall corrugated-metal fence. To one side was a barrel-shaped cedar hot tub. "Let's take a bath," she said, beginning to slide off the cover to the hot tub.

"I don't have a bathing suit," Ingrid said.

"Be naked. Be free." Sun-mi stripped off her clothes and dropped them to the ground. She raised her arms, twisted her hair into a bun, and walked up the steps to the tub. Her body was quite lovely.

Ingrid turned her back to Sun-mi. She disrobed, then

climbed into the tub, covering her breasts and genitals with her hands. Sun-mi watched her openly, amused, examining the tattoos on Ingrid's arms. The water was scalding at first, especially in contrast to the chilly air, but slowly she became adjusted to the heat and felt her body slackening.

"Watch for this," Sun-mi said. She pressed a button on a remote, and all the lights inside and outside the house dimmed until it was completely dark. "Now look up."

Ingrid did, and saw more stars in the night sky than she'd ever seen in her life, no moon, no city lights, the constellations sparking across the firmament.

"So relaxing, right?"

It was, and the two of them sat silently in the hot tub, Ingrid sliding down and leaning her head back and staring up at the stars.

"You know I am lesbian," Sun-mi said.

"What?"

"This is why I keep asking if you are lesbian. I have a small attraction for you. You know your look—haircut, clothes, like a tomboy—is very popular in Korea. Many K-pop singers look like you. Maybe you have a small attraction for me?"

Unsettled, Ingrid wondered if Sun-mi was going to try to extort her into having a sexual relationship to earn her favor. "I'm afraid I don't," she said.

"Min-yeong, my character in *The Partition,* is lesbian. You did not realize this, did you?"

Ingrid was startled, and aghast with herself for missing such a major character attribute. "No, I didn't."

"Why did you make so many things in my book different in your translation?"

The entire time Ingrid had been in Colima—really, ever since she'd gotten the summons from the literary agent until now—she had been waiting for this, for Sun-mi to chastise her, yell at her, condemn her for her negligence, and the moment had finally arrived. "I'm sorry," she said.

"Translation is important. It is a great responsibility. It is about a country, a culture, how you represent an entire people to the world. If you are not careful, if you make everyone into stereotypes or portray all the feelings with a Western perspective, it is like imperialism. It is like ethnic cleansing."

"I'm sorry," Ingrid said again. "My Korean wasn't good enough. My translation was incompetent."

"No, I don't think so."

"What do you mean, you don't think so?"

"You wanted to be a writer one time," Sun-mi said. "Professor Oh says in your file you studied at Johns Hopkins University to be a fiction writer."

"I dropped out. It was just a phase. It wasn't for me."

"Maybe translation is easy for you, attractive for you, because you don't have to create story or characters. You don't have to be original. You never have writer's block with translation."

"I'll admit that's one of the appeals."

"But with my book, you wanted to be more than translator," Sun-mi said. "You wanted to be coauthor."

"No."

"Yes. You didn't make just mistakes. You didn't make just errors. You intentionally changed my book because in your opinion you thought it was not good. You thought you could make it better."

"No."

"Yes. Maybe other people cannot tell, because they are not writers, but I can tell. Give me the truth."

In the dark, Ingrid couldn't see Sun-mi's expression or even her face very well—only able to make out an outline of it, not any of its features.

Ironically, one of the reasons she had been drawn to *The Partition* in the first place was because she'd believed it was a book she might have written. But she had decided she would have written it differently.

"The tone of the novel felt off to me," Ingrid said. "It was too inconsistent, unclear. It was largely morbid, but sometimes wandered into farce. I thought it needed to be a dark satire all the way through. So I rewrote parts of the book."

"Many parts."

"Yes."

"You were wrong to do this," Sun-mi said.

"Yes." Sun-mi had never planned to endorse her translation, Ingrid realized. She had brought Ingrid to Colima to force her to confess, and repent.

"You were—what did you say to me before?—ridiculously presumptuous."

"Yes, I was. I see that now. I'm sorry. I'm so sorry."

In her mind she had justified the changes as being part of the translation process. But all along, she knew she wasn't being faithful to the spirit of the original. She wasn't translating. She was transposing—privileging her own ideas of what the book should be over Sun-mi's—and that was another big problem with translation. It was impossible for a translator to remove his or her or their or hirs/

zirs subjectivity, and therefore it was impossible to resist subjugating a work.

"But you were also right," Sun-mi told her. "The tone was off. You made the book better."

"What?"

"I will send your college a letter and say I accept your translation." She pushed a button on the remote to turn back on the exterior lights in the garden. "But I want something from you."

"What do you want?"

"I am going to divorce Dong-joo. I am going to expose my real name and be known as an author in Korea. I will get revenge against Dong-joo and his family."

Han, Ingrid thought. Han.

"Gu-yong says a publisher in New York is interested in reading my new novel when it is finished. I think the foundation did something. I think they gave *The Partition* to the publisher. So this is what I wish to ask you: when I am finished with my new novel, will you translate it for me?"

She leaned forward, lifted her hand out of the water, and brushed Ingrid's bangs aside with her fingers. Ingrid felt a few drops of water trickle down her temple.

"Maybe they will be interested in my old novels also," Sun-mi said. "Maybe we will work together for many, many years."

Ingrid stared at Sun-mi, at her large, rounded eyes and narrow nose and flawlessly contoured jawline, and thought perhaps it wasn't that synthetic of a look after all. In this light, it appeared almost natural—as natural as the idea of forming a partnership with her, and attaining a semblance of jeong.

"What do you say?" Sun-mi asked. "You think maybe you will want to do this?"

"Yes," Ingrid told her. "Yes, I think maybe so."

CONFIDANTS

• • • • • • • • • •

NOTHING GOOD CAN EVER COME when someone asks you, as Solveig asked me one summer evening, "You know, don't you?"

"Know what?"

"Oh, you don't know," she said, and her face louvered through all the pleasures of an inveterate gossip—glee, malice, titillation, relish.

I was grilling flank steaks. Kate and I were hosting some of her friends for a Labor Day barbecue at her row house in Rodgers Forge, a residential neighborhood just north of Baltimore. The party was a valediction to a good summer in which Kate's divorce had become final and we'd gotten engaged to become engaged.

What I didn't know, what Solveig now revealed to me, was that Kate was talking to Charley Rusk again. Charley Rusk, the founder of a company that produced something called "host access" software, applications for mainframes and legacy systems that were quickly becoming obsolete. Dinosaurs. Nonetheless, Charley Rusk had been able to sell the company not too long ago for a bundle of money— enough to buy a small share of the Baltimore Orioles.

He and Kate had had an affair. Somehow, her ex-husband never learned about it, though Rusk's wife had. She'd made Rusk break it off, and Kate had been heartbroken. They hadn't spoken in three years. Or so I'd thought.

"Kate told you?" I asked Solveig.

"Charley did." In addition to being, ostensibly, Kate's best friend, Solveig was also, ostensibly, Rusk's best friend. Could she have dreamed of being in a more delightful position?

"He called her?" I said. "Or the other way around?"

"Neither."

Apparently, a week ago, Rusk had ambushed Kate in the parking lot of the new Trader Joe's on Kenilworth Drive as she was opening the trunk of her car. "I still love you!" he had cried. "I still love you!"

"Don't," she'd told him, and had jumped in her car and driven away, leaving her groceries behind in the shopping cart.

As she was speeding out of the parking lot, he began texting her, and he kept texting her, *Will you talk to me? Please talk to me. I still love you. I never stopped,* and after an hour Kate had texted him back, *You can't do this to me,* and then he had texted, *Elisabeth left me.*

This had been news to Solveig, Rusk's putative best friend—that his wife had left him. "I can't believe he didn't tell me!" she whispered to me beside the grill.

I looked across the backyard at Kate. She was sitting in the shade of the patio umbrella, chatting with her friends, not betraying that anything was amiss.

"They've been talking on the phone ever since," Solveig said. She put her hand on my forearm and bugged her eyes in concern. "What are you going to do?"

★ ★ ★

I didn't want to do anything, afraid of what might emerge. I wanted Kate to do something—fess up on her own accord and explain, dismiss the conversations as inconsequential.

We cleaned up after the party, gathering plates and glasses, washing pans, and loading the dishwasher. I watched Kate for signs of nervousness or guilt, but there were none. She affected good humor, doing a postmortem about the party, recalling a few boastful announcements and working out who was mad at whom. Someone was always mad at someone in her circle—a perceived insult, an inferred snub.

She had interesting friends. One was an artisanal clothing designer, another—Solveig's husband—a ceramic artist. There was a transgender poet, an admissions officer for MICA, and a pediatric heart surgeon who, on the side, made abstract sculptures out of discarded plastic bottles. Another woman, a jazz cellist, ran an organization advocating music in the schools with her husband, a former drummer and professional duckpin bowler. All had advanced degrees. Kate herself was no slouch. She had a PhD in literature and taught at Johns Hopkins.

There were a couple of things, though, that set Kate and me apart from her friends. The first was that we were Asian Americans, while they were all white. Heretofore, her ethnicity as a third-generation Japanese American had never seemed to make much of an impression on them, perhaps because she had spent ten years in the UK and had a soft English accent, most noticeable when she said words like "job." Or maybe it was simply because she was an Asian female, so often accepted as a benign accoutrement to white men. (Her ex-husband was white. Charley

Rusk was white. Every man she'd ever dated before me had been white.) Yet everything about me was a curiosity to her friends.

Foremost was the way I talked. Her friends' nickname for me was Roget, after the thesaurus—perplexed and amused by my highfalutin vocabulary, syntactical flourishes, and funky enunciation, especially when I didn't have any kind of pedigree or even an undergraduate degree. Also, except for Kate, who was thirty-nine, I was younger than everyone else by a good ten years, thirty-four to their mid- to late forties, and in far better shape than all the men. I worked out at an MMA studio in the same building as my shop, and I looked like a fighter, a featherweight, with a buzz cut and tats, though none were too garish or visible—everything faded indigo, nothing on the neck or face.

I had been in a gang as a kid. This had been in Dorchester, south of Boston, when I was twelve, thirteen. I'd been raised in Lowell, my old man a mechanic who bounced from one garage to another, continually getting fired because of his drinking. My mom and I moved to Quincy after they divorced, then to Dorchester after she got a bookkeeping certificate from Bunker Hill and was hired as an accounts payable clerk at Devon Lumber.

My first day of school in Dorchester, I heard *chink, gook,* witnessed the usual slanty-eyes gestures, and was coldcocked in the lunch line. All my life I'd been undersized, which invited abuse. The gang offered me protection, even though they were mostly Vietnamese and I was Korean. I gladly took it. All I had to do in exchange was participate in some minor antics: a few beatdowns, robberies, vandalism, a little dealing, i.e., cannabis, ecstasy, nothing too serious, really, before I managed to get out.

You see, while never very diligent with my homework, I always aced my exams and scored off the charts on every standardized test. A school counselor took note of this. He was an alumnus of St. Paul's in New Hampshire, and after a protracted process I was offered a scholarship to the boarding school. I never graduated—I kept getting into fights and was expelled at the end of my junior year—but maybe it's not an exaggeration to say that going there likely saved my life.

Kate's friends knew none of these particulars, just that I was not a model minority—say, like her. Raised in Danville, California, a serious ballerina until she was sixteen, Princeton undergrad, PhD from the London Consortium, her dissertation entitled "The Aesthetics of Modern Vulgarity in the Contemporary Novel," a tenured professor at Hopkins, and now an assistant dean.

After we finished with the dishes, I went to the basement to clean out the cat's litter box, then took out the trash. By the time I climbed the stairs to the bedroom, Kate had changed into a tank top and flannel shorts—her usual sleepwear—and was applying coconut butter lotion to her legs. She had wonderful legs. She still did barre exercises and worked out nearly every day at a women's-only gym in Belvedere Square. And her skin—white as heroin, as if she'd never ventured outside in her life. She'd had a melanoma on the bottom of her foot as a teen, and she studiously kept out of direct sunlight, wearing sunscreen even during the winter and carrying a parasol during the summer.

"Is something bothering you?" she asked me. "You seem distracted."

Are you and Charley Rusk doing more than talking? I thought. Are you still in love with him? What other secrets have you been keeping from me?

A month ago, we'd started discussing marriage—a conversation I'd initiated—but Kate had said she wasn't ready yet to become officially engaged. When would that be? A year? Two? Who knew. We didn't live together. I still had my rental apartment in Hampden. I came over to Kate's house on Tuesday, Friday, and Saturday nights, as if following some sort of court-appointed visitation schedule, with the occasional holiday thrown in for good behavior. There was no suggestion that I move in anytime soon. It was clear she preferred living alone.

"I'm just tired," I told her.

We had met five years before, in 2012. She came to my shop in the Mill Centre to order a broadside of a poem for her friend's fortieth birthday, and she was, like most people uninitiated with letterpress, confounded by the process, especially when it came to the prices.

"All I want is one print, though," she said.

"It doesn't matter. A one-off will cost the same as a hundred. It's the design, setting the type, doing the makeready, that's the bulk of the work. Running the prints is actually the easiest part. How long is the poem?"

She pulled a printout of it from her messenger bag.

I read the poem over carefully. "This is pretty good," I said. "Yours?" There were lesbian themes in the poem, and I was trying to ascertain if she was gay or straight, attached or single.

"My friend's. The one who's turning forty."

"You're going to give your friend her own poem for her birthday?"

"Yes. It's *their* poem, by the way, not *her*. They're non-binary. Why's it strange? It won a big award."

It seemed narcissistic to me, to hang your own poem up in your house, regardless of whether or not it was a gift. "I'll have to charge you forty-five dollars extra for the additional text."

"What?"

"The base rate's for fifty words."

"All right, fine."

We began sketching out the layout and design with a pencil, discussing typefaces, ink colors, stock, sizes, deckle vs. straight-cut edges, possible ornaments, fleurons, rules, and vignettes.

She removed another printout from her bag, this one of an elaborate pen-and-ink drawing of a tree. "What about adding an image like this?"

"I can't do that," I told her.

"Why not? I have the JPEG for it."

I had to explain to her that I didn't do digital, I eschewed computer-generated polymer plates and magnesium etchings. I hand-set and hand-pulled everything and used only antique wood or authentic foundry metal type, along with vintage image cuts and embellishments.

"You're kind of a strange bird, aren't you?" she said.

We settled on the typeface Perpetua in dark blue on an all-cotton, cream BKF Rives. She came back the next week to look at a proof, I ran off ten prints for her, and she seemed satisfied. I didn't see her again for another two and a half years. By then, her entire life had been destroyed.

She had a daughter, Julia. One afternoon, Julia developed a slight fever. She complained her ear ached, and Kate and her husband assumed it was an ear infection. They gave her some Tylenol, and she fell asleep, but awoke a few hours later and began vomiting. Her fever spiked. Dehydrated, she was slurring her words, slipping into incoherence. At the ER, they hooked her up to an IV and ran a slew of tests. They couldn't figure out what was wrong with her. She started having seizures, then became unresponsive. They did a spinal tap, and then a CT scan. There was massive swelling in her brain, which was bulging into her spinal cavity. By morning, Julia was declared braindead. Within sixteen hours, she had gone from a healthy, happy eight-year-old to a corpse. They never determined the cause. Possibly a virus, maybe a bacterial or fungal infection. No one really knew.

What can you say to something like that? There's nothing you can say.

Did I mention my name? It's Jay, short for Jae-hwan. To my shame, I was largely responsible for the Americanization. I'd wanted to fit in as a child, although that impulse fell away quickly enough.

I have a confession to make here. I've never much cared for white people, which, I suppose, makes me a racist. This whole experiment of multiculturalism in the United States, the desire for integration and diversity—I think it's folly, a colossal mistake. It's never worked anywhere in the world, at any time in history. Trying to foist such a grandiose, fruitless concept upon a society only brings about hardship, tragedy, and fury. Then again, maybe the oligarchs know this well and good. Maybe they insist on imposing this burden because a) nothing erases identity and disempowers minorities more efficiently than assimilation and miscegenation, and b) political correctness is a brilliant way to sow discord among liberals and people of color.

Case in point: all the times Kate's white, supposedly progressive friends would utter some stupid generalization, e.g., "That's because Asians have stronger familial networks than any other ethnic group," and then, after I called them on it, would trip over themselves trying to walk it back and prove they weren't being racist, e.g., "My college roommate was Chinese. I was the best man at his wedding."

Their most egregious faux pas, though, were reserved for African Americans. They'd never slip and say anything explicitly racist. Instead they'd talk about switching dentists because the waiting room at the clinic had been "like a bus stop downtown," or they'd tell a story about following up on a Craigslist ad for an old Martin D-18 guitar and not paying attention to the address plugged into their car's GPS and then slowly realizing, holy shit, they'd wandered into Four by Four (a Black neighborhood) and getting the fuck out of there lickety-split.

None of them ever talked about Freddie Gray. None of them had a single Black friend.

The worst of the perpetrators was Solveig. Once, she recounted standing behind an "idiot woman" in the self-checkout line at Giant, and mimicked the woman's "Baldamore" accent: "Aye-yo, how you dew this shit? Wholetime, you know, I just want a fugg and half and half and walk my dug down to get a lor chicken box, woe."

I despised Solveig. I thought her vain, frivolous, a drunk, an obvious bigot. It dumbfounds me to this day that I came to rely on her as a confidant.

Sunday morning two weeks after the barbecue, I was about to run the trails around Loch Raven Reservoir when I paused to tie my shoe. Solveig jogged past me on the path, then backtracked to where I was kneeling.

"I didn't know you ran," I said to her. She was wearing sculpted compression shorts and a sports bra—tall with elongated legs, flat-chested, Nordic blond. She was in decent shape, yet I'd assumed it was from yoga and Pilates and purging.

"Not as much as I used to," she said. "Run with me?"

To my surprise, I had a hard time keeping up with her, particularly on the hills, where she bounded ahead of me. We did the entire six-and-a-half-mile loop together, and by the time we reached Dulaney Valley Road, where our cars were parked, I was completely winded.

"You kicked my ass," I said.

"We can all use a good ass-kicking once in a while."

It turned out she had run track in college, the 400. It'd been only Division III, but still. She'd hustled me.

"I'm sorry for what I told you the other day," she said. "About Kate. Someone made those gimlets way too strong. I shouldn't have said anything."

I doubted very much she was sorry. As a gossip, her abiding impulse was to create drama. In fact, at that moment I wondered if she'd somehow followed me to the reservoir to foster more trouble. Meeting her here seemed too coincidental. "I'm glad you told me," I said.

"You are? Did you bring it up with Kate?"

This was disingenuous of her, too, I knew. If anyone had heard that I'd confronted Kate, it would have been Solveig. "Not yet."

"Are you planning to?"

"I don't know. Are they still talking to each other on the phone?"

"Oh, Jay," she said. "You poor man."

We began running together every Sunday morning so Solveig could share what she'd learned, but as it got colder, we ditched the pretense of the runs and simply rendez-voused at a café during the week. Like me, Solveig wasn't bound to regular hours at an office. She was a freelance decor photographer—more of a hobby than a job. Her husband, the ceramic artist, didn't earn all that much, ei-ther, but they had family money.

She told me that, subsequent to the initial calls, Kate had met Charley Rusk for coffee somewhere in Timo-nium, and then the following week for a drink.

"A drink?"

"Maybe not literally," Solveig said. "It might've just been a figure of speech."

"What does he know about me?" I asked. "Does he know Kate and I are together?"

"Well," she said, "you have to understand: he's my friend, he asks questions. He's asked questions about Kate nonstop for the last three years, how she's been, what she's been doing."

"So he knows everything."

"Yes."

And yet Rusk had chosen not to respect that I was in Kate's life. As if I were not a threat to him at all.

Solveig filled me in on parts of their history, the out-
lines of which I'd known, but not the specifics.

Johns Hopkins had wanted to build a literacy center in
Better Waverly, east of its main campus, and Kate and Rusk
had been on the steering committee. Evening meetings
segued into drinks at Gertrude's restaurant in the BMA.
Rusk was an alcoholic, and Kate, after Julia's death, was fast
becoming one.

They soon moved the cocktail sessions to the Valley
Lodge in Brooklandville, an out-of-the-way former road-
house frequented by the Greenspring horse crowd, post-
commute lawyers, and divorcées on the prowl—not a
few from Kate's own neighborhood. (Rodgers Forge was
known as Divorce Forge. When couples from Stoneleigh,
Roland Park, and Guilford separated, women often down-
sized to Rodgers Forge. The English cottage–style row
houses were affordable and located in the county, not the
city, meaning their kids could go to good public schools
for free. Never mind that Baltimore County was one of the
most segregated areas in Maryland, and that many deeds in
Rodgers Forge still had Jim Crow–era covenants attached
to them that stated, "No person of any race other than the
white race shall use or occupy any building on any lot.")

The Valley Lodge was notorious for aiding and abet-
ting trysts, with its dark lighting, discreet booths, and prox-
imity to a string of motels up I-83. Indeed, it had been up
there, in a Red Roof Inn, after a sloppy night of negronis
at the lodge, that Kate and Rusk had first fucked.

Kate's marriage was disintegrating—too much sadness—
and her husband, with nothing to hold him in the US
anymore, decided to repatriate to the UK. Every week for

the next year, Kate and Rusk snuck in an hour or two at her house, and occasionally took trips together. He'd sold his company by then, but he served on the boards of several corporations, including a few international ones, and he sometimes got Kate to accompany him when he traveled to board meetings—once to Berlin, another time to Geneva.

He said he wanted to leave his wife for her, but it would be—as philanderers always contend—complicated. First, there were his four kids to consider. And then there was the issue of money. They hadn't done a prenup. He would lose a fortune.

How much of a fortune?

"I was over at his house once," Solveig told me, "and he had his bank statement on the coffee table, just lying there, right out in the open. So I took a peek at it. He had a balance of over two million dollars. Not in an investment account or a brokerage account, not even a savings account. A regular checking account, accruing zero interest, for everyday expenses. Can you imagine?"

I couldn't, of course. It explained some things, however. Namely, what could be at all appealing about him to Kate. He was not a handsome man. I'd looked him up on the internet and had found various articles and photos of him at tech conferences, philanthropic events, and Orioles games. He was short, disheveled, and woefully out of shape, with a pronounced belly. A homunculus. But money begat power begat charm. Not that Kate, by nature, was materialistic, yet that sort of casual wealth tended to make people—men in particular—more winsome.

Okay, given his business success, he was presumably

ambitious and smart as well—he had a PhD in physics from MIT—but what did he and Kate really have in common? He wasn't artistic, like so many of Kate's friends, like me. What did they talk about?

"I don't know," Solveig said. "What does any couple talk about? Nothing and everything."

"Does he read? Do they talk about books?"

"Some, I think."

"What kind of books? Novels?"

"I'm not sure. He has a lot of different interests."

Once, I had snuck into the back of the lecture hall for one of Kate's classes, "The Great American Novel Since 1945." She had stood in front of the lectern, not behind it, occasionally pacing across the floor or leaning against a table, on which lay one sheet of paper. She gave an entire fifty-minute lecture on Thomas Pynchon's *The Crying of Lot 49* as if she had memorized a script—not a single stumble or lull—only pausing to read passages from the book or ask the class some well-timed, incisive questions. She cut a sexy, stylish figure with her high-waisted pin-striped pants, boots, and tucked-in dress shirt. I'd been transfixed, as were most of her students. I asked her later what was on the sheet of paper, and she'd showed it to me. A cursory outline, nothing more. Had she written out the lecture at some point earlier and committed it to memory? No, she said, most of it had been extemporaneous. She was a gifted, brilliant teacher. I thought it a shame, a waste, that she rarely taught classes now, with her position as an assistant dean.

The affair had ended three years ago in the most banal, predictable way. Rusk's wife, Elisabeth, saw a text from

Kate flash on his cell phone. He had password-protected the phone, but hadn't disabled the feature that showed previews of texts on the screen.

"People are morons," Solveig said. "No one ever thinks they'll get caught. It's being in love that makes them stupid. It's physiological. You know how loud people can be when they're having sex? A scientist figured out that your auditory canals become engorged and close up when you're near orgasm. You think you're being quiet, but you aren't. It's the same thing when you're cheating. Your neurotransmitters go all haywire, and you think you're being careful, but you're not."

After seeing the text, Elisabeth hacked into Rusk's computer (not difficult; his password had been "mannymachado," the name of the Orioles' star third baseman at the time) and read through all their emails and texts. She gave Rusk a choice. He could promise never to speak to Kate again, or he could leave the house at that very moment and wait for her to massacre him in court, as she'd surely be able to. She'd arrange it so he'd hardly ever see his children. Naturally, as cowards always do, he took the easier option.

I looked through Kate's checkbook. I opened her file cabinet and flipped through her credit-card statements. I didn't find anything suspicious.

I tried to break into her laptop, typing in character names from *Lolita,* one of the novels Kate had written her dissertation on, as the password: "humberthumbert" (too obvious), "clarequilty," "blancheschwarzmann," and, Kate's favorite, "viviandarkbloom," which was an anagram for Vladimir Nabokov (and what Kate had named her cat).

I tried unlocking her phone, using various combinations of 342, 42, and 52, the numbers that recurred in *Lolita* as addresses, ages, dates, and room numbers. Nothing worked.

"Are you drinking again?" I asked her during dinner one night.

"What?"

For some reason, the possibility that she was drinking again worried me as much or even more than the possibility that she was going to resume her affair with Rusk. Maybe because the first would ensure the latter, because of what drinking alone would symbolize: deceit, lies, betrayal. I'd already checked through her purse and drawers for mints, gum, and mouthwash, and through the house for bottles, but hadn't found any, which did not mean anything. No one was as cunning or as wily about keeping secrets as an alcoholic.

"What makes you ask that?" she said. "Did someone say something? Solveig?"

I suppose I could have simply confronted her about Rusk then, about why she had been lying to me about talking to him and seeing him, if she was still in love with him, but I didn't want to ask. I didn't want to know the answer. I already knew the answer.

Kate did not love me. She did not want to get married to me. She had been waiting for something to break us up. She couldn't do it herself. She wanted me to do it.

All along, I'd been waiting for this to happen. I had been sure it'd happen, and I didn't want it to happen, but I knew it would happen, although I hadn't known how it would happen.

"I'm not drinking," Kate told me.

It'd never made any sense for her to be with me. What could I give her? A temporary respite from grief, a sense of kinship with another Asian American, help with her sobriety. Or maybe just sex with someone younger, someone from a decidedly low-rent background, as opposite as she could get from anyone she'd ever known. Maybe instead of being good for her, she had chosen me because I was bad.

After I was expelled from St. Paul's, I moved to Medford, north of Boston, and got a job at a medical laundry facility. My title was production associate (a joke). I worked the third shift, eleven p.m. to seven thirty a.m., sorting hospital scrubs and sheets that were soiled with blood, ointment, vomit, urine, shit, medicines, and iodine, stuffing them into bins and then industrial washers and dryers and then folding and packaging them, being subjected to all the detergents and bleaches and chemicals that were used to try to sanitize the germs. Needless to say, it was a terrible job. On top of everything, workers got sick all the time with colds and flus and afflicted with sudden skin ailments like pimples and boils. Everyone was afraid of getting a staph infection that'd be resistant to antibiotics (I've always wondered if something like that had killed Kate's daughter, Julia).

But it was a job, and mostly kept me out of trouble. I shared a shithole two-bedroom apartment on the ground floor of a triple-decker with four Tufts University students, the smells in that dump not much different from the laundry facility. During the day, bored, I began auditing courses at Tufts. When I say "audit," I mean that I ghosted them, sneaking into large lecture classes. I'd wanted to take art classes—I loved to draw—or architecture classes, but they were too small for me to go incognito. In lectures, though, they didn't take attendance. All I had to do to blend in was wear a baseball cap, if that.

I thought I'd mainly be interested in philosophy or ethics courses, but it ended up that poetry, of all things, appealed to me, and I took introductory survey classes in literature. It was in one of them that the professor invited a guest speaker, Andrew Mortensen, to talk about Victorian printing technologies. Mortensen was the proprietor of what he called a "printing office," Ascender Press, which specialized in letterpress.

What struck me at once about him was his voice—a deep, stentorian baritone, with the most eloquent and precise enunciation of the English language I had ever heard, crisp and beautiful.

"When it comes down to it," he said to the class, "there are really only two ways with which to approach any task. The first is to grasp whatever shortcuts are available to you, to have everything quick, easy, convenient. The other approach is to appreciate that details do matter, that they are important, they are not trivial or superfluous, and to care about getting them right. This is, obviously, a much more difficult path, being rigorous, meticulous, to go above and beyond what's merely adequate and strive for perfection, but ultimately I believe it makes for a much more rewarding journey. This pertains not just to typography. I would venture to say that this applies to every aspect of life."

At the end of his talk, Mortensen mentioned offhandedly that his press was looking for a summer college intern; anyone interested could inquire in person at the printing office over the next few weeks.

The following morning, I walked into Ascender Press, and I was immediately taken by the smell of ink and paper and the rhythmic clanking of the machines, which were being operated by two employees working alongside Mortensen.

"I'm not exactly a student at Tufts," I told him.

"What exactly are you, then? A vagabond? A scofflaw?" Mortensen said.

"Well, kinda yes."

He grimaced. "In all honesty, your academic status doesn't matter one iota to me, yet what does matter is that you avoid phrases like *kinda* and *sorta*. They're expressions of tenuity and indecision, which indicate a lazy mind. There's no place for that here. Understood?"

All summer, while continuing to work the graveyard shift at the medical laundry facility, I interned at Ascender Press for four hours a day, unpaid. For the first two months, all Mortensen allowed me to do was clean—clean blocks, brayers, type, trays, cans, tables, platens, presses, and the floor. No surprise, he was a stickler for cleanliness and order.

"What you have to comprehend is that this ink knife has five sides, the two flat surfaces of the blade, of course, but also three edges—here, here, and here—all of which need to be scrubbed assiduously."

Slowly, though, Mortensen began to tutor me on the mechanics of hand composition and presswork, demonstrating, for instance, how to mix inks with that very knife. "You see how I keep drawing it through the ink, stirring it and blending it? You want the motion to have a continuous flow. It's very similar to the technique of scrambling eggs."

Finally he let me take a few runs on a press. It fascinated me to no end, arranging and locking type into a chase, inserting leads, slugs, and quads. I would stay for hours after the shop closed to practice. By the end of the summer, Mortensen was letting me do small jobs, and then he offered me a paid position. I quit my job at the medical laundry facility and worked as Andrew's apprentice for the next nine years.

Ascender Press was doing great business, thanks to, of all people, Martha Stewart. She had extolled using letterpress for wedding invitations, and the industry suddenly found itself in a renaissance. We were so busy, we routinely turned away jobs. We did everything from invitations to stationery, business cards, broadsides, CD packaging, cocktail napkins, gift tags, certificates, birth announcements, and greeting cards.

Contrary to what Andrew had asserted in his talk at Tufts, you couldn't seek perfection with letterpress, which never produced pristine edges. Yet that was part of its art and charm. It was a fiddly, laborious craft. Laypeople were attracted to the tactility of letterpress, wanting to feel deep depressions on paper, thinking divots were desirable. In fact, excessive debossing was frowned upon. Heavy impressions wore down machines and type. "What you want," Andrew said, "is the gentlest of kisses, little pecks of lipstick, if you will, while somehow avoiding smearing or grooving."

I learned a tremendous amount from Andrew during my time at Ascender, and not just about printing.

He lent me books. Hundreds of them. A lot of Romantic and Victorian poetry, but also novels, biographies, and reference books such as *Fowler's Dictionary of Modern*

English Usage and *Farnsworth's Classical English Rhetoric.*
Little wonder I began talking like him. What's more, he
made me obtain my GED and attend continuing education classes at night as an official student, paying for them.
I even took a few courses at Harvard.

He also taught me something else. He taught me how
to drink. Granted, I was already a pretty practiced boozer,
binge-drinking beer with my roommates every weekend,
but Andrew introduced me to the hard stuff, albeit very,
very good hard stuff—single-malt Scotches. Nearly every
evening after we closed down, Andrew would pour a dram
into a Glencairn whiskey glass for each of us, always neat,
and school me on the subtleties of each batch as we took
dainty sips.

What I'd discover later was that Andrew would then
go home and get blackout-pissed every night—not with
Lagavulin or Glenmorangie or Bruichladdich Black Art,
but with a bottle, a whole bottle a day, of Old Crow, one of
the cheapest bourbons around.

I had a secret, too, back then. I'd stayed in that shithole
apartment in the triple-decker while roommate after
roommate from Tufts graduated or flunked or dropped out.
Something those roommates and their friends kept asking
me was if I could cop for them. Eventually I complied. I
called up some old acquaintances in Dorchester. First it
was grass, then bennies, coke, shrooms, then MDMA, ket-
amine, and opioids. I did it because I wanted the money,
and because I myself was using—the cardinal sin of dealing. I was lucid and productive during the day at work, as
Andrew was, but the nights and weekends were a private
debacle for both of us.

Or maybe it hadn't been so private after all. One day, Andrew mentioned to me that a friend of his in Baltimore was retiring and wanted to offload his printing office—a small, one-man operation, with a Chandler & Price platen press and a Vandercook proof press, along with a cache of well-preserved lead type. The lease for the shop in a converted mill was transferrable as well. "It's a good opportunity for someone who wants to strike out on his own," Andrew said to me.

I was confused, because I had never expressed to him the desire to strike out on my own. I had hoped, actually, that I might apprentice for Andrew forever, and then, when he died, learn that he had left Ascender Press to me in his will.

He was effectively firing me. He was kicking me out. He had caught wind that I was dealing and getting jacked every night, and that I was associating with some less-than-savory characters, and that I had recently acquired a gun, a Glock 22. He was ashamed of me, scared of me.

But maybe not.

"If you'd like," he continued, "I'd be happy to stake you with a loan."

Maybe he didn't know? Or if he did, was he trying to help me escape?

I never found out. I took the loan and bought his friend's business and moved to Baltimore. It took me a long time to reform. I weaned myself off drugs, but not alcohol. After closing the shop for the day, I'd walk to a gastropub called Rocket to Venus and eat something with a couple of beers and shots of Bushmills, then go to a string of other bars in Hampden before reaching my apartment, where I'd crack open a bottle of Old Overholt.

It went on like this for years, until finally I'd had enough. There was no tipping point, no culminating moment that made me decide to quit. I just did. I knew I had to. I guess I got tired of waking up hungover and not remembering things I said or did the night before and feeling sick all the time and getting fat. Drinking was going to kill me, one way or another. I had kept the Glock.

Whereas for Kate, something did happen. She was trashed and driving down Charles Street one night and ran into a light pole. She totaled her car. The cops came, but for some reason they didn't arrest her (because she was sobbing in contrition? or because she was attractive and not Black?). They let her wait for her car to be towed and get a ride home from Solveig.

Two and a half years after Kate visited my shop, I saw her again at a recovery meeting at First and St. Stephen's United Church of Christ. Neither one of us liked AA, the idea of having to turn your life over to God. This particular group—despite meeting in a church—was secular and based on self-reliance. Unlike twelve-step programs, they allowed for the possibility of leaving addictive behavior behind and not attending meetings anymore. A member could be "recovered," not perpetually "in recovery," not always "an addict." I didn't quite believe this. I am certain I'll always be an addict. But the program fit my temperament, as well as Kate's.

Andrew Mortensen died a few years ago of a coronary. He didn't leave Ascender Press to me in his will. He left it to a daughter I never knew he had. They'd been estranged since her early twenties. She didn't come to the funeral in Medford, and I heard at the wake that she planned to sell the printing office and donate the proceeds to ISPCAN, the International Society for the Prevention of Child Abuse & Neglect.

I don't know what to make of this. Andrew was, like all of us, a flawed human being. Was he guilty of deeper depravities? I hope not. He gave me a trade, and he rescued me more than once. I never fully repaid him the loan, and his will specified that the balance should be forgiven. It goes without saying that I thought of him as the father I'd always wanted to have. I loved him.

A jacket was hanging in Kate's foyer closet. A man's field jacket, one of those coats treated with wax that cost an arm.

"Whose jacket is this?" I asked, thinking her and Rusk very careless.

"What?"

"This jacket. Whose is it?"

"Let me see." She stood up from the living-room couch, walked over to the foyer, and took the jacket from me. "Oh, this must be Thomas's."

Her ex-husband's? "But he never lived here." Kate hadn't moved to Rodgers Forge until after he'd left for the UK, whereupon she had dumped all his leftover belongings and sold their house in Stoneleigh.

"He came this summer. Don't you remember?"

To make their divorce official, Thomas had had to fly to the US and appear in person with Kate at the courthouse in Towson.

"I guess he forgot it," she said.

"I thought he stayed at a hotel."

"He did."

"So how'd this end up here, then?"

"He stopped by. He wanted to see the new place." She gave the jacket back to me and returned to her spot on the couch, where she'd been reading a magazine.

"Why would he have needed such a warm coat?"

"You don't know how cold London can be in June."

"Are you going to mail it back to him?" I asked.

"Why should I?"

"These things are usually four, five hundred dollars."

"His loss. You want it? Take it. I think it'd fit you. Try it on."

She was being very clever. I was surprised that she could remain so unrattled. "Give me his address," I said. "I'll put it in a box and take it to the post office."

"Why would you want to do that? You don't owe him anything."

"Just to be nice," I said.

"That's not like you."

"Funny."

"All right, fine. I'll give you his address." She grabbed her cell phone and tapped in her four-digit passcode, which unfortunately I didn't catch, and opened her contacts list. She wrote down Thomas's address on a subscription post-card from her magazine and gave it to me.

I looked down at the address in London. It occurred to me that if the jacket wasn't Thomas's and I mailed it to him, I wouldn't be able to confirm my suspicions. He wouldn't call me or send me an email or text to say, *What's this? This isn't mine,* since we didn't know each other; we'd never even met. He'd simply contact Kate directly, and I'd never discover what he said. I thought of inserting a note in the box. What kind of a note, though? *I am engaged to become engaged to your former wife. Regrettably I think she's cheating on me. I believe this coat, which I found in her house, belongs to her lover. She claims it's yours and that you forgot it when you visited last summer. Could you tell me if she's lying?* It would appear foolish either way, whether the jacket was his or not. And no doubt he'd call Kate and tell her about the note. If I was wrong, it'd be especially disastrous to include an addendum: *By the way, she cheated on you with the same man.*

I didn't mail the jacket. I decided to keep it. It fit me pretty well. It was warm, and the wax coating repelled rain and snow nicely.

The next week, there was a strange, unfamiliar smell in the first-floor powder room of Kate's house. It was sickly sweet, pungent. Was this a new soap? A floor cleaner? A weird deodorant that Kate was trying? I couldn't for the life of me figure it out. The smell was overpowering, nauseating. Then I recognized it. Aftershave. Men's aftershave.

"Who came to visit you?" I asked Kate.

"What do you mean? When?"

"I'm guessing pretty recently."

"What? No one's visited me."

"Did a repairman stop by?"

"No. Why?"

"What's the smell in the bathroom, then?"

"What smell?"

"Aftershave."

"What are you talking about? That's impossible. No one's been in the house."

"Go in there yourself and tell me that's not aftershave."

She disappeared into the bathroom for a couple of seconds—I could hear her sniffing in investigation—then she came out and threw a matchbook at me. "I took a shit, all right?"

The matchbook was a special incense type, with a potpourri scent. Kate sometimes lit kitchen matches in the bathroom after shitting to mask smells with sulfur. She had decided, evidently, to make a slight departure from the regular matches.

"What the fuck's wrong with you?" she asked me.

I was beginning to think I was just being paranoid. Perhaps Kate had seen Rusk a few times, but nothing untoward had occurred.

Solveig didn't have any insights for me. "All of a sudden they're being very cagey—Kate first, now Charley. It's like they've decided to shut me out. Maybe they know we're in cahoots."

I ignored her. Kate and I had had a good month. Things had relaxed between us, and her parents had bought tickets to come to Baltimore for Thanksgiving. I would finally be meeting them. Maybe there was nothing to worry about. Maybe I could even bring up something that I'd been harboring since we'd first begun dating—I wanted us to have a kid together.

I knew this was nonsensical. Kate hadn't indicated any desire to have another child after losing Julia. Even if she did want a baby, why would she have wanted one with me, when I was convinced that she didn't love me, that she was going to break it off with me? Yet irrationally I thought having a child might change things for us. Whatever the case, I was ready to work on keeping us together somehow and to let go of my preoccupation with Charley Rusk.

Until the first screw appeared.

When I started my car one morning, the tire indicator came on. I walked around the car and didn't see a flat, but it wasn't unusual for tires to lose pressure after a sudden temperature drop, and it'd gotten significantly colder of late. I drove to a gas station and parked in front of an air hose and attended to the tires one by one. The first two didn't seem to need air, yet the third was underinflated, and for good cause. A sheet-metal screw was embedded in the tire between the treads. Nonetheless, I didn't think much of it at the time—just bad luck, a chance thing. I drove to a tire shop on 41st Street and had them plug the tire for $14.52 and promptly forgot about it.

Until two days later, when the second screw appeared.

It was impaled in exactly the same tire, the driver's-side front, in exactly the same location, the second groove between the treads, and it was exactly the same type of screw, I saw, when it was extracted at the tire shop: a stainless-steel, Phillips-pan-head-drive, #8 sheet-metal screw that was three-quarters of an inch long.

"You been going past a construction site?" the guy at the tire shop asked.

Not that I knew of. Yet I was willing to chalk it up to an extraordinary coincidence, one of those mystical flukes that defied probability and would never occur again.

Until the third screw appeared the next day.

Same tire, same location, same type of screw. "Who

you pissing off?" the guy at the tire shop said. "Cause it sure looks like someone don't like you."

It had to be Charley Rusk. Who else could it be? He was taunting me. He was laying claim to Kate. He was telling me he could fuck with me as much as he wanted, and there was nothing I could do about it. He was saying, Screw you, I'm not afraid of you.

"Where does Rusk live?" I asked Solveig.

"Why?"

"His wife stayed in the house, right? Where'd he move to? An apartment somewhere?"

"No, he bought a house down the street," she said. "What're you thinking of doing? Are you going to confront him or something, man to man?" The prospect of this excited her, obviously.

"Just tell me where he lives."

"Are you going to beat him up?"

I was thinking, actually, I might have to kill him.

"Jay," Solveig said, "were you really in a gang once?"

He was in Ruxton, in a neighborhood called Four Winds, which could never be confused with Four by Four. Most of the homes were enormous, worth well over a million dollars. Rusk's two-story house was a big, new, midcentury modern affair, with flat-roof overhangs and walls of windows, wood cladding, and stacked stone. It was perched on top of a knoll on at least an acre of land, perimetered by a low wrought-iron fence and a driveway gate—not impenetrable, by any means, but the house was in plain view from the street and had a multitude of exterior accent lights. I would be exposed walking up the driveway to hammer a screw into the tire of Rusk's car, which sat outside the garage—a Tesla with a custom matte-orange paint job, almost certainly an homage to his beloved baseball team.

It wasn't a street, either, where I could loiter without attracting attention. In Hampden I could pass as a hipster, but here I would be taken for a thug. I needed to find another place to lodge the screw. I needed to figure out Rusk's routine.

There was one liquor store in Ruxton, next door to the lone grocery store. I began waiting in the parking lot there at four in the afternoon, when people typically begin shopping for dinner, and when bourgeois alcoholics typically stock up so they're prepared for five o'clock, the magic hour to begin drinking. It took several days. Even in the large parking lot I wasn't completely inconspicuous, so I kept switching locations, parking on side streets and in front of other businesses.

Finally I sighted Rusk's Tesla. Only, he didn't stop at the liquor store. He kept going. I almost missed him. I just happened to catch a glimpse of the Tesla's distinctive matte-orange paint in my rearview mirror, and I scrambled to catch up to him. He drove down Falls Road toward Lake Roland, then veered up to a long warehouse-like structure, windowless and constructed out of corrugated steel. He parked almost immediately upon entering the lot that ran the length of the building, which was strange, because there were plenty of spaces and, judging from the location of an awning, the entrance seemed to be in the center. Then I got it. He was fastidiously parking his Tesla away from everyone else to avoid door dings.

I made a U-turn and sidled to the curb across the street.

In the few seconds it took for me to make the maneuver, however, I somehow lost track of Rusk. I no longer saw anyone sitting inside the Tesla, and there was only one person walking in the lot toward the building entrance, a trim-looking man in athletic wear, carrying a small duffel. Then the man glanced back at the Tesla. It was Rusk. He had transformed himself. He'd lost his belly, his carriage now upright and self-possessed, and he'd done something to his hair, which was neatly cut and blow-dried. At the same time, I saw a sign on the building that identified it as an indoor tennis club and gym. Rusk had been working out—vigorously, it seemed. I realized that none of the photos I'd seen of him on the internet had been newer than four or five years, when he'd sold his company and become a minority owner of the Orioles.

Why hadn't Solveig mentioned this? Had Rusk lost weight and gotten into shape to try to win over Kate? To compete with me, a younger, fitter man? Or had he quit drinking—another sacrifice made in his quest? I remembered when I first got sober, I had had so much time all of a sudden, so much restless energy. That was when I had begun training at the MMA studio.

There were a couple of closed-circuit security cameras mounted to the side of the building. None of them were too close to the Tesla, but the place was not ideal. In addition to the cameras, it was unpredictable when other members might enter or exit the lot.

Rusk stayed in the gym for about an hour, and when he came out, he was sweating through his warmups. Apparently he didn't like showering in public. He drove directly back to his house.

Over the next two days, I continued my stakeouts in Ruxton, hoping to spot Rusk going to a more suitable locale, but I only saw him driving to the gym, parking in the same space, always around the same time, four thirty-ish, staying until five thirtyish. He must have had a regular session with a personal trainer.

I decided to chance it. I'd already wasted too much time on this. There was never much activity in the gym parking lot, and what were the odds of getting caught, anyway, when the whole thing would take me less than a minute?

The next afternoon, after Rusk entered the gym, I turned my car into the lot, then backed up so my driver's side was adjacent to the Tesla's. This way I'd be partially shielded from the cameras by my car when I got out.

I opened my door, and, holding my hammer and a #8 three-quarter-inch sheet-metal screw below my waist, I stepped toward the trunk in a half crouch. Then I squatted down and drove the screw into Rusk's tire, in the second groove between the treads, with one firm strike of the hammer. When I stood up, I found myself face-to-face with Rusk.

"What are you doing?" he asked. He must have forgotten something in the Tesla and returned for it.

I thought I'd be taller than him, but we were the same height. "You're having an affair with my girlfriend, aren't you?" I said.

"Who's your girlfriend?"

He genuinely did not seem to recognize me, nor was he particularly agitated or fearful, even though I was gripping a hammer. He simply appeared befuddled. For a moment, I wondered if Solveig had fabricated everything.

Maybe, dementedly, she had made it all up to amuse herself. Or maybe, now that I thought of it, she'd always been in love with Rusk and jealous of Kate, and this had been her way of exacting revenge, to blow everything apart for Kate and me.

"Kate Yamazaki," I said.

"Oh," Rusk said. "I thought so. I've never seen a picture of you."

It was all true, then.

"Do you want to go somewhere and talk?" he asked.

We were standing close enough for me to catch a whiff of something, his deodorant or aftershave. It smelled more than a little like the potpourri incense. "No," I said. "Let's do it here."

He glanced down at the hammer. I opened the rear door to my car and dropped the hammer onto the seat. I kept my Glock wedged in the waistband behind my back, underneath my waxed field jacket.

"What'd you put in my tire?" Rusk asked. "A nail?"

"A screw."

"You know, Teslas don't come with spare tires," he said. "No tire, no jack, no crowbar, nothing. You get a flat, you have to call Tesla or AAA. There're various theories as to why: the lug nuts are torqued too high to remove without a power wrench, Telsa's afraid if you try to jack it yourself, you'll damage the battery pack under the car. Or maybe it's just that they assume owners are too spoiled and clueless and lily-livered to change a fucking tire. Turns out it's an industry trend. All car manufacturers are beginning to eliminate the spare to save weight and improve fuel economy and, by and by, increase profits."

"This doesn't interest me one iota," I told Rusk.

"No? It kind of fascinates me. Everything's changing so rapidly. Everything's disappearing. I didn't even want to buy this car. It seemed too flashy, too midlife. But I needed a new car, and I wanted to do something for the environment. That was my reasoning. But who was I kidding. I could've gotten a Prius. It's always been about impressing other people, about bigger, better, brighter. It's relentless."

"Listen, you asshole, I don't give a shit about any of this."

"I'm not allowed an existential moment? I'm not—"

"Are you fucking Kate?"

"Why don't you ask her?"

"I'm asking *you*."

"This is the thing I've learned," Rusk said. "Human behavior is immutable. It doesn't follow trends. It's not disrupted by innovation, like so many industries now. You think you can change, you do everything you can to change, but no one ever really changes. You can no more change who you are than change the color of your skin."

I pulled out the Glock and racked the slide and pointed the gun at Rusk. "Turn around."

"Don't be ridiculous."

"Get on your knees."

"No, I won't. You're not going to shoot me. Put that away."

I noticed then that the sky around us was lightening. (I hesitate to mention this because it'll sound like an epiphany, when it was nothing of the sort.) It'd been overcast all day, but now it was clearing a bit, and the edges of the clouds were torching red. Nature always surprises you like this, with unexpected beauty. It'd be a magnificent sunset.

Rusk was right: people don't really change. I'd always been a punk, and I'd always be a punk. Nothing I did would ever change that. Nothing really mattered. I pulled the trigger.

I would never find out who put the screws in my tire, or—if it wasn't Rusk—why. Nor would I find out definitively if Kate was having an affair with Rusk. I assumed so, and still do, yet she would neither confirm nor deny it for me, despite my demands.

He didn't press any charges. I'm not sure what the charges would have been. Stalking and harassment? Vandalism, destruction of property? Making threats? Was there a law for that in Maryland? I suppose I could have been arrested for illegal gun possession. The Glock hadn't been loaded. I'd just wanted to see the look on Rusk's face, how he'd react—a juvenile gesture on my part, I concede. He'd flinched, but not a whole lot, and then he'd walked away. (I attribute this to shock. No fucking way it was nerve.)

Kate, of course, was infuriated and appalled. She broke up with me posthaste. I told her she'd just been slumming, anyway. She said it was all my doing, that I'd sabotaged everything because I could never be convinced that I was good enough for her. I didn't argue with her on that point.

They're together now, she and Rusk. I have to admit, from a purely objective standpoint, they're a pretty good match for each other, and it's almost sort of sweet that they ended up together after everything they'd been through, although I will forever maintain that the guy's a total dickwad.

As for me, I've been going to school at night, working

toward my undergraduate degree. I'm determined—I'm a little embarrassed to say—to get an advanced degree someday, although it may take me until I'm fifty.

I've also been seeing a little of Solveig. I'm not sure how this came to be. There are still things about her I despise. We go trail-running together, and once in a while we'll stop by the Valley Lodge, where I'll have a dram of single-malt—the one drink I allow myself a week—before we head up I-83 to the Holiday Inn.

She keeps me entertained with gossip about Kate's friends. The funniest tidbit has been that the pediatric heart surgeon–cum–bottle sculptor is now going out with a Black oncologist on staff at her hospital, and everyone keeps taking self-congratulatory photos with him at barbecues and dinner parties and posting them on social media. Solveig, naturally, doesn't understand why this amuses me so much. What titillates her more is her latest revelation, which is that Kate might be pregnant. It's still an unsubstantiated rumor (Kate and Rusk no longer confide in her), but I trust Solveig implicitly. In turn, as an audience for her gossip, I don't think she'll ever find anyone more receptive, or deserving.

YEARS LATER

• • • • • • • • • •

IT WAS HER LAST NIGHT IN TOKYO, her last night with Junichiro, and although they had promised to see each other again, somewhere, sometime very soon, Emily knew this probably wouldn't be the case, and she thought Jun knew this, too. Maybe that was why the evening was infused with such delicious melancholy, a well of yearning and nostalgia—false as it may have been—that made it hard to swallow, nearly bringing tears whenever one of them dislodged the blandest statement.

"The train is very crowded today," Jun said to her, and they almost crumbled.

They were riding the Yamanote Line to Meguro, to a tonkatsu restaurant called Tonki's. They had decided not to do anything particularly special tonight—well, with one exception—thinking it would be more meaningful to do what they'd always done. It was the summer of 1982, the year of the Falklands War, the US embargo of Libya, Israel's invasion of Lebanon, the deaths of John Belushi and John Cheever. The latter had affected Jun greatly. He loved Cheever's short stories. He was finishing his junior year studying literature at Tokyo University, and dreamed of a career translating American fiction. For a few months this winter, Jun had taken private lessons with Emily, who had spent the past year after college teaching at one of Tokyo's many conversational English schools.

As always, there was a wait at Tonki's, but they didn't mind. It was all part of the experience. While they were in line outside, a waiter took their orders, and once they were inside the door, they sat among the chairs against the walls and happily watched the cooks working in the open kitchen. It was a wonderful bit of theater. The men rapidly breaded and dipped the pork cutlets with maniacal precision and the most profound solemnity. When Emily and Jun were seated at the counter, they were served cold beers and peanuts, and, in less than a minute, their orders came—the tonkatsu and sauce and miso soup, the pickles and rice and shredded cabbage. The tonkatsu was heavenly, crunchy on the outside, moist inside, so good they couldn't slow down to savor the meal, eating and eating. Still ravenous, they looked at each other, laughed, and ordered an extra cutlet.

From Tonki's, they got back on the Yamanote Line for two stops to Harajuku, then meandered down Omotesandodori to walk off the meal. It was a stifling summer night— oh, the humidity. Within a block, Emily's shirt was damp, and Jun was sweating rather heavily in his suit jacket, a Kawabuko knockoff. He was dressed in all black. The jacket had upside-down pockets, sleeves that extended past his fingers, and looked as if it had been turned inside out, frayed seams exposed. Needless to say, Jun—in contrast to Emily, with her practical suburban tastes—was quite the fashion plate. He kept tugging her to windows of boutiques along the boulevard.

Finally they made it to Minami-Aoyama, down a narrow alley that led to a cramped, steep staircase, at the bottom of which was their favorite bar, North Beach. It was a funky neo-beatnik place modeled after Vesuvio's in San Francisco. Years later, Emily would go to the real Vesuvio's with her first husband and see how close an approximation this bar was, down to the worn wood chairs and café tables, the memorabilia and curios, the murals of Baudelaire, Rimbaud, and Bob Kaufman, even the sign from Jack Kerouac Alley that read, *Beware pickpockets and loose women.* And, of course, they had the drink here, Vesuvio's famous Jack Kerouac drink, tequila and rum mixed with orange and cranberry juice. Jun asked the waiter for two Jack Kerouacs after they found a table near the back, and then they relaxed in the air-conditioned dimness and talked, fingers twined.

"Tell me what you're going to do with your life," Emily said.

"I am going to have many, many adventures," Jun said, and he vowed that he would go to Yale and get his doctorate and become friends with many writers, and then live in the Village, where he would translate books, traveling frequently to Europe, occasionally accompanying authors to Tokyo on their tours. "What I like about American literature," Jun had once told Emily, "is that it is subversive. Japanese literature cannot be so subversive."

Now, in the bar, over the Coltrane playing on the turntable, he said expansively, "I will bring the infection of American books to the Japanese people!"

At first, Emily—still the teacher—thought "infection" was a malapropism, but then she reconsidered. It was the perfect word, a clever if unintended metaphor.

"Tell me what you will do," Jun said.

Emily had so many plans. She was a humble, big-boned, second-generation Korean American from Fairfax, Virginia. Her father was a pharmacist, her mother worked in an insurance office. Her brother managed conferences at a hotel. One sister was a housewife, the other fielded calls at a mail-order company. Yet Emily's parents, former campaign workers for Bobby Kennedy, had instilled in all their children a respect for public service, a passion for progressive, humanistic values, and Emily would be going to the University of Minnesota for her law degree in two months. She wanted to become a civil rights attorney. She wanted to argue discrimination cases in front of the Supreme Court. She wanted to help pass the Equal Rights Amendment.

"I will bring the infection of equality to the American people," she told Jun, to which he raised his clenched fist into the air and said, "Ganbatte!"

"When we are fifty," he told her, "we will meet and have an affair."

"I'll be fat," she said.

"No," he said. "Never."

They were a little drunk when they left the bar. Emily remembered her camera. She had taken so few photos in her year in Tokyo. Originally, after graduating from George Mason University, she had wanted to go to Morocco, or Turkey, or India, somewhere truly exotic, but her parents worried for her safety, and her cousin, who had once taught at the same school, reassured them that Tokyo, if anything, was safe, in spite of the historical enmity between Japan and Korea. A little too safe, Emily reflected, not challenging her comfort levels much, although maybe this was specious hindsight, a form of braggadocio. After all, before Japan, her only excursions outside the US had been family trips to Canada.

She got Jun to pose on Aoyama-dori and snapped a shot with the flash, after which he pretended to have been blinded, shuffling toward her with outstretched arms.

They caught the subway at Omotesando for the short ride to Akasaka and walked up the hill to Palace Wales. Jun lived at home, and Emily had been staying at a gaijin house in Suginami, so this love hotel was an indulgence of privacy. Palace Wales indeed looked like a Welsh castle on the outside, but inside they had their pick of themes. In the lobby, they examined the lighted panel of room photos, and after careful consideration they pressed the button for Sunset Strip, an homage to art deco. In the room, it was all pastels and black marble. There were zebra-patterned wing chairs and George Nelson bubble lamps, and the bathroom featured a huge claw-footed tub, which, despite its faux-antiquity, incorporated hidden pressure jets.

They got into the tub, and, facing one another, did things beneath the surface with their feet, smirking. When they dried each other off with the hotel's plush towels, Emily admired Jun's body. He was her first Japanese lover, her first lover ever, in fact, who was not white—a bias that now shamed her. Except for Jun's head and the profusion of coarse, straight strands in his armpits and on his genitals, he was completely hairless, his skin smooth and unblemished, paler than her own. His body was muscular but without definition, without shape or protrusion, thin and rectilinear, an unearthly, exquisite plank. He had only one distinguishing mark, a birthmark that looked like an indigo inkblot on his lower back. Jun had told her it was called a Mongolian blue spot, common among Asian babies, something she had not known. The spots, which could resemble bruises, usually shrank and disappeared by adolescence, but Jun's never quite did, leaving a vestige the size of a nickel. Many years from now, this information would prove useful to Emily. A Korean client would take her baby to the hospital because of a fever, and a callow intern would summon child protection services after seeing the blue spots, thinking Emily's client had been abusing the baby.

They sprawled onto the French bed, which had scalloped head- and footboards made of burr walnut. There was no mirror on the ceiling, thank God, with which the hotel equipped most of its rooms, but as Emily and Jun began to make love, they discovered, to their shock and hilarity, that the room was rigged with lasers that shot over the bed when one of them moaned.

"Turn it off, turn it off!" Emily laughed as Jun scampered about, looking for the sensor switch.

"Kuso," Jun swore, starting to lose his erection. He located the control console and said, "Hayaku, hayaku"—hurry, hurry—and leapt back onto the bed.

Years and years later, Emily would find the photograph of Jun on Aoyama-dori that night, grinning at the camera. Because of the flash and his black clothes, he would be disembodied, only his face and right hand, raised in a victory sign, visible. She would, of course, wonder what had become of him then. They would have stopped writing to each other long ago. She would know that he had studied for a brief time at the University of Texas, and though he'd enjoyed the music scene in Austin and was popular with the girls, he had felt dislocated. He would have moved back to Tokyo and found a job at a publishing company, albeit not involving literature, and then quit and begun working in advertising for the fashion industry, and that would be the last Emily would hear of Jun.

He scooted down on the bed for what she liked best. He had a special technique that demented her. After repeated inquiries, he revealed what he was doing down there. With his tongue, he was lightly tracing the hiragana and kanji characters that comprised the translated opening for *The Great Gatsby:* "In my younger and more vulnerable years . . ."

There was so much that Emily didn't know yet. She did not know that she would go to the Twin Cities for law school and never leave. She did not know about her father's Parkinson's or her best friend's son being blown apart by an IED or her sister's car getting T-boned by a drunk driver and leaving her a paraplegic. She did not know about the mindless infidelities and small heartaches and everyday betrayals—ordinary tragedies that abused and ravaged one's faith, yet constituted a life. She would never file an appellate brief or work for the ACLU or the Southern Poverty Law Center. She would be an attorney, part-time, for a small legal aid center in Minneapolis and specialize in immigration law, most of her clients Hmong, Laotian, Somali, Korean, and Mexican. It would be noble, important work, but so often tedious, processing applications for green cards, work permits, deportation stays, asylum claims.

Her commitment to multiculturalism and social justice would extend to her choice in lovers. She would marry and divorce twice. First a public defender (African American), then a photojournalist (Chicano), with whom she would have one son each. During the second birth, she would nearly hemorrhage out, and then two months later would almost die again because of a missed piece of placenta. They would tell her that, because of the scars in her uterus, she would never be able to conceive again, which would make her pregnancy with a daughter eight years later a surprise. She would not marry the girl's father, an ESL teacher (Bengali American), skittish about the institution, but would live with him, reasonably happy, hoping she was doing some good, doing her part, however small it might be. But occasionally, although she would try not to, she would be struck more by what she hadn't done than what she had. She would forget sometimes that she also knew about love, the virtue of patience and forgiveness, and about joy, the pleasure of being with those closest to her, family, friends, comrades, these beautiful mixed-blooded children people often assumed could not be hers, picnicking with them alongside Lake Nokomis on a warm, clear, breezy day, hearing their easy laughter, the reassurance of their safety.

Jun sensed where she was and pressed a little faster, harder. She wanted it to last forever, this feeling—youth, time, glory, everything still before her, waiting, her extraordinary life—but she felt it rolling over her and gave in to it.

"Oh, that was good," she said. "That was so good."

UFOs

• • • • • • • • • • •

FOR THE MOMENT, VICTORIA CRAWFORD had two lovers—
one who was married, one who was not. The latter, the one
who wasn't married, he was new, a mistake, really, a charity
case of sorts. She didn't know what she was doing with
him. The other, the one who was married, he was safe,
predictable, familiar. He was, until recently, her boss.

They worked together at WFTN, the NBC affiliate
in Boston. Richard Early had brought Victoria aboard
in January 2008 as a nightside reporter, but after a tepid
February sweeps, a media conglomerate took over the
station and cleaned house, demoting Richard to special
assignments producer. He had more time than he knew
what to do with now, free to leave the newsroom whenever he wanted to conduct "research," which for the last
four months had happened to land him, every Tuesday and
Thursday, in front of Victoria's door.

This particular Tuesday in July, he was loaded down
with groceries, out of breath from the three flights of stairs
to her one-bedroom on Marlborough Street.

"You're sweating," Victoria observed.

"It's hot out."

"There's a news flash."

Eleven thirty in the morning, and it was already ninety-three degrees, no breeze, no letup in sight to the week-long heat wave. New England weather. Victoria was sick of it. When she first got to Boston, practically all her assignments had required her to don her blue Storm Watch parka for stand-ups in front of the Mass Turnpike's sand and salt depots as crews prepared for nor'easters, half of which never materialized, or shivering in Copley Square, asking wind-whipped passersby what they thought of the cold. Now it was about the heat, the never-ending heat and humidity and dew point, which always seemed to be higher in her apartment than out.

"Come in the bedroom," she told Richard. "I'm living in the bedroom now." The apartment didn't have central air-conditioning, just a window unit in the bedroom. She'd bought a second air conditioner for the living room, but it had tripped the circuits, the wiring in her building apparently inadequate for the load.

She was still in her nightgown, unshowered, having awakened just an hour ago to read the newspapers with the half a cup of coffee she allowed herself a day. Caffeine was bad for the throat. After Richard put away the groceries, he stripped off his clothes and climbed into bed with her, and within minutes they were fucking.

Richard was twelve years older than Victoria, at forty-two the oldest person in the newsroom, but he was, without a doubt, the best lover she'd ever had, ready to go at a moment's notice. He was a rice chaser, California slang for a white guy with a fetish for Asian women. In that parlance, Victoria, who was 1.5—born overseas, in Korea in her case, but raised in the States—was a yellow cab, or a lu. As a general rule, she only dated white guys. Of course, Richard, after a lifetime of Asian girlfriends, had married a Wasp attorney, Bettina, who had ended up being unable to conceive. In the midst of IVF rounds, Richard had attended a seminar called Healing Love. He'd dabbled in tai chi over the years, as well as in other martial arts, and he had thought the seminar would be a session on qigong, focusing on fertility. Instead, it was about arousing the kundalini and awakening the chakras. It was about opening up the qi channels and recirculating sexual energy up the spinal fire channel and down the yin water channel. It was about *semen* retention and jing and the Microcosmic Orbit. It was about *testicle* breathing. Or some such nonsense. Richard had tried to explain it to Victoria once, and she didn't understand a word. She only cared about the end result, which was that Richard could maintain an erection for hours, coming but not ejaculating, and he made Victoria flop and fish in eye-white delirium.

More and more, though, there was only so much she could take. After thirty minutes, she was sore and, truth be told, a tad bored.

This was just sport, they had agreed. Neither of them expected or wanted him to leave Bettina, and they were never going to fall in love. She had had affairs like this—with EPs and editors and reporters—at almost every station she had worked. Who else would tolerate such hours? But the repetitive hump and run, the monotony of whack and smack, was becoming, the multiple orgasms notwithstanding, old. It was so dispassionate. She was beginning to—oh God, was she really going to admit this to herself?—feel that it wasn't enough.

They shifted positions, and she glanced at herself in the mirror. Supine, her breasts looked disturbingly saggy, deflated. In general, she hated every aspect of herself—her body, her vanity, her utter lack of conscience and compassion. She was an unlikable person, she knew, yet she seemed incapable of change. Nearly everything she did, in fact, only made her hate herself more, so she concentrated solely on the tangible, taking pride, for instance, in the definition of her ribs, each one of which she could see in the mirror, the happy result of five days a week at the gym and consistently skipping dinner. Lunch was her only real meal now, and she wondered what Richard was planning to make for her today. He loved to cook—a passion in which he could no longer indulge at home. Bettina had taken over the kitchen, ever since they had adopted a Korean boy two years ago. Now she made exclusively Korean food. She took the boy to Korean church and Korean culture classes. She enrolled herself in Korean-language school and had formed a network of Korean-adoptee families. She knew more about Korea than most Korean Americans. And Richard—who, for all his wonton, rice-chaser, vanilla-Asian proclivities, had argued they should Americanize the boy, immerse him in English and purge him of his roots—had been shut out as an unwelcome Caucasian wheel.

Victoria watched Richard squeeze his eyes shut, concentrating on circulating his qi or jing or whatever it was. "What time is it?" she asked him.

He stopped moving and looked down at her. "You're hungry, aren't you?"

"Famished," she said.

★ ★ ★

Yung-duk proved to be of no help whatsoever. The previous weekend, he had gone to the store with Victoria and lugged the new air conditioner up the stairs to her apartment and installed it into her living-room window, but this weekend, he told her he couldn't do anything about the wiring.

"You don't have enough amps," he said.

"¿Qué?"

"This circuit's connected to your refrigerator and stove. You need an electrician to increase the capacity. You should call your landlord."

"I *have,*" Victoria said. "There's nothing you can do?"

"Sorry."

"What good are you, then?"

He took the air conditioner out of the window and packed it in the box and carried it downstairs to his car and returned it to the store. Afterward, they decided to see a movie, and, to kill time before the next show, they went to a café on Newbury Street.

"Everyone's looking at you," Yung-duk told her.

She peered around the café. It wasn't everyone. A few people sneaking peeks.

"They recognize you," Yung-duk said.

"Maybe," she said, unimpressed.

"You have that aura, you know. You have this light, this radiance. It's impossible to ignore."

Victoria grimaced. It irritated her whenever he spoke like this. So corny. "Stop," she said, more convinced than ever she should break it off.

"What?"

"Don't you know sincerity is boring? Haven't you ever heard of irony?"

They had been seeing each other for three weeks, a setup by her uncle in LA, who, ever since Victoria's father died of pancreatic cancer, had taken it upon himself to find her a husband. When her uncle had first told her about his middle-school classmate's son, a 1.5 surgeon at Mass General, Victoria had assumed, of course, that he was another UFO, another Ugly Fucking Oriental. Korean men were generally the most unattractive and noxious of the lot. They were short and bowlegged, with disproportionately long torsos and no asses. They had enormous heads and pancake faces. They were macho and rude, and they had the same creepy stereotypes about Asian women as rice chasers—namely, that their women should wait on them hand and delicate foot, do all the cooking and cleaning and laundry, be quiet and submissive, essentially a maid, which was exactly how Victoria's father had treated his second and third wives.

And that name, Yung-duk Moon? Was her uncle kidding? *Yung-duk Moon?* Was there a more ridiculous, Old Country, Charlie Chan caricature of a name? Her uncle had persisted, though, and Victoria finally gave in. One drink. It couldn't hurt.

He wasn't as bad as she'd imagined. He had passable looks and was articulate and smart. He'd asked about her work and spoke movingly about his own. At Mass General, he was the attending plastic surgeon in Bigelow 13, the burn unit ICU. She might have gone out with him a second time, if only he hadn't called her again so quickly, if only he hadn't seemed so interested. Didn't he know anything about dating, about women? On the phone, he had asked if he could see her the next weekend, and she had said her toast was burning in the kitchen, could she call him right back. Needless to say, she didn't call him right back. She caller-IDed him and ignored his voice mails and emails, and after a few days he desisted.

But then the mice appeared. Everyone had told her that the Back Bay was the place to live in Boston, that Marlborough Street was the most fashionable address to have. It was a lovely, quaint street, all right, and her brownstone apartment was charming and roomy, a through-and-through, but with parking it cost her two thousand a month—exorbitant in 2008—and it lacked the most basic amenities: no dishwasher, no garbage disposal, no central air. Quaint. They could have quaint. She'd take prefab, wall-to-wall, unadorned square box any day. What she couldn't take were mice.

Technically, she supposed, it was just one mouse. As she walked into her kitchen one night, it skittered across her foot and underneath the stove. She used an entire roll of packing tape to seal off the bottom of the appliance, and still she couldn't fathom sleeping there that night. She called Yung-duk Moon and drove across the river to his condo in Cambridge. Maybe it was the adrenaline, or the wine. Sitting on his couch with a glass of Merlot, she found Yung-duk, dressed in his scrubs, strangely attractive. She forgot herself and slept with him.

Each time she saw him thereafter, she meant to end it. Yet he was so useful. He plugged up the hole in the wall behind the stove where the mouse had come through. He got her car inspected. He assembled a bookcase for her.

He mailed some boxes. It was nice having someone to rely on, someone to go to the movies with, to take as a date to the occasional benefit party. In those situations, standing with a champagne flute or a canapé, Yung-duk acquitted himself well. He was polite, empathetic, a great listener. It was only sitting down with him, when the small talk had been exhausted, that the void emerged. A void of personality, nothing there except sunny solicitude, the exact representation of another stereotype about Asian men that she despised—diffident, emasculated, ever so accommodating with a toothy Hop Sing smile.

"Tell me the weirdest thing about you," she said one night, and he thought and thought, and came up blank.

"Like what?"

"Let me ask you this, how come you use your Korean name?" she said. Most 1.5s ditched their Korean names in favor of American ones at the first opportunity. "Weren't you teased mercilessly about it as a kid?" He had grown up in Davenport, Iowa.

Unbelievably he said, "Not really."

"You didn't go through the usual period of self-loathing and Twinkie denial?"

Unbelievably he said, "No."

He was completely at ease being Korean. He was close to his family. He had Korean friends, whom she refused to meet, and he belonged to a Korean church, which she refused to attend. He wanted her to go to Korean Culture Day with him. She laughed and laughed when he had first suggested it.

"What about you?" he said.

"What about me?"

"Did you change your name because of your job?"

This was the other problem with Yung-duk Moon: he knew too much about her, thanks to her uncle. He knew her name was Hyo-son, not Victoria; Cho, not Crawford.

"Yes," she lied.

"And your—" He gestured to his eyes. "The blepharoplasty?"

She couldn't get this past him, either, as a plastic surgeon. Everyone, including Richard, assumed she was a hapa, but she was full-blooded Korean. She had begun dying her hair brown when she was in junior high school in San Marino, California. She had had a blepharoplasty (her lids creased to make her eyes look rounder) when she was in high school, a rhinoplasty (nose) when she was an undergraduate at USC, and a genioplasty (chin) after her third on-air job in Binghamton, New York. At first, it had been an advantage in the business, being Asian, yet as she bounced from one small market to another, she discovered that female Asian reporters were a dime a dozen. You could be ethnic, but not too ethnic. It was better to blur your origins, a little bit of this, a little bit of that, not too distinctly other. Multiracial was very hot.

If anyone was to blame for all of this, it was her father. He had taken her to her first cosmetic surgeon when she was seven—two years after their arrival in America, one year after Victoria's mother died—to have a frenectomy, snipping the thin band of tissue underneath her tongue to facilitate her English, freeing her mouth to say "rice" instead of "lice." The day she'd died, her mother had gone to two pharmacies and had tried to explain, in her halting English, what she wanted. Victoria's father, out of grief and guilt, believed that if she had been able to communicate with the pharmacists, she wouldn't have committed suicide. She used to suffer from awful migraines, he told Victoria, and she must have been in terrible pain, unhinged. If only she had been able to describe her condition and gotten triptan or ergotamine, he said, she would never have killed herself.

From that point on, he told Victoria to forget her Korean and speak only English. He hired tutors and made Victoria join the debate team and the choir and the drama club. By the time she became a broadcast journalism major, she already knew all about pitch and duration and intonation, about what the French called liaison—linking words together properly. She also acquired a reporter's inquisitiveness, an insistent need to find out why people did the things they did, although she had long ago figured out that her mother had not been at the pharmacy for her migraines, but for sleeping pills, something tidier and gentler than having to, as she did, go home and shoot herself with her husband's gun.

She wasn't asking the right questions. Her reports were coming out tepid. She had never been much of a writer to begin with, and she had always relied on sound bites and video for her packages. As much as Richard railed against the station's slick new tabloid format, the style suited Victoria. WFTN was all about pace and presentation now. Flashy sets, graphics, music, a minimum of chatter, an emphasis on breaking news, especially crime. It was aggressive, in-your-face, with plenty of live shots and dramatic camera angles. Rather than the classic stand-up, it was walk-and-talk, everything always *moving,* fast, entire wraparounds timed out to a minute fifteen. Who couldn't fill a minute fifteen?

There was a fire in Roxbury, five alarms. A mother and her baby boy were standing on a fire escape when it gave way, and for ten agonizing seconds, the mother hung on to her baby with one arm and to the fire escape with the other, until the remaining support bracket snapped off the wall. They fell onto a lower level of the building that was already engulfed, crashing through the roof. The woman died, but the baby, miraculously, was still alive, shielded by his mother from the brunt of the fall and fire.

There were witnesses, but Victoria couldn't locate any who could provide the histrionics she needed. She looked for the woman's husband, relatives, friends, neighbors. She wanted weeping and caterwauling, breathless descriptions and lurid excitations, convulsions and collapses, cheap sensationalism and sentimentality. Instead she got dull pronouncements from policemen and the fire chief and worthless hypotheses from a few syrup-brained bystanders. "Where were you when it happened?" Victoria asked. "What did you see? How did you feel?" She finally corralled a woman who was willing to go on camera. She was crying, distraught—perfect. "What were you thinking when you saw them fall?" Victoria asked.

The woman frowned. "I didn't see them fall."

"What?"

"Didn't see it."

Nothing came to Victoria's mind except that familiar mantra, *How do you feel? How do you feel?* "Well," she said, "how do you think you would have felt if you *had* seen them?"

"Huh?" the woman said.

Victoria turned to her cameraman, Milos, and sliced her finger across her throat. She did a quick, uninspired VO-SOT for the six o'clock and then went back to the station, where she caught the predictable flak. The other channels not only got interviews with the family, one of them had *film* of the fall, taken by someone with a camcorder. "We got completely shellacked on this story," the nightside EP told her. "Come up with something we can sell for the eleven."

Richard was still at the station, editing a feature on STDs. It was July sweeps, which meant special reports on sex, drugs, violence, and communicable diseases, with bonus points if religion could be thrown into the mix: "Are Your Children Dying to Get High?" "Is a Terrorist Living Next Door to You?" "Is Your Priest a Pedophile?" The perfect story for today's if-it-bleeds-it-leads newscasts, Richard once told her, was a love triangle between a politician, a priest, and a prostitute, the latter ideally a fourteen-year-old heroin addict who'd contracted HIV and given birth to a deformed baby, over whom there was a custody battle and a fugitive warrant, ending with a crash and a shoot-out after a live car chase on the interstate, tragically resulting in an innocent driver being decapitated or impaled by pipes.

In the editing room, Victoria told Richard about the evening debacle. "I wish I was perky enough to be an anchor," she said. "It'd be so much easier—and more lucrative." She had held various stints in her career as a weekend anchor, but research directors always said she wasn't ebullient enough, particularly evident when she had to gab on-air with other broadcasters, her jokes and retorts falling flat.

"You don't want to be another Kewpie-doll talking head," Richard said. "You're better than that."

Was she? Victoria was beginning to wonder. But she was touched that Richard thought so. For all his anti-quated ideas about ethics and journalistic integrity, she respected Richard enormously. He was a real newsman, with more local Emmys than all the other producers combined at WFTN.

"It's the damn people angle," Victoria said. "If I didn't have to deal with people, I'd be fine. Give me some advice."

"There's no secret to interviewing. You just have to reserve judgment. You might think you know what's going on, but there's always a story within the story. Be open to it. Stop thinking so much and try to feel what they're feeling. The key is to care."

Victoria was disappointed. She had expected more from Richard in the way of pearly wisdom, not platitudes. Granted, he had pinpointed her exact problem. She rarely cared, she could hardly ever imagine what people were feeling.

Luckily she didn't have to for the eleven o'clock up-date on the Roxbury fire. She found out the baby had been transferred from Boston Medical to Mass General's burn unit, and Yung-duk was on duty.

She talked to him in the stairwell outside Bigelow 13.

"You know the HIPAA rules," Yung-duk said. "I can't tell you anything other than his condition. You shouldn't even be up here without Public Affairs."

"How badly is he burned?"

"Come on."

"Is he going to survive?"

"Are you listening?"

"As a personal favor to me?" Victoria said. The other stations would only have the official statement that the boy was in critical condition. If she could say whether he'd live or die, it'd be a small scoop. She put her arms around Yung-duk's waist, interlaced her fingers, and gazed up at him.

"This is very transparent," he said.

"I'll make you dinner."

"You can't cook."

"I'll do that thing you like."

"A tempting offer, but no."

"I'll go to Korean Culture Day with you."

"Again, nice try, but this isn't something I can negotiate."

"Even if it's off the record? Is he in bad shape?" For a moment, she felt an uncharacteristic pang of sympathy for the baby. Even if he were to survive, he would be an orphan, and probably disfigured for life. But she quickly put aside the thought. "Don't you want to help me?"

"You won't use anything I say?" Yung-duk asked dubiously. After listening to her promises, he told her the baby presented with sustained 40 percent TBSA deep partial and full thickness circumferential burns, then rattled off some vital signs and potassium and hemoglobin lab values and finished with a flourish of acronyms.

"What?" Victoria said. "Start over with TBSA."

He went slower, but grudgingly. He was being downright surly, actually. This was a side of Yung-duk she hadn't seen before. Where was that moon-faced jollity of his, that hop-to, chop-chop servitude?

"Is the baby going to die?" she asked.

He sighed. He talked about the debridement and grafting they'd do in the next two weeks, about the possibility of sepsis, renal failure, pseudonomas infection.

"So he's going to live," she said.

He looked at her, then said, "Probably."

"Is it safe to say that on the air? I won't name you as my source."

"Victoria, please don't do this."

"You don't have to say a thing to me," she told him. "But if I were to report that hospital sources have told me they believe the boy has a good chance of survival, would I be wrong? Let's just stand here for ten seconds. I'll count to ten, and if you're still here, I'll know I wouldn't be wrong."

It was the oldest ploy in the book. In the stairwell, Yung-duk crossed his arms and leaned against the wall and stared at her churlishly, but he did not leave, and she had her story.

Ninety-two degrees out, and she began, of all things, sneezing as soon as they arrived at the park in Sudbury.

"Allergies," Yung-duk diagnosed as they unloaded the car.

"I don't have allergies," Victoria said, then sneezed again.

"I've got some antihistamines in the glove box."

"No can do," she said. Antihistamines, along with peanut butter, pretzels, and all dairy products, dried out the vocal tract. "Tequila would be good, though. Anything to get me through the afternoon."

They were a little late, and everything was already in full swing—soccer and volleyball games, a tae kwon do demonstration, all sorts of arts-and-crafts activities under tents. A hundred Korean children were running amok in the park, parents looking at them fawningly, nary an Oriental face among the adult crowd.

Korean Culture Day was not for Koreans, per se, but for adoptees and their white parents, an opportunity for the kids to "bond" with one another and expose them to Korean culture and alleviate, for one day, the guilt their parents felt for plucking them from their homeland and hauling them halfway across the world to the white-bread suburbs of Boston.

They had barely reached the end of the slope from the parking lot before Richard's wife, Bettina, spotted Victoria. "Oh, I'm so happy you're here," she sang.

This wasn't quite the reception Victoria had been expecting. Earlier that week, knowing Bettina would be here, then learning she was one of the day's organizers, Victoria had asked Richard if he would find it awkward if she came. Bettina had to suspect something by now. But Richard had said, "Why would it be awkward?"—exactly the answer Victoria had wanted, and one that had depressed her profoundly.

"I've been badgering Richard to get you to attend," Bettina said.

Victoria sneezed.

"Bless you," Yung-duk said at the same time Bettina said, "Utchoo," the Korean equivalent. Glancing at Victoria and then at Yung-duk, Bettina asked, smiling slyly, "You two came together?" They knew each other from previous summers. Yung-duk had been participating in Korean Culture Day ever since he was an undergrad at Tufts and a member of the Korean Student Association.

Bettina dragooned Victoria into playing MC for a fashion show, and as she escorted her toward one of the tents, she hooked Victoria's arm inside hers and said, "I would have set you up with him a long time ago if I'd known you were looking."

One by one, children in hanbok, ceremonial Korean costumes, walked out from behind a curtain for the fashion show. Victoria's job was to read off their names and, courtesy of a script Bettina had written for her, describe the garments, the boys' paji and magoja, the girls' chima and jeogori. Victoria knew she should have summoned a little more enthusiasm and cooed over the kids, exhorting the audience to do the same, but it wasn't in her. That low percolation factor. Bettina didn't seem to mind, however, beaming from her chair with a little Korean boy, obviously her son, on her lap. What was his name? Richard must have told her at some point, but she couldn't remember.

"He has a Korean name and an American name," Bettina said after the show, the boy hiding behind her. "You want to tell her what they are, honey?"

"Mark," he said, barely audible.

"And your Korean name?"

"Chung-ho."

"Victoria's half-Korean. She's a reporter at Daddy's station. Don't you think she's pretty?"

The boy wiped his nose on her dress, then said, "Curate."

Bettina brushed aside his bangs. "You've had so much Kool-Aid today. Just one more cup, all right?" The boy bolted.

"He's cute," Victoria said, although she didn't think he was.

"I know," Bettina said, and launched into a story about

something funny the boy had done the other day, which Victoria didn't find all that funny but laughed at, anyway. "I'm worried about him, though," Bettina said. "He's so shy. You notice he wasn't in the fashion show. He wanted no part in that. He has a little speech impediment."

Victoria almost told her about frenectomies and phonemes and exercises for ending consonant plosives—"Fat lazy cat," "Put a cup," "Drink buttermilk"—but checked the impulse.

"We've been sending him to a speech therapist," Bettina said. "The other kids are teasing him that he's a foreigner and saying I can't be his real mom. I'm dreading when he starts school in September. He's going to ask me, What's wrong with me? Why didn't my parents want me? And even though I've been steeling myself for those questions ever since we adopted him, just the thought of it breaks my heart."

Victoria suddenly felt herself well up. Allergies, she told herself. "Kids are more resilient than you think," she said to Bettina.

Yung-duk was under the crafts tent, showing kids how to make kites out of bamboo and paper, and Richard was in the adjacent cooking tent, watching kids prepare mandu dumplings. He waved Victoria over. "That's right, fold them over just like tacos," he said to the children, then steered her toward the field. "I met your new boyfriend, *Yung-duk*. So, if you get married, you might have Young-Yung-duklings?"

"You've been drinking," she said.

"I've been sampling a little of the soju. What were you and Bettina talking about?"

"How all men are shits. How everything awful you ever suspected about them is true."

"You're in a mood."

She was, inexplicably. Despite everything, she liked Bettina, and meeting her and her son made Victoria wonder about Richard. What was this whole coming-but-not-ejaculating thing about? Why was he *withholding* himself from everyone in his life? Why wasn't he more supportive of his son?

She joined Yung-duk in the crafts tent, and he introduced her to several of his friends, most of whom were American-born Korean classmates from Tufts and BU, where he'd gone to med school. Nice enough, although a bit too enthralled with her, as most people were when meeting a friend's new romantic interest, one who also happened to be a minor celebrity. They chatted for a while, and then everyone moved in front of the main stage for a recital.

In the middle of the second performance, Yung-duk and his friends began slipping down the aisle in a crouch. "Where are you going?" Victoria whispered.

"A surprise," he said, and winked.

Twenty minutes later, he and his crew of friends reappeared, this time onstage and in costume. Yung-duk's hanbok was the most elaborate among them, topped off with a black gat, a wide-brimmed cylindrical hat made of horsehair. He knelt down and placed a six-stringed zither on his thighs and began plunking out a Korean folk song, his friends accompanying him on dulcimer, oboe, drum, and gong. A group of college students came out and performed a couple of traditional dances, and afterward Yung-

duk began *singing,* swaying in time as he urged everyone
to join him for two famous ballads, "Sae-ya, Sae-ya" and
"Arirang."

Heritage camp, Yung-duk told Victoria as they stood in
the buffet line. He had gone to heritage camp in Colorado
every summer throughout high school and learned, among
other things, to play the zither. "Mostly," he said, "I learned
who I am."

They sat down at a picnic table, and Yung-duk dug into
the piles of bulgogi, kalbi, and japchae on his plate. A boy
and a girl were chasing each other and circled the table,
trailing a busted kite that bounced up and grazed Yung-
duk on the shoulder, knocking his hat atilt. He laughed
and said to them, "Careful," and adjusted the brim. "I love
kids," he said to Victoria. "Don't you?"

She looked at him looking at her, waiting for an answer,
smiling, blissfully unaware, thinking she was his girlfriend
and that they were heading toward something meaningful
enough to produce Young-Yung-duklings. What could she
say to him? How could she make him see the things she
had seen, educate him that the world was a terrible place,
a den of tragedy and heartache where lovers betrayed each
other and innocents were impaled by pipes? She looked at
him looking at her, and she pitied him.

An ambulance raced by the park, followed by two fire
trucks, sirens bawling. Victoria stood up from the table and
called the station on her cell phone. She asked the assign-
ment editor if they were picking up anything on the scan-
ners for Sudbury, and he said a car accident at Willets Pond.

"Where's Willets Pond?" she asked Yung-duk.

It was only half a mile from the park, but when they

got to the scene of the accident, a wide, gentle curve that opened to the pond, the victim had already been pulled from the water and taken away in the ambulance. Within minutes of their arrival, another car appeared. Several men rushed to the water's edge, and there was a commotion, one of them—a beefy, handsome blond—yelling. After talking to the firefighters, the men got back in the car and peeled away.

By the time her cameraman, Milos, reached Sudbury with the news truck, Victoria was working on her script: "A beautiful family outing was shattered by a tragic accident today." The couple, Frank and Amanda Mahoney, was among the parents at Korean Culture Day—Victoria thought she remembered seeing them now, arguing, but she couldn't be sure—and Amanda had left to find a store with hot dog buns. Not all of the children were that enamored with the Korean food. Apparently she had lost control of her car and had driven into the pond. An anonymous caller reported seeing it go under. Amanda was pronounced dead at the hospital, leaving her eight-year-old adopted Korean daughter, Jileen, with her husband, who was, ironically, a firefighter in nearby Watertown.

Milos took some footage of Amanda's car being dragged out of the pond. Victoria said goodbye to Yung-duk, and she and Milos drove first to the hospital and then to the Mahoneys' house. Victoria knocked on the door and unfurled the usual soft sell to Mahoney's brother, trying to convince him that it'd be a tribute to Amanda, an honor to her memory, to have him or Frank describe her on camera, talk about what type of person she was, how deeply she would be missed, that it might even be cathartic to share their sorrow, but Mahoney's brother, Tim, would have none of it. Watertown was decidedly blue-collar, far less posh than the suburbs of Lincoln, Sudbury, Concord, and Lexington where most of the adoptive parents lived, and Tim Mahoney, a firefighter as well, didn't bother with any bourgeois formalities. "You people are a bunch of fucking vultures. Keep the fuck away from us," he said.

They sat in the news truck, waiting to see if they could snare any relatives or friends or neighbors on their way to the house. The standard grief watch. It was a humid night, and Victoria fanned herself with her notebook. She started to feel her bladder expand, and she tried to calculate how long it would be before she had to pee. This, among other humiliations, was one of the worst parts of the job: figuring out where to go to the bathroom. Out here, the choices were asking neighbors for use of their facilities or sneaking behind a tree.

Something bumped against the door of the truck. Victoria leaned out the window and saw, down below, a little Korean girl.

"You were at the park today," the girl said.

Victoria stepped out of the truck. "Yes, I was."

"You're Korean."

"Uh-huh."

"I've seen you on TV."

Victoria crouched down so she was eye level with the girl. "Your name is Jileen, isn't it?"

The little girl nodded.

"I'm Victoria." The girl was in a white dress, a church dress, and—this was very odd—Victoria noticed she was wearing makeup. Blush and lipstick. "I'm so sorry about your mother, Jileen," Victoria said.

"Will you put me on TV?"

"What?"

"I want to talk about my mommy. I want people to know what kind of mommy she was."

Milos didn't like the idea. They should get her father's permission and have him present, he said, but Victoria knew Frank Mahoney would never give his consent. "Let's tape it and see where it goes," she told Milos. "We don't have to use it. If it's iffy, we can show it to the Mahoneys and let them decide."

They were walking a very thin line, which they tacitly acknowledged when they agreed to set up the interview by the side of the truck and shoot it with a small Cool-Lux light, lest they be seen from the house or by the two other news crews parked down the street. Both Milos and Victoria got on their knees, and after he checked the sound level, she said to Jileen, "Why don't you tell me about your mommy? Whatever pops into your head."

"She was nice," Jileen said.

"What kinds of things did you do together?"

"We went to Ireland," she said, and she recounted a family trip to Dublin earlier that summer, then a week they spent at Lake Winnipesauke last year. The girl was rambling, but nonetheless was composed, not yet comprehending what had happened. Victoria, her bladder about to burst, shifted on her knees. She wondered what Frank Mahoney had told Jileen, or if, as her own father did, he had let his brother break the news to her that her mother had died.

"What about things you did every day?"

"We read books, and we baked cookies."

"Chocolate chip?"

"Oatmeal raisin."

They had gone to a church picnic for the day, just Victoria and her father, her mother excusing herself because of a headache. When they had come home, they had registered a funny smell—metallic, sulfuric. Her father had gone into the bedroom, then the den, then had sprinted out, his face a rictus of terror. He had swooped Victoria up and out of the house, and had had an assistant from his office drive her to her uncle's place in Mission Viejo, where she'd remained until the funeral.

"Is that your favorite food in the whole world?"

"No, grilled cheese. Mommy made the best grilled cheese."

"What was her secret? Did she have a trick to making them?"

Jileen described her mother's special method for preparing grilled cheese sandwiches, grating cheddar and brushing white bread with melted butter and sprinkling slices with a dust of paprika, and as she talked, Victoria intuited an obvious fact, something she should have gleaned much earlier, which was that Amanda Mahoney did not lose control of her car, but had intentionally driven it into the pond.

"Do you know why she was so unhappy?" Victoria asked.

Jileen stared at her uncertainly.

Victoria was no longer thinking. Her consciousness had become viscous and was recirculating through her body, urinating all decorum. She was feeling what the girl was feeling—if not now, then what she would in the years to come. "Why do you think she didn't want to live anymore?"

Jileen inhaled sharply.

"Do you keep asking if somehow it was your fault?"

The girl began to wail and ran to the house.

Victoria, finger to her throat, turned to Milos, but he was already packing his camera back into the truck.

After the eleven o'clock broadcast, Victoria went home, and the phone rang. "Long day, huh?" Yung-duk said.

She was tired and in no mood to chat.

"My friends really liked you," he said.

She switched on the window air conditioner in her bedroom and took off her shoes.

"We were talking about getting a house on the Vineyard, Labor Day weekend," Yung-duk said. "What do you think?"

"You don't know everything," she said.

"Hm?"

"I hate kids. They're a pain in the ass. They're a nuisance. They ruin everything. I never want to have kids."

"Oh," Yung-duk said after a pause.

"You say you know who you are, but you don't know anything," Victoria told him, hating herself as she spoke. "You're pathetic. I've been fucking Richard Early the entire time we've been going out. He makes me come five ways to Sunday, and I've never had a single orgasm with you."

He stayed on the line a few seconds, silent. "I'm sorry it didn't work out," he said finally, adding, "I hope you find happiness someday," then hung up.

Victoria set down the phone and wept.

★ ★ ★

The following week, Jileen's uncle, Tim Mahoney, called Victoria at the station, but not for the reason she had expected. Jileen, it appeared, did not tell anyone about the interview. Mahoney had a proposal: as a public service, he and his brother, under the auspices of the Watertown Fire Department, wanted to film a demonstration on how to escape from a submerged car. He apologized for his language the other night—the heat of the moment, he said—and told her, "We figure if something good can come out of this, we ought to do it. Maybe we can save a few lives."

The station loved the idea, as did Victoria. Participatory journalism always pulled in great ratings. They assigned Richard to produce the segment. "Wonderful," he said to her. "I suppose if this goes well, I'll have to do an entire series of 'Get Out Alive' specials. Burning buildings. Lost in the woods. Attorney-infested waters."

Two afternoons later, they gathered at a boat launch along the Charles River in Watertown, and while the fire department prepared the demonstration, Milos shot Victoria's introduction to the segment. "You're driving in your car, and your accelerator sticks. Or maybe the roads are slick, and you skid off a curve into the adjacent river. Would you know what to do? Every year, more than eleven thousand drivers find themselves trapped underwater in their cars, and an estimated three hundred people drown, many of them needlessly. Today, I'm going to show you how to escape and avoid becoming another victim."

Tim Mahoney put on scuba gear. His brother, Frank, stood to the side, watching, but he wasn't in uniform.

"You're sure this is safe?" Victoria asked Tim Mahoney.

"Piece of cake," he said.

There would be four other divers alongside him, and she would have an air tank and a regulator and a center-punch on the seat next to her. The car would be attached to a fire truck by cable in case they needed to winch it out, and they had a rescue boat and an ambulance standing by.

Milos and Richard mounted two fish-eye cameras inside the car, a rusty Oldsmobile junker. "If I die," she told them, lifting a can of hair spray, fuming the air, "at least get my good side."

They did another stand-up beside the car. "The first thing to remember is don't panic. The firefighters have told me that cars usually stay afloat for a few moments, and that's when you should remember the acronym POGO: *push* the button to release the seatbelt, *open* the window, and *get out*."

"Ready?" Tim Mahoney asked.

She strapped herself in the car and gave everyone a thumbs-up. She wasn't at all nervous. This was looking to be a terrific segment. A firefighter tapped on the window and again asked if she was ready, and she again brandished a thumbs-up. Then she put the car into neutral, and they pushed it down the boat ramp. The car bobbed rather gently away from the shore. She had plenty of time to escape right then, but they had all agreed it would be more instructive (and dramatic) to wait until she was fully submerged. The water began filling the interior, and Victoria gasped, surprised the river was so cold, even in early August. The weight of the engine tipped the car down, and, as prepared as she was for this inevitability, she was taken aback by how quickly it went down, barely able to swallow

a last breath. She saw lights in front of her. Another cameraman who was a recreational diver was filming with an
underwater housing.

POGO, she thought to herself, and she pressed the
seat-belt release button and grabbed the window crank
handle. It came off the door. She sat mystified for a moment, staring at the crank handle in her hand. Tim Mahoney had said when the car was completely flooded, the
pressure would be equalized and she'd be able to open the
door. She lunged for the door handle, but it, too, came off
in her hand.

She panicked. She blew out her air and tried to scream
and banged on the window. She was going to die. Tim
Mahoney swam up to the car and, suspended before her,
his eyes dull and emotionless behind his mask, he watched
as she caterwauled and convulsed and flailed. Then he
smashed the glass with a crowbar and dragged her out.

She rolled onto the concrete of the boat ramp and
retched. On her knees, spluttering water, she said to Tim
Mahoney, "You son of a bitch. You set me up. You rigged
the car."

He stared as she dry-heaved. "I don't know what you're
talking about. You were never in any danger."

"I'm going to sue your ass. I'm going to press charges.
I'm going to get you all fired."

His brother, Frank, stood over her, hands in his pockets.
"Who's the one who should get fired?" he said. "Because
of you, my daughter thinks her mother killed herself, you
bitch."

"What's he talking about?" Richard asked as the Mahoney brothers walked away.

Hair in her face, she looked up at Richard from the ground, shivering in the heat of the day, a wet helpless heap. She realized she had pissed herself.

Milos pressed his lips together in disgust. "Go on. Tell him," he said.

The news business was full of ironies. It turned out that Amanda Mahoney had, in all likelihood, committed suicide. There were no mechanical problems with her car, and there was no evidence—no skid marks or evasive tracks on the muddy embankment, no alcohol or drugs in her system—to suggest she did not speed straight into the pond. Yet Richard would not have anything more to do with Victoria, despite her attempts to explain, pleading that there was more going on than he knew, a story within the story. Intending to embarrass her, he convinced the station to air the segment as an example of what not to do when trapped in a sinking car.

It was a big hit. Instead of ruining Victoria's career, it landed her, four months later, at ABC News in New York and then, a year and a half after that, with her dream job—network correspondent in London.

In the fall, before leaving Boston, she called Yung-duk Moon and asked to see him again. She felt bad about the way she'd treated him, and, surprisingly, she missed him. He had been nothing but kind to her. But he told her no, he didn't want to see her. He said she represented the exact stereotypes of Asian women he had always despised—spoiled, bloodless, vain, fake.

Victoria was thinking about what he had said one day in her rental in Kensington, one of the more fashionable districts of London. Her one-bedroom suite was in a hotel for extended stays, posh and well appointed, the building offering many amenities, including central air-conditioning, but unfortunately no room service. She watched a video-tape of the previous night's broadcast, a massive brushfire in California one of the lead stories. She was waiting for her current lover, the London bureau's assistant news di-rector, to arrive. This lover, he was married, naturally, and for a moment she felt weary and alone. All the cities and towns, all the men.

She fast-forwarded the tape to her report on the PM, and she admired the cut of her blouse as she stood in front of 10 Downing Street, the perky plum shape of her breasts, which she'd had augmented before going overseas. She wondered whether she needed a mini brow lift, and also whether she should pursue a new procedure she had heard of—a nerve behind the knee could be severed to atrophy the radish-like bulges in calves, to which Asian women were prone. She had come this far, and she didn't fore-see any limits to her future. Although she was no closer to knowing why people did the things they did, she had everything she ever wanted, she supposed, and she looked happily at her face on the tape. Granted, it was a face she might never truly learn to love.

There was a knock on the door, and she went to open it, hoping her lover had picked up lunch for her on the way, perhaps something from the Indian restaurant down the street, a nice little curry.

LES HÔTELS D'ALAIN

I

THE SANNO

· · · · · · · · · ·

WE WERE SUPPOSED TO STAY at the Sanno Hotel for only a week or so while my parents looked for an apartment to rent, but we ended up spending the entire summer there. For me, fourteen at the time, there could have been nothing better, having the run of the sprawling hotel, being overseas again.

This was forty-five years ago, in 1974. The Sanno—located in the Akasaka district of Tokyo—was called a transient billeting facility, meant to house US military personnel on R&R (Rest and Recuperation), TDY (Temporary Duty), or, as with us, in Japan for a PCS (Permanent Change of Station). Although my father was classified as an Air Force civilian, he was not actually employed by the military, however. He was in the CIA, something I'd learned two years earlier and was still trying to puzzle out.

The Sanno had a pool, an arcade of stores, beauty and barbershops, a spa, a cocktail lounge, a movie theater, and several restaurants that featured a continuous rotation of buffets. Much of it was staffed by non-Japanese Asians, mostly Filipino and Korean. There were also quite a few non-Japanese Asian women, mostly Thai and Vietnamese, who served as the dates or girlfriends or wives of the officers and GIs in the Sanno. Yet there were very few Asians like us—Asian Americans—at the hotel, a situation that was not unfamiliar to me.

My father was Korean American, born and raised in Lincoln, Nebraska, until he moved to Honolulu for high school. My mother, who'd never left O'ahu before meeting my dad at the University of Hawai'i, was your typical Hawaiian mixed plate of Asian ethnicities: Korean and Okinawan, with some Chinese, Filipino, and Japanese thrown in there, along with a trace of Portuguese, maybe a freckle of Scottish. Apart from haoles, i.e., the white minority, practically everyone on the island was just like us. Nearly everywhere else in the world, though, we were viewed as anomalies, objects of flagrant curiosity, especially in the countries to which my father was posted (local boys would often trail after me in astonishment, yelling, "Bruce Lee! Bruce Lee!").

My father had studied Korean, Japanese, and political science at UH, but absurdly, after recruiting him, the CIA had assigned him to the Middle East desk. Thus, we were sent to Turkey, Egypt, Lebanon, Iran, and Oman, with queer detours to Yugoslavia, Greece, and Zaire. We never stayed anywhere longer than two years, sometimes leaving after just one. In those days, these were not desirable or even very tolerable overseas posts, although they were relatively safe. Pretty much all of them were considered hardship assignments, meriting additional pay. "Shitholes," my mother called them. "The armpits of the Third World. Why is it we never get to go anywhere *nice*?"

Another one of her perennial complaints was about my dad's covers. Almost without exception, his covers were

DOD-related—some sort of military attaché or advisor or liaison officer, often with the USIA or Army, not as a full-fledged diplomat in the State Department. So, we never got a fancy house or a maid, or a luxury sedan or a chauffeur, or a nanny or a gardener. We never got blue diplomatic license plates that would allow us to park anywhere with impunity, or black diplomatic passports that would let us bypass security at airports and enter lounges and get upgraded to first class. Generally speaking, we never got to be, as my mother desired, "big shots."

Tokyo was supposed to be a major change for us, a substantial step up, but my father's office wasn't even in the US Embassy building. He was in the Provost Marshal Liaison Detachment (PMLD) for the Fifth Air Force at Hardy Barracks, a little outpost in Nogizaka that contained offices for the *Stars and Stripes* newspaper and the Office of Naval Research (which might have been the NSA), a helipad, a tiny Navy Exchange store, and a lone gas pump. And we wouldn't be living in the Grew House, the embassy housing compound near Roppongi, either. We had to find a civilian apartment somewhere in the city.

This task was challenging for several reasons. First was the meager budget my father had been given. Second was that many Japanese landlords didn't like renting to gaijin, or foreigners. Third was that though we were American, we were Korean by blood, which didn't play well with a lot of Japanese.

"This is *ridiculous*," my mom would say to my father after another fruitless day of searching. "This is impossible!"

We were beginning to go stir-crazy in the Sanno. Initially I'd been thrilled just to be half a world away from

Falls Church, Virginia, near CIA headquarters, where my father had been posted for a year. It'd been the first time I'd ever lived in the States for an extended period, other than our usual home leaves to Hawai'i every other summer. As expected, being the new kid in Virginia—one who happened to be "Oriental"—I'd been bullied and taunted. I couldn't wait to get out of there. But as the summer wore on in Tokyo, I was running out of ways to entertain myself.

After breakfast with my parents, I'd usually go to the small bookstore near the front entrance and read for a while in the lobby. I liked spy thrillers. I'd watch the comings and goings of guests and imagine clandestine meetings and assignations. The hotel was busy. Although the Vietnam War had almost completely wound down by then, there was still a large US presence in the Pacific Rim, and a lot of personnel came through the Sanno. Eventually I'd meander from the lobby into the game room and play pinball until I ran out of quarters, then I'd go upstairs and change into my trunks and head to the swimming pool, where I'd eat a cheeseburger and fries for lunch at the snack bar. By one o'clock, I'd be bored.

My father often had to go out at night for his job, so when dinnertime rolled around, my mother and I would eat at one of the buffets and then amble into the cocktail lounge, where there was sometimes live music. I would have a Coke with five maraschino cherries and she would have a glass of Mateus Rosé before shifting to Rusty Nails—Scotch with a dash of bitters and Drambuie liqueur floating on top, garnished with a twist of lemon.

"Promise me something, Alain," she said to me one

night. "Promise me you won't end up to be a useless panty like your father."

I didn't know how to respond to this. Panty was Hawaiian pidgin for wimp, wuss.

"Promise me you'll stand up for yourself once in a while, be a man," she said. "Promise me you'll have some *balls.*"

A Filipino couple—husband on electric guitar and wife on synthesizer—was performing on the little stage in the lounge, butchering Beatles songs in broken English.

I wasn't sure if my mother was expecting an answer from me. Thankfully, by the time the Filipino duo finished singing "Lucy in the Sky with Diamonds," she'd moved on.

"Want another Coke?" she asked me. "I think you do. I think it's high time for another round, yeah?"

The apartment my parents at last found for us, a few days before school was to begin, was in the Minami Aoyama Dai-ichi Mansions. The name was a misnomer. Granted, the large main building—twelve stories with bay windows and balconies, the exterior walls clad in a mosaic of tiny orange tiles—was quite fancy, and celebrities were rumored to be among the residents, yet in Japan the word *manshon* simply signified a structure that had been constructed with reinforced concrete (and was therefore more resistant to earthquakes), opposed to the wood frames of an *apaato.* In any event, we weren't in the fancy part of the Dai-ichi Mansions. We were in an annex of sorts, a little six-story wing that had just two apartments, one on each of the top two floors. A prominent drawback was that the elevator didn't open onto private hallways, but to the fluorescent clatter of offices. Businesses were the main tenants of the annex.

Our two-bedroom apartment on the sixth floor was nice enough, but it was small. It had beige textured wallpaper and gray wall-to-wall carpet, and almost all the windows looked directly into an office in the building across the street.

Yet these were not the main reasons why the apartment was affordable and available to us. It was because the place was a jiko bukken, or a "stigmatized" property, otherwise known as a "black" property, a "psychologically harmful" property, in which a former occupant had died of unnatural causes, such as murder, suicide, fire, neglect. Real estate agents were legally obligated to divulge that an apartment was jiko bukken, and usually offered a substantial discount to renters, 30 percent in our case.

The previous tenant, an eighty-two-year-old widow, had killed herself by ingesting paraquat, an herbicide, in the apartment, and it had taken a month for her body to be discovered. Despite the increasing putridity, the salarymen and OLs (office ladies) on the sixth floor had been too polite to alert anyone.

"It's a good thing we're not superstitious," my father said to me, winking behind his gold-rimmed aviator eyeglasses.

There was a mad rush to unpack our household goods, which had been sitting in storage at Yokota Air Base, and move in our government-issued furniture—ugly, blocky faux-Colonial oak dressers and tables that buttressed a brown and orange tartan sofa and matching chairs. Then we had to figure out how I would get to the American School in Japan, which turned out to be an hour and fifteen minutes away in Chofu via a subway and three different train lines. The last possible subway I could catch to make the 8:05 bell was at 6:49. My mother and I purchased a train pass for me, went to school orientation, and charted out my ninth-grade schedule. Then I began my daily commutes, getting up at six twenty a.m. and returning home around four thirty—closer to seven if I had sports practice.

As far as schools went, ASIJ was better than most. It was a well-maintained private international school, unlike so many of the DOD schools I'd attended, some of which had been in Quonset huts. It boasted high educational standards, yet was progressive and relaxed (and coed). It stressed community over discipline. We were allowed to wear whatever we wanted and could have long hair. I'd grown mine out further over the summer, down near my shoulders, after an unfortunate incident at the Sanno, where a barber had lopped off a lock of my hair without bothering to ask how I wanted it styled.

Maybe the hair partly explained how I fell in with a couple of stoners at ASIJ, a freshman named Wood Strong and a junior named Dave Knapp.

There were kids of all nationalities and races at the school, embassy brats and expat children whose parents worked for corporations like Deutsche Bank, Proctor & Gamble, IBM, and British Petroleum. Moreover, nearly a third of the pupils were Japanese nationals. Students drifted into the usual cliques—jocks, nerds, freaks, preppies, etc.—but there were less than four hundred kids in the high school, and it was such a diverse group, everyone tended to get along. In previous places, I'd gravitated mostly toward the jocks (I played soccer and ran track), but it hadn't

been uncommon for me to hang out with the druggies
and rebels, because I was a skater. A cousin in Mililani had
introduced me to skateboarding one summer, giving me a
Sims fiberglass deck with Tracker trucks.

So I'd already smoked my share of pakalolo, beginning
in seventh grade, but nothing prepared me for the stuff
Dave Knapp was getting: Buddha stick, also known as Thai
stick. The strain was grown by tribes in the hills of northeast Thailand—dense, seedless sinsemilla. The buds were
wrapped around bamboo sticks and wound with hemp
string and then, according to rumor, dipped in hash oil or
opium for a truly outrageous, trippy high. The doob was so
potent and pure, you could throw it against a wall and it'd
lodge there, it was so sticky. I spent most weekend nights
that fall absolutely baked.

We also smoked a lot of cigarettes and drank a shitload
of beer. Dave's father, a Foreign Service Specialist who was
a facility manager for the US Embassy, would buy cartons
of Camels for him from the little commissary in the basement of the Grew House, but we didn't need anyone's
help to acquire contraband. We could buy cigarettes from
any kiosk or vending machine in the city. You could get
practically anything from vending machines on the street:
Marlboros and the Japanese brand Seven Stars, umbrellas,
batteries, cans of film, men's ties, condoms, porn magazines,
used women's underwear, live rhinoceros beetles (popular
with Japanese kids as pets), Sapporo beer, Suntory whiskey.
We also went to bars occasionally. The minimum age for
drinking and smoking in Japan was twenty, but no one
seemed to care, especially if you were a gaijin.

I'd stumble home, and once in the apartment my

mother would say, "Eh, are you drunk, Alain? You are, aren't you?" She'd have me swallow two aspirin, drink a tall glass of water, pee, and go to bed. "You gotta puke, do it in this bucket, ku'uipo."

I wasn't the only one coming home hammered. My dad would trundle in at all hours, soused, his disguise in disarray.

The first time my mother and I had seen the disguise, we'd collapsed in guffaws. "You look ridiculous, Ed!" my mother had told him.

He'd been putting on his coat to go out, and was wearing a wig and a fake mustache and some kind of pancake makeup to hide his acne scars.

"What are you thinking?" my mother had said. "You're not going to fool anybody like that!"

It was true. It was an obvious disguise, absurd in its ineptitude. So, too, was his secondary cover, which apparently superseded his main cover as a liaison officer in the PMLD office. He was supposed to be a nisei, a second-generation Japanese American, named Bob Saito. I didn't know anything else about Bob Saito's backstory. All I knew was that if someone called the house and asked for Mr. Saito—or any other name—we were supposed to say, "Just a minute, please," and go get my father.

"You don't look Japanese at all. You look Korean," my mother said upon hearing these instructions. "How stupid can people be? Who in their infinite wisdom assigned you to Japan in the first place, when the Japanese hate Koreans so much?"

I didn't understand anything about my father's job. Who was he meeting and drinking with? Japanese poli-

ticians, bureaucrats? What was he trying to do? Influence
policy? Get them to leak information, hand over smuggled
documents? Was he consorting with Soviets and North
Koreans, too, maybe trying to inveigle them into becoming double agents or possibly defecting, as I read about in
spy novels? Did he go on stakeouts and peer through tele-
photo lenses and eavesdrop with bugging devices? Did he
do dead drops with microfilm? Did he interrogate people?
Carry a gun?

"I don't carry a gun," he said when I tried to probe
him for clues. He wouldn't tell me anything more. He had
taken an oath of secrecy, which I was supposed to follow by extension. Anyway, he was, by nature, remarkably
taciturn. To this day, I can't recall a single conversation of
any import in which he'd asked more than a smattering of
questions or imparted more than a couple of declarative
statements. He wasn't uncaring or indifferent, I don't think.
He just wasn't very talkative. He was impervious, even, to
my mother's verbal assaults, buttoning up further when she
launched into her grievances.

"Say something!" she would squawk. "Why don't you
ever say anything? This is why you haven't gotten anywhere in the Agency, why we get these crap assignments.
You're not the least bit clubbable."

This was a word she invoked frequently. She had taken
a business course at UH in which the professor had lec-
tured on the value of being clubbable in corporate hier-
archies. The term had been coined by Samuel Johnson for
a man who was sociable, lively, good company, someone
who'd be a welcome addition to a club. The notion of
clubbability—being a leader, a man's man, the life of the

party—had stuck with my mom as the single most important attribute for success in any field.

"That wouldn't change anything for us," my father once said to her.

"What would, then? If you were haole?" she asked, and he'd only shrugged.

When my father had first revealed to me that he was in the CIA (I'd begun asking questions about his many job titles), I had been thrilled. I felt a newfound respect for him. All of a sudden, he'd elevated himself into the same sphere as the characters in my favorite TV shows, *Mission: Impossible* and *The Man from U.N.C.L.E.,* a world of suave men, ingenious gadgets, and sly tradecraft. Yet my mother methodically chipped away any fantasies I might have had about my father as a secret agent, and by the end of that fall in Tokyo, I was inwardly starting to belittle him as much as my mother did.

"This is one of the hard lessons of growing up, Alain," she said. "I know you love your father, but the sad truth is, he's a doofus."

Odd as it may seem, this was all just background chatter to me at the time. Maybe I had become inured to my mother's constant disparagements of my father. Or it could have been that I simply had other things on my mind—predictably, sex. I was fourteen, almost fifteen, in hormonal agony. I was desperate to have sex, even though I didn't know exactly what transpired during the act itself, fuzzy when it came to the anatomical details. By today's standards, I was incredibly naive. These were the days before sex education was routinely offered in schools, before the internet, before hardcore pornography became readily available. In junior high, I'd played Spin the Bottle and Truth or Dare a few times and had kissed a couple of girls—nothing more. I had seen *Playboys*, but the airbrushed triangles of pubic hair on the women in the centerfolds did little to clue me in. Neither did the copy of *Penthouse* Wood Strong got from somewhere, nor a Japanese porn magazine I bought from a vending machine, which had all the genitalia censored with black bars.

In the Dai-ichi Mansions one night, while my parents were out to a dinner party, I found a hardcover book of color photographs in my father's closet, tucked into a manila envelope. It showed a naked couple having intercourse, engaged in all sorts of positions, yet again there was nothing graphically exposed in the photos, nothing truly edifying.

Nonetheless, whenever I was alone in the apartment, I took the opportunity to pull out the book, and—often wearing my father's wig—I would study the photos, staring at the tan bodies of the models, who were young and vaguely hippieish, the woman with long straight blond hair parted in the middle, the man with curly brown hair and sideburns. Of course I would masturbate to the photographs. Not right then, with the book in hand, because I didn't want to accidentally rip or stain the pages, but after replacing the book in the manila envelope and carefully aligning it back on my father's closet shelf and returning the wig to its stand. Then I would masturbate while taking a shower or on my twin bed with a sock over my penis to collect the ejaculate—a nightly ritual regardless, sometimes twice nightly. "How many pairs of socks can you possibly wear in a day?" my mother would ask, perplexed, as she did the laundry.

I urgently wanted a girlfriend. There were girls I liked at ASIJ, but I had no idea how to approach any of them. The situation seemed dim. Then one afternoon that winter, Dave Knapp and I were cutting through Aoyama Cemetery toward Omotesando, when Dave said, "Hey, look. There's Leigh Anne."

Across the intersection, a teenaged girl, sixteen or seventeen, was riding a bicycle in the parking lot of Oji Homes, another mansion with orange tiles a quarter mile down the street from mine. She was pedaling in a slow circle, following a kid on a skateboard, presumably her younger brother, the two of them laughing.

"Talk about a babe," Dave said to me.

She was cute. First there was her russet-colored hair, the top half tied back with barrettes, the other half falling freely in waves down her shoulders. Second was her face—broad cheeks and a little pug nose. Yet these were incongruities, the rest of her very different. Even with a jacket on, I could see she had a figure on her, shapely, womanly, not at all girlish, and she carried herself with the confidence of an adult. I found her undeniably sexy.

We walked up to them, and she and Dave exchanged hellos. Her brother, perhaps unnerved by the new audience, stumbled off his skateboard. He didn't know what he was doing. To circle, he was having to step off and redirect the deck.

"Alan skates," Dave said. "He's pretty good."

I had everyone call me Alan back then, not Alain. Simpler that way. Too often, people said, "What? Ellen? Your

name is *Ellen*?" I was born in Beirut, where French was
spoken along with Arabic. Most of the films at the cinema,
where my mother had spent much of her time, had been
French, and she became a devotee of the New Wave, fond
of Jean-Paul Belmondo and especially Alain Delon, after
whom I'd been named.

"Yeah?" Leigh Anne said. "Show us some moves."

"Maybe later," I said. I hadn't skated in a while. Apparently it was against the law to skateboard on the street in
Japan. A few months ago, a cop had stopped me in Harajuku and taken me to the corner koban, or police box; he'd
kept asking me for my alien registration card, which I'd
never been issued, just an Air Force ID, and he'd detained
me for over an hour, pointing at my skateboard and shouting at me in Japanese, which I didn't understand, until finally he let me go. If I'd had an embassy ID, he wouldn't
have apprehended me at all—diplomatic immunity.

"Come on, show us what you got," Leigh Anne said.

Mind you, this was 1974, before the ollie was invented,
before everything went aerial. Skating was mostly confined to cruising then, making slalom turns. But I knew a
few freestyle tricks. I hopped on her brother's board and
pushed off and built up some speed and kickturned a couple of times and did a manual, a wheelie.

"That all you got?" Leigh Anne said.

I pumped toward her and did a bertslide right in front
of her feet, squatting down and planting a hand on the
ground and kicking the tail so the wheels slid out and the
board whipped around, and then I stood and kept going in
one unbroken motion.

"Okay, that was all right," she said.

I flew through a bunch of end-overs, 180-degree pivots, one after another.

"That's kind of cool."

I performed my coup de grâce, walking the dog, standing with one foot on the middle of the board and using the other foot to spin it underneath my shoe a half-dozen times so it looked like I was moonwalking.

"Not bad, not bad."

Some people have good hands. I had good feet, which contributed to my soccer, skateboarding, and, later, dancing skills.

I gave the board back to her brother, who was a bit slack-jawed. "Can you teach me some of that?" he asked.

"I don't know, maybe."

"Hey, be nice to Scotty," Leigh Anne told me. "You're nice, maybe there'll be some fringe benefits."

As we left Oji Homes, Dave said to me, "You hear that? She was coming *on* to you."

"Naw."

"You kidding? She was practically propositioning you!"

Dave told me Leigh Anne Pruitt had moved to Tokyo just two weeks ago from Connecticut. He'd met the Pruitt family at the Franciscan Chapel, the English-language Catholic church in Roppongi. Dave's mom and dad were lax about nearly everything in regard to parenting, except they insisted he go to Mass with them every Sunday.

Leigh Anne's brother was attending St. Mary's, the Catholic boys' school in Setagaya, and she was going to Sacred Heart, the Catholic girls' school in Hiroo. "She's no prude, though," Dave said.

Newly sixteen and in tenth grade, she was rumored to have had sex with five guys already.

"No shit?" I said.

"Her brother told me."

"He's, what, twelve? What does he know?"

"Enough to know she's a slut."

I felt intimidated, but also emboldened. I began going to Oji Homes once or twice a week after school, hanging out there until Leigh Anne's father, who worked for Johnson & Johnson, and her mother, who had a job as well, as an editor for *Time* magazine, were about to return home. Ostensibly I was there to teach Scotty how to skateboard, but it was a thin ruse. I'd demonstrate a trick, watch him fail at it, give him a tip or two, and tell him to go off and practice. Then I'd join Leigh Anne in a glass-paneled gazebo in the back garden of the apartment building. We quickly moved from smoking cigarettes and chatting awkwardly to making out on the bench.

"Look at me," she said. "I'm in Tokyo three weeks, and already I'm fooling around with a Japanese boy."

"I'm not Japanese," I told her. "I'm from Hawai'i. I'm American."

"You know what I mean," she said.

I chose to ignore what she meant. I was besotted with what we were doing, and I wanted more. "Can we go up to your room?" I asked. "Please?"

Oftentimes she would still be in her school uniform: navy-blue V-neck sweater, white dress shirt, green and blue plaid skirt, black tights, and Mary Janes. I spent hours on her bed over the next few months trying to wedge, tug, jimmy, and pry those items of clothing off Leigh Anne.

Eventually I got her to remove the sweater, after which I worked on the shirt, a campaign that took weeks, first extricating the tails and sliding my hand upward along her stomach and cupping her bra, then cramming my fingers underneath the underwire, then unhooking the clasp, then rolling up her shirt and sucking on one nipple while rubbing the other nipple between my thumb and index finger until, startlingly, I heard her moan.

I'd been proceeding instinctively from memory. Mornings as a child, I had padded into my parents' room and climbed into their bed and as a matter of course rolled up my mother's nightgown and sucked on one nipple while rubbing the other nipple between my thumb and index finger. I had done this nearly every morning until the age of ten, when I suddenly found the door to their bedroom locked.

I had known and not known that nipples and breasts were erogenous zones, but until that moment with Leigh Anne, I'd never considered that what I had done with my mother might have been erotic. If I had felt any shame or weirdness about the morning ritual, it had been about how long it'd taken for me to be weaned, not about the act itself. Now, hearing Leigh Anne groan, I wondered for the first time if it was possible, during all those mornings, all those years, that I'd been turning my mother on.

Years later, I confided in a girlfriend about this, and she angrily accused my mother, who was long dead at that point, of sexual abuse, incest. I refuted the charge, but since then, I've thought about it, and I've concluded that my mother (and father) had been, at the very least, irresponsible, letting me suckle her like that, and she might

have fucked me up in terms of women for most of my
adulthood.

When I was a toddler, she had dressed me in suit jack-
ets with matching shorts and knee socks and jaunty hats. In
Cairo and Athens, she had hired me out as a fashion acces-
sory: I held hands with models and walked down runways
at shows. She always encouraged me to appear in school
plays and go out for sports. She enjoyed seeing me onstage
and on the field.

"Who's my handsome little boy?" she'd say to me.

"I am," I'd say.

I doted on her. I liked watching her get ready to go
out—plucking her eyebrows and upper lip with tweezers,
using a curler for her eyelashes, applying powder and lipstick, rolling nylons up her legs and clipping them to her
girdle. I liked the way she smelled. When she and my father
were gone for the night, I sometimes took out her nightgown and brought it to my face.

I said nothing to my mother about Leigh Anne, but
she noticed something was different. "Why are you coming home so late all of a sudden?" she asked. "What're you
doing after school?"

I made excuses. Shortly afterward, though, she saw me
walking up the street from Oji Homes and asked, "What
were you doing in that direction?"

I told her I'd been visiting a friend.

"What friend?"

A new friend.

"Is it a girl? You're seeing a girl? Is that what you've
been hiding from me?"

I shrugged. We were standing outside the entrance to

the Dai-ichi Mansions annex, and I stepped aside to let people walk through the automatic glass doors.

"Who is she? What's her name?"

I gave her the briefest of biographies.

"Sacred Heart. She's Catholic?"

I nodded.

"You're still a virgin, aren't you, Alain?"

I winced.

"Has your father talked to you about girls?"

I squirmed.

"Of course not. Do I need to tell you about protection?"

I grimaced.

"Okay, then, I want you to know something. Girls—especially Catholic girls—might play hard to get, but secretly they like it when boys take charge. Understand?"

I want to say a few things about my mom (her name was Suki, by the way). She didn't grow up with a lot of money. Her mother cleaned houses, and her father was a baggage handler at Honolulu Airport. Often he moonlighted as a house painter and a handyman to make ends meet. She had three brothers, and they lived in a termite-infested house with jalousie windows. My mother called it a jungle house. Yet her father made sure they were never wanting for anything essential, meals or clothes or school supplies.

Although she didn't finish her degree, my mother was the first in the family to go to college. She studied hotel and resort management, hoping to get a job at a Waikiki hotel that was part of a worldwide chain, then transfer to other locations on the Mainland and in Europe. She wanted to get off the island and see the world. She had wanted a glamorous existence.

The itineracy of Agency life was not what she had expected. She couldn't really work. Most of the time, she was precluded from pursuing any outside jobs because of visa, language, or cultural issues. Pretty much the only thing she could do was work part-time in the embassy in the CLO, the Community Liaison Office, which was supposed to provide support for FSO (and CIA) families abroad. She didn't fit in with the other wives, maybe because she wasn't white and lacked the proper sort of pedigree, maybe because she attracted the notice of the other wives' husbands—undoubtedly a little Asian fetish there. She enjoyed the attention and flirted back, which of course didn't win her any favors. (I don't think she ever had any affairs, although this may be enormously naive on my part.)

Hence, not only was I my mother's best friend during our ever-changing posts, I was often her only friend. Although she would have never admitted it, during the entire time she was married to my father, I think she was very lonely and depressed.

In late February, my father came home and said he had news for us. He was eligible for a promotion to the rank of GS-11 in April, and he had been told that not only were the chances good for the promotion, but that it might also come with a transfer to Paris.

"Ed Kweon!" my mother squealed. She ran up to him and vised his face between her palms and kissed him on the mouth.

She began taking private lessons in French, which she

hadn't spoken in years, and also enrolled in French cooking classes. Truth be told, she was a terrible cook. Loco moco, the traditional comfort-food plate lunch in Hawai'i, was her "specialty" for our dinners: two burger patties accompanied by two scoops of white rice and two scoops of store-bought macaroni salad, everything smothered with "gravy" (made by heating up Campbell's cream of mushroom soup with a little water and a lot of salt) and topped with two eggs, sunny-side up. As a variation, she would sometimes substitute the burger patties with slabs of fried Spam, a staple in Hawai'i. Another recipe in frequent rotation was chicken cacciatore, thighs and sliced onions baked with Campbell's cream of tomato soup poured on top.

Her lack of culinary skills could have actually jeopardized my father's career. I would learn years later that, in CIA officers' performance reviews, there was a section that assessed spouses' ability to entertain, to host dinners and cocktail parties. This was why my parents always hired a cook or had food catered when they had guests.

None of this deterred her from trying to tackle Julia Child's *Mastering the Art of French Cooking,* and over the next couple of months, we were treated to botched renditions of boeuf bourguignon, cassoulet, bouillabaisse, and cherry clafoutis, all largely inedible. Nevertheless, my father and I indulged her, forcing ourselves to swallow as much of the dreck as possible, because we'd never seen her happier, and that made us happy.

We should have known then what would happen. If there's one thing I have learned in the intervening forty-five years, it's to be wary of happiness. Sure enough, there were soon harbingers that things would be going awry.

We heard footsteps, heavy footfalls, above the apartment, someone stomping. Only, we were on the top floor of the annex, and on the roof above us were mechanical systems and HVAC units—nowhere for anyone to walk on. One day, without explanation, all the house plants in the living room died. Blackened, flopped over, shriveled. We came back from dinner out another night to find that the door to the apartment was locked, from the inside, with the chain. We had to get a maintenance man to chop it off with bolt cutters. There was no evidence that anyone had been in the apartment, or had left. All the windows were cranked shut. Occasionally we smelled something odd, a whiff of something malodorous, first chemical, then akin to a decomposing body. Jiko bukken.

After slow but steady progress with Leigh Anne, removing all the items of clothing except her panties, dry-humping in three positions that were displayed in my father's book of color photographs, once even slipping my hand underneath the waistband of her underwear and inserting my middle fingertip into her vagina, she abruptly wouldn't let me go any further.

"Stop," she said, wriggling away from me on her bed.

"Why? What's wrong?"

"You just waltz in here whenever you feel like and immediately go for my crotch. You've never even taken me out on a date."

"What do you mean, a date?" The concept was completely foreign to me.

She sat up and put her clothes back on. "Like to dinner or a movie."

"I'd take you to the Sanno, but you're always with your family on Sundays."

The Sanno screened a movie every Sunday at three o'clock, and I rarely missed a show. It was difficult to see American movies overseas at the time, and the ones at the Sanno were only a few months old, projected onto a large screen in the basement ballroom of the hotel, which was set up with tables and chairs and had a bar in back. After standing for the national anthem, I'd settle into my seat with my Coke and popcorn and watch the previews and then the main feature, enthralled. It was the golden age of American cinema, the 1970s: *The Conversation, The Last Picture Show, Chinatown,* innumerable others. I saw many of those films at the Sanno. Often the next morning I would recount and act out parts of the movies on the train to school for the benefit of classmates who couldn't go to the Sanno. I developed a terrific memory, able to recall entire scenes. No doubt this all contributed to my becoming a theater geek the following year, and then pursuing an acting career.

I would have gladly had Leigh Anne accompany me to the movies at the Sanno, and we could have eaten dinner at one of the buffets as well, but on Sundays she went to church, then had brunch with her family at the American Club, an elite, members-only facility for rich expats near the Tokyo Tower, and afterward they'd spend the day together at Oji Homes, reading books or magazines or playing cards or board games—a family ritual.

"We never talk," Leigh Anne said to me in her room.

She got off the bed and straightened her clothes in front of her wall mirror. The Pruitts' apartment was bigger than ours, with three bedrooms, and had much nicer furniture—modern, made of teak.

"What should we be talking about?"

"I don't know. We hardly know anything about each other. Like, what's your dad exactly do in the Air Force?"

"He's a pilot," I said. I didn't know why I was lying.

"Really? I thought you said he was an attaché, whatever that is. Didn't you say he's an attaché? What does he fly? Does he fly jets?"

"They don't fly jets out of Hardy Barracks. A helicopter. He flies a Huey."

"That's cool. You see, I didn't know that. What about your mother? Does she work, too?"

"Yes," I told her, unable to stop myself. "She's a translator. She translates French. Right now, she's translating Julia Child's new cookbook."

Leigh Anne nodded, then said, "Wait, isn't Julia Child American?"

Was she? I had assumed she was French. "She's translating the cookbook from English to French," I told her, impressing myself with my quick thinking.

"Oh, okay," she said. "All right, you ask me some questions now."

I wanted to ask her if it was true she'd had sex with five boys already, and if so, why, then, she wouldn't have sex with me. Was it because I wasn't white?

"What's your favorite color?" I asked.

"Come on, you're not even trying. Ask me something serious, something deep."

"What kind of music do you like?"

"Not much better, but the answer might surprise you. I like the blues."

"Like B.B. King?"

"Like Sonny Boy Williamson and Muddy Waters. Like Robert Johnson," she said. "My dad's a big blues fan. He plays guitar and harmonica. A little piano, too." She told me that wherever her father went, parties, family gatherings, holidays, he'd get everyone to sing the twelve-bar blues with him and jam. He'd have people grab whatever was around and play—kazoos, bongos, maracas, tambourines, spoons, Tupperware, tin cans, bottles—making up lyrics as he went. "It goes on for hours sometimes. It's unbelievably fun."

Clubbable, I thought. Her father was the definition of clubbable.

"Lately I've branched out into blues rock," she said. "I'm really into acts like the Allman Brothers, the Marshall Tucker Band, and Eric Clapton now. You like any of those bands?"

"I love Eric Clapton," I said, although I was barely familiar with him. But I happened to know two people who were Clapton fanatics, and instantaneously I formed a plan to win over Leigh Anne.

"I'm not giving you one of my tickets, man," Dave Knapp told me in the cafeteria at ASIJ.

"Me, neither," Wood Strong said.

Clapton was playing three concerts at the Budokan arena the following week, and Dave and Wood were planning to see two of them, the first and last nights; they'd been talking about it for months. I wanted to surprise

Leigh Anne with tickets, but I'd learned all the shows were sold out.

"I'll pay you double," I told them.

"No."

"Triple."

This persuaded them.

"There's one more thing I need your help with," I said to Dave.

I never knew where Dave got his weed. I'd assumed it was from a local dealer, a Japanese hustler he'd met somehow. But it turned out he was being supplied by a US Marine. The embassy was protected by fourteen MSGs, or Marine Security Guards—all surprisingly young, between nineteen and twenty-one—and the MSG detachment's barracks were on the grounds of the Grew House, down the hill from the pool. A PFC was selling Buddha stick to people in clubs in Roppongi, Shibuya, and Kabukicho. He was getting it from a network of marines and sailors in Iwakuni air station and Sasebo naval base. By chance, Dave went to make a buy from the PFC at a disco called Uterus the night the police were making a coordinated sweep of the operation.

"What about diplomatic immunity?" I asked Wood when we rendezvoused in Yoyogi Park. "He's the dependent of an embassy employee."

"That's why he's not in jail."

Wood filled me in on the drug laws in Japan. Possession alone could garner a sentence of five years; importing and distribution, ten years. Dave and his parents had been deported immediately upon his arrest, not even allowed to pack a suitcase.

"Here," Wood said, surreptitiously handing me a box of Marlboro Lights. "There're a couple of joints in there. I've been hoarding them. You take them. I don't want them anymore."

"You sure?"

"You kidding? Mr. Knapp's career is over. He'll never work for the government again. My dad would kill me if that ever happened to him."

My father would have as well, but that didn't stop me from taking the joints. Leigh Anne had only toked some pitiful schwag in Connecticut, pure crabgrass that barely had any effect on her, and she'd told me she wanted to get high for real. "This is all my fault," I told Wood. "He was getting the stuff for me. I ruined Dave's life."

"He wasn't doing it just for you. He was doing it for himself. He got unlucky. Wrong place, wrong time, wrong country."

I took Leigh Anne to dinner at Shakey's Pizza on Omotesando-dori, and then we boarded the Chiyoda Line subway for six stops, transferred at Otemachi, and rode the Tozai Line for two more stops to Kudanshita. (It was a marvel we could navigate the transit system as we did, when we didn't know Japanese, the written characters indecipherable hieroglyphics to us, and there weren't as many signs in English or even Romaji back then. Yet that was the nature of being a military or diplomatic brat, an expat kid: you feigned nonchalance, as if nothing could ever rattle you; you figured things out; you adapted. You did everything you could to pretend that things were *normal,* when things were far from normal, when you felt dislocated and fragmented all the time in one strange land after another.)

Emerging from the station, we crossed the moat to what was formerly Edo Castle, passed through a couple of ancient gates, and then we were there, in front of the octagonal concrete edifice that was the Budokan. Dave and Wood's tickets were quite good, the seats in the second row of the lower balcony. It was actually my first concert of any kind. Leigh Anne's father had taken her to a few blues clubs, but this was her first arena concert. "I'm so excited!" she said.

There was an opening act with a hard-rock band that I remember nothing about. Then Clapton came out, wearing a full beard, jeans, and an Edwardian shirt with puffy sleeves and a ruffled neck that was open to reveal most of his chest. The first half of the concert was strange. There were several countryesque songs, and one that was reggae. Preternaturally laid-back, Clapton seemed stoned and/or drunk. But the second half got livelier, louder, bluesier, and he launched into soaring solos on "Can't Find My Way Home" and "Have You Ever Loved a Woman?" and then he played "Layla" in the encore, a huge wall of lights illuminating behind him to raucous cheers.

"That was fantastic!" Leigh Anne shouted at me, our ears ringing as we walked out of the Budokan. I thought so, too, vowing at that moment to learn the guitar.

We went to a little bar called Flashbacks that Dave had introduced me to. It was in Akasaka, down an alleyway and up an elevator to the seventh floor, completely unmarked, impossible to find unless someone showed you. We ordered beers, and Leigh Anne told me the story behind "Layla," how the song was written for Pattie Boyd, who at the time had been married to George Harrison, Clapton's best friend. Clapton asked Pattie to meet him, played a demo tape of "Layla," and professed his love for her. Harrison found out what was going on and demanded Pattie make a choice: him or Clapton. She chose Harrison, breaking Clapton's heart. For three years after that, he didn't record anything and was a veritable recluse. This tour was his comeback.

"The best thing is that he and Pattie are together now," Leigh Anne said. "Who says there're no happy endings."

We got drunk. When we left Flashbacks, we began kissing in the elevator, and I kept pressing the buttons for the top and ground floors so we could persist.

Holding hands, we took the subway to Nogizaka and then walked into Aoyama Cemetery, wobbling down the sidewalk adjacent to the central two-lane thoroughfare.

"You know how all the gravestones are vertical blocks?" Leigh Anne said. "How close they are to each other? That's because land's so scarce in Japan, they have to bury people standing up."

"Nooo."

"Okay, that's not true," she said, and laughed. "They cremate everybody."

The cemetery was manicured, without a speck of trash, like everywhere else in Tokyo. "It's so spooky here at night," I said. There were no other pedestrians, hardly any cars.

"Do you believe in ghosts?" she asked.

I hadn't, but the weird occurrences in the Dai-ichi Mansions were making me reconsider. I wondered if the ashes of the former tenant, the eighty-two-year-old widow, were interred here.

"There are stories about this place," Leigh Anne said. "Taxi drivers pick up fares who ask to be taken here. When they arrive, the driver looks in the backseat and no one's there." The same thing happened with buses, she told me. The cord was pulled for a stop in the cemetery, but no passengers were on board. According to one theory, the problem was with the Chiyoda Line. The subway ran right underneath the cemetery. Sometimes when a train went by, the souls of the dead got accidentally whisked away to remote districts, and then they needed to find a way back to their graves.

"You're making all this up," I said, and shivered. I now regretted choosing the cemetery as a hiding place—dead drop, indeed. I led Leigh Anne down a side lane and made a series of turns down paths, counting my steps. Aoyama was the largest cemetery in Tokyo, notable for having a section for foreigners and a gravestone for Hachiko, the faithful dog who had been memorialized with a bronze statue outside Shibuya station.

"It's here," I said. "I think."

"Why'd you hide it here?"

She hadn't heard about Dave yet. "Paranoid, I guess." I reached into a crevice between two marble gravestones and pulled out the pack of Marlboro Lights.

How much of what we remember is true? I tried to do an internet search recently for Leigh Anne, Dave, and Wood, and nothing relevant appeared in the results. Did I get their full names wrong, or the spellings? Am I mixing things up? I'm sure I've confused a few minor details, but beyond that? Did things happen as I recall? I was curious about their whereabouts, how they turned out, what became of them. (I do know, however, that Eric Clapton, that brilliant motherfucker, is still going strong at seventy-four, after all the heroin and alcohol and cigarettes, after Pattie Boyd divorced him, after his four-year-old son died falling from the fifty-third-floor window of a Manhattan condo tower—unimaginable, unspeakable—after getting married a second time to a hapa of Korean and Irish descent who was twenty-two when they first met, after having three daughters with her . . . and he's still touring, despite continually saying he won't tour anymore.)

What I remember: Already drunk, Leigh Anne and I got awfully high—higher than I'd ever been. The Buddha stick in these joints, it must have been dipped in opium. We lay on a patch of grass and looked up at the sky, the passing clouds, glimpses of haloed crescent moon. The wind ruffled through the hedges and the canopy of cherry trees, through their gnarled limbs. We could smell the remnants of blossoms from earlier in the month, the flowers and sprigs of Japanese star anise and spent bundles of incense that had been left at graves. We heard leaves whispering, crickets chirring, the shush of cars passing on the outskirts of the cemetery. It was so peaceful, serene. My mouth and lips were unbelievably dry. I couldn't feel my tongue. The streetlamps pulsed, the lights in the nearby skyscrapers gyrated with orange and red contrails.

I turned my head and looked at the nearest gravestone, where, as offerings, someone had left a can of green tea, a can of beer, and a can of sake, perfectly spaced apart in a neat row. On the ledge below was a package of rice crackers; another of pancakes filled with red bean paste; a bunch of bananas; a tiny toy bus, which drove up to the edge and put on its blinkers and opened its front and rear doors yet didn't have any passengers to disembark; and a little hamster plush doll, which began singing in a thunderous baritone, *"I woke up this morning, feelin' mighty blue / I woke up this morning, feelin' mighty blue."*

Only, it wasn't the little hamster plush doll but Leigh Anne, wearing a toupee and a fake mustache and chin puff, singing in the thunderous baritone, *"There ain't no sunshine here, baby"*—but no, it was just the shadows, no toupee, no mustache—*"When I can't begin to make due."*

"Sing with me!" she said, and I did.

She was so beautiful. We kissed. *"I woke up this morning,"* she sang softly. We kissed and kissed. I rolled her shirt up and unhooked her bra and sucked on her nipple, and she moaned. I unbuttoned her jeans and slid my hand beneath the waistband of her panties and inserted my middle finger into her vagina, and she gasped.

This night. Tonight. At last, I thought. If there were any lost spirits in that cemetery, I was sure they were cheering me on.

Unhurriedly I turned onto my back and rummaged in my front jeans pocket. I gazed up at the sky and sang, *"I woke up this morning"*—I thought for a second—*"blowin' a kazoo"*—I chuckled—*"I woke up this morning"*—I paused again—*"cookin' barbecue."* I laughed. I found the condom I'd bought weeks ago from a vending machine and tugged it out of my pocket. *"There's lots of sunshine in here, baby"*—I propped myself up on my elbows—*"Cause I'm goin' to make love to . . ."*—and discovered that Leigh Anne was no longer beside me, nowhere anywhere in the cemetery, as if someone or something had whisked her away from me.

She wouldn't talk to me the next day, nor for days after that. I didn't know what was going on. She wouldn't come to the phone. I kept calling her apartment, until Mr. Pruitt, whom I'd never met, happened to pick up. "Who is this?" he asked. He put down the telephone for a minute, then returned and said, "Apparently she doesn't want to talk to you, Alan. Could you please stop calling this number?"

I began going to Oji Homes directly from school every day, only to be turned away each time by the concierge after he tried to summon Leigh Anne on the intercom for me. Finally one evening, her brother, Scotty, came down and said, "She wants you to stay away."

"Why?"

He didn't have an answer for me.

I didn't understand. Until she'd disappeared, it had been such a perfect, romantic night. What had happened to spook her? Did the ghost stories get to her—tripping out on the Buddha stick, hallucinating she was seeing ghouls? Was she overcome with guilt about being with another boy, one with the wrong skin color? Had I done something to turn her off?

"What'd you do?" my mom screamed in the Dai-ichi Mansions. "What'd you do?"

At the start of the week, my father had revealed that he'd been passed over for promotion, and we were not going to Paris this year, or any year, most likely. Ever since he'd given us the news, my mother had been haranguing him nightly.

"Answer me!" she said to him. "You must have done something to fuck this up!"

He sat stonily on the brown and orange tartan sofa in the living room, smoking a Kent and drinking his usual—Jim Beam and 7UP.

When I first heard he'd been denied, I worried it was connected to Dave's arrest, to the Knapps' deportation; that the CIA, in vetting my father for promotion, had investigated me as well and found out I was a dopehead. But no. The embassy had distributed a flier warning dependents about the dangers of drug abuse, and my father—unaware I'd been anything more than classmates with Dave—had handed me a copy of the flier without ceremony.

On Sunday morning, I waited outside the Franciscan Chapel. The church didn't look like a church, particularly a Catholic one. It was sandwiched between other buildings on a narrow side street, and there were no gargoyles, gables, spires, or flying buttresses. Rather, the façade was a plain gray three-story cube, nondescript and a little sad, with windows in the center that were covered with black vertical slats and a discreet white cross.

Leigh Anne and her family arrived in a taxi, the left rear door swinging open automatically to let them out, Mr. Pruitt rising from the front passenger seat. He was quite tall.

I called to Leigh Anne, and everyone turned to me. Her father said something to her, and then Leigh Anne walked over to where I stood on the sidewalk while the others went into the church.

"What're you doing here?" she asked.

She was wearing a beige crochet dress with pockets

sewn over the hips, white pumps with block heels, and a pink hair band.

"Why won't you see me?" I said.

"You can't figure it out?"

"No."

"Then you're an idiot. An asshole and an idiot."

"Why'd you run away? What happened?"

"You tried to drug me so you could have sex with me."

"What? No, that's not true. You said you wanted to get high. You asked me to get us—"

"You tried to trick me."

"No, I didn't."

"You were trying to get me wasted so you could fuck me."

"No."

"I wanted you to slow down," she said, "but you pulled out a condom, anyway."

"Wait. It wasn't like that."

My memory of that night was crystalline to me, every detail, every sensation. We were being tender and affectionate. We were making out, and she was giving me every indication she wanted to keep going. The mood hadn't turned ugly like she was describing.

"You didn't care," she said. "If I hadn't run away, you would've probably raped me."

The accusation horrified me. "No." Why was she saying all of this? I was in love with her.

"I thought you were different," she said. "But you're just like every boy I've ever known. I never want to see you again."

"Please, Leigh Anne. I'm sorry. This has gotten all turned around. Can't we just go on?"

"Go on?" she said. "Go on to what? You don't give a shit about me. You just wanted to use me. You're moving to Paris this summer. Did it cross your mind for one second you might miss me? No, it didn't."

"We're not moving to Paris anymore," I said stupidly.

"You ruined everything," Leigh Anne told me. "I really liked you. Why couldn't you have waited?"

Years later I would consider that, subconsciously, I had done to Leigh Anne what I surmised my father did to recruit agents. I had targeted her from the start. I knew her vulnerabilities, and I thought I could manipulate her. I had lied to her, sweet-talked her, gotten her drunk and high, and tried to take advantage of her. In the end, it didn't matter exactly what had happened in the cemetery, or why. I was guilty regardless, and I'd always feel ashamed. The fact was, I had orchestrated the entire night with the aim of getting laid.

For days, my parents argued—or rather my mother did, berating my father mercilessly.

"No one has any respect for you. Not one bit," she said later that week while he was watching the *CBS Evening News* on FEN, the Far East Network. "It's because you won't ever fight for anything."

Glum about Leigh Anne, I was eating dinner alone at the table—fried Spam, rice, and macaroni salad that I'd fixed myself. My mother had stopped experimenting with French dishes, had stopped cooking entirely.

"We're always going to be treated like shit," she said to my father.

He ignored her.

"You've got no spine whatsoever!"

He continued staring at the TV.

She delivered several more salvos, culminating with "You're such a loser!"

I blurted out, "Leave him alone."

They both glanced at me. "What'd you say?" my mother asked.

The outburst had surprised me, too. "Leave him alone. He didn't do anything wrong."

My father focused on the TV again.

"Stay out of this," my mother said. "You don't know what you're talking about."

"Maybe it's you," I said. "Maybe you're the reason nothing ever works out."

"What?"

"You don't know the first thing about being a man."

"You shut up," she said.

"Quiet," my father told us. "This is *important*."

The news broadcast was about the final American withdrawal from Vietnam the day before. The correspondent, Ed Bradley, was doing a report about the fall of Saigon, just before the Viet Cong were to move into the city. Everyone was looking for a way out. Hundreds of Vietnamese surrounded the US Embassy, trying to climb the walls, getting shoved back down by Marine Security Guards. Inside the compound, helicopters were picking up evacuees from the roof and ferrying them to American ships off the coast. South Vietnamese pilots were trying to land their own helicopters on the carriers and frigates, but apparently they'd never been trained to land on mov-

ing platforms. They floated above the ships and had their
families and passengers jump off, then flew to the side and
ditched their helicopters, leaping into the sea just before
they crashed. Other pilots simply smashed down onto the
decks, and, once empty of passengers, the disabled helicopters were pushed off the ships to clear the way for the next
round of evacuees. The final image of the report was of the
US ambassador leaving the country. "After so many long
and bitter years," Ed Bradley concluded, "the American in-
volvement in Vietnam was over."

I looked at my father and realized he was crying.

"Don't you see?" he said to my mother and me. "Don't
you see?"

I didn't understand then exactly what he wanted us to
see, and I still don't, really, though I can guess. The scale of
real human tragedy. The futility of colonialism. The atroc-
ities of war. All the lives displaced and ruined and lost. Although those are my politics, not his. He never disclosed
to me what his were precisely; he maintained he was apo-
litical. For all I know, he was crying about the humiliation
of America losing the war and having to retreat in such an
ignominious manner.

After that one year in Tokyo, we were transferred to
Tehran—our second posting in Iran—and we were sta-
tioned there for two years, getting out in 1977. The Iranian Revolution occurred in 1979, the Shah leaving for
exile and Ayatollah Khomeini returning to the country
and Muslim students storming the US Embassy and taking
fifty-two Americans hostage for 444 days. Many of those
hostages, of course, had been in the CIA. They no doubt
had been complicit in prolonging the Shah's brutal re-

gime, and I'm sure my father had had a hand in that, too. Who knows what else he was involved in. Assassinations? Coups? At the very least, he had helped suppress democratic movements in the name of US national security and economic interests. Policies I protested against as an adult.

Yet his job, his actions, had had real consequences. Life-and-death consequences. If that hadn't taken balls, I don't know what would have.

He didn't get very far in the CIA, remaining a case officer and never rising to management, as it were. I give him credit for never complaining that he was held back because he wasn't haole, even though it was obvious that being white would have benefited him enormously, more so than going to Yale and belonging to Skull and Bones. My mother discounted racism as a principal factor in my father's career. I don't know why, when it was so apparent. It's something I became very familiar with, being typecast as an actor.

He was never the same after we left Tehran. My mother divorced him then, and the hostage crisis—obsessively tracking it from afar—seemed to break him. He kept taking overseas assignments, so I didn't see him that often. I spent my senior year of high school with my mother in Mililani, then I went to college on the Mainland. My mother died at fifty-nine of ovarian cancer. My father retired at sixty-five and returned to O'ahu, buying a one-bedroom condo in the Discovery Bay Towers in Ala Moana. He never remarried. I can't account for how he bade his time. He never took up any hobbies.

He has Alzheimer's now, and whatever secrets he was keeping, he'll take with him. I've put him in an assisted care facility in Hawai'i Kai and call him once a week. I'm lucky if he remembers where I'm currently living. Every so often, though, he'll surprise me. He'll begin reminiscing about one of our posts when I was a kid. His memory is sometimes better than mine about those years (which, given Alzheimer's links to heredity, concerns me). He'll keep me on the phone and get downright chatty and nostalgic. "Do you remember that one time in Tokyo, your mother tried to make a flaming crêpe suzette and almost burned down the apartment?" he'll say. I'll laugh with him, and then he'll ask, "How's she doing these days? Have you talked to her lately?"

II

REENACTMENTS

• • • • • • • • • •

THE PROBLEM WAS ALL THE BLOOD. There were a lot of dead bodies sprawled about, perforated by gunshots and encrusted with immense amounts of blood, and everyone was cooking in the high desert heat, the blood attracting a slew of unwanted insects—namely, ants. Hungry ants. We were getting eaten alive out there.

We'd finished the shoot-out the day before—ostensibly a straightforward handover between ALEX RUDD and JE-SUS BELTRAN, the Mexican drug lord's righthand man, who had been flanked by a dozen cartel henchmen. It was supposed to have been a simple exchange: the ten million in bearer bonds for "the girl" (as she was referred to in the screenplay, though the character was said to be in her late twenties). It'd been a setup, of course. Beltran had never intended to deliver "the girl." Rudd had assumed as much and had booby-trapped the basin in the Chihuahuan Desert with M18A1 Claymore antipersonnel mines. He was an ex–Navy SEAL. He'd also hidden in strategic spots a Heckler & Koch MP5K submachine, a Benelli M3 Super 90 shotgun, and a Cobray M11/9 semiautomatic. Underneath his jacket was a SIG-Sauer P220 handgun and a crisscross of ammo bandoliers. Despite this firepower, he was outnumbered and eventually would have been dispatched if not for my intervention.

The fact that I, the hit man from Hong Kong known as EL MANO SILENCIOSO, The Silent Hand, would protect Rudd was a surprise to everyone, when I'd been trying to eliminate him for days. Yet I was a contract killer, and my contract with the Wo Shing triad, which had been smuggling chemicals from Chinese factories to the cartel in Mexico for the production of meth, had changed overnight. With my help, Rudd was able to escape, but Beltran got away as well. I wasn't as lucky. Shot up good, I was left for dead on the desert sand with all the henchmen, our bodies strewn among a cluster of souped-up monster trucks and SUVs.

Today, the script called for:

EXT. DESERT BASIN — DAY

Just after sunrise, a ragtag family of THREE
ILLEGALS cautiously approaches the corpses,
surveying the horrific scene. The FATHER
nudges one of the henchmen's bodies with
the toe of his shoe. Finding no response,
he begins rifling through the man's pockets
and pillages his wallet and cell phone. The
MOTHER follows suit with another body.

Their little BOY goes to El Mano Silencioso
and stares at the hit man's face, then the
gleaming gold Rolex on his wrist. He starts
to reach for the watch, when suddenly El Mano

opens his eyes and grabs the boy's arm. The
boy SCREAMS hysterically.

El Mano somersaults to his feet and draws his
two Beretta 92FS pistols and points them from
the boy to the father to the mother. They
freeze, terrified.

Calmly, El Mano lowers his guns and nods
sideways for them to vacate, and they scram-
ble away as quickly as they can.

Once they are gone, he collapses to his
knees, drops his guns, and rips open his
shirt, revealing a Kevlar bulletproof vest,
which trapped several slugs. But two bul-
lets bypassed the vest at the waist and the
shoulder, and another grazed the side of his
head. He is weak and in pain and bleeding
profusely.

At least, that was what we were supposed to have
filmed in the desert between El Paso and Colima, Texas.
But the scene had required us to lie repeatedly on the sand
for hours in the scorching heat, and insects—fire ants!—
had quickly appeared, lured by the sugary fake blood. We
squirmed, we winced, we twitched and grimaced. We
couldn't stay still. Production had to be halted for the day.

We were in the last ten days of filming. It'd been a long,
complicated shoot, over two and a half months on the road
now, moving from Arizona to New Mexico to Texas. The

director/writer, Lucius Royal, had insisted on doing everything on location, no soundstages. Yet supposedly we were on schedule and on budget, and supposedly Warner Bros. was happy with the way things were going. This was in July 1999, when I was thirty-nine, when I still thought I could have a career as a Hollywood actor, although I no longer had any illusions that I'd be appearing in *good* films.

Days of Scorn was decidedly a B-movie. Lucius talked a good game, describing it as an existential, postmodern neo-Western about the nature of evil and survival in a primordial, unforgiving world, and how he wanted it to be an homage to the director John Woo, who had originated the gun-fu genre of action films in Hong Kong (hence, the reason why Lucius had written a Chinese character into the story). However, while *Days* would, like Woo's *A Better Tomorrow* and *The Killer,* marry gunplay and martial arts, Lucius intended to amp everything up and make this motherfucker even more intense. Opposed to the stylized, slow-motion ballet of violence in Woo's films, the fight sequences in *Days* would appear real. Hyperreal. This was going to be a gritty, visceral, brutal film, Lucius promised us.

That being said, we all knew that *Days* would not be up for any awards upon its release. It was a pretty standard narco/border thriller. It'd be regarded as no more than a serviceable entertainment. All of which was fine with me. This was the biggest part I'd ever landed in a studio film, fourth billing in the main titles, single card. Granted, El Mano Silencioso, whom all the characters assumed to be a mute, had yet to speak a single line, but he was a presence—stealthy, deadly, ruthless, yet honorable, with a roguish sense of humor. He also cut quite the figure, hair slicked back, always impeccably dressed in a dark Armani suit, accessorized by a funky pair of oval sunglasses with purple lenses. He was, in short, cool, a quality that never could have been ascribed to any of my previous characters. It'd been a fun part to play so far, and I had hopes *Days* would lead to other roles that were the same size or bigger.

We drove back to El Paso to the Esperanza, one of the few hotels downtown. Usually anyone above-the-line (principal actors, the director, department heads, etc.) got put up in four-star hotels, but there were no four-star hotels in El Paso, just a DoubleTree and two "historic" hotels, the Esperanza and another called the Drysdale, both of which, purportedly, had once been grand but had fallen into disrepair. There wasn't much to boast about the rest of the city, either. Hardly any restaurants or stores, no one walking on the sidewalks, a bland skyline of ten- to fifteen-story office buildings that emptied out at the end of the workday and left the place a ghost town on nights and weekends. We'd been marooned in the Esperanza for nineteen days now.

After I showered, I joined Kevin Burr (who was playing Alex Rudd) and Tommy Navarro (who was playing Jesus Beltran) in the hotel bar/restaurant. We had trained together for months before principal photography—martial arts in the morning, tactical weapons and stunt driving in the afternoon—and had gotten close, even though I was not nearly as prominent of an actor as they were.

They were drinking mojitos and snacking on pork rinds at a table. "Al, you got a spot of blood there," Tommy told me when I sat down. He motioned to an area underneath his right earlobe.

The makeup department was usually responsible for removing everything at the end the day, but sometimes they didn't get to every cranny. I dipped a napkin into a water glass and began to lift it to my right ear.

"Other side," Tommy said.

"You know the best thing to get fake blood off?" Kevin asked.

"Baby wipes," I said.

"No."

"Rubbing alcohol. Hydrogen peroxide. Toothpaste." I'd learned a few tricks in my time.

"Shaving cream," he said. "The cheaper, the better—like Barbasol. Just rub it into your skin, wait a few minutes, rinse with warm water. It'll stop it from seeping into your pores, and it's a surprisingly good moisturizer."

"You know Chloe Taylor?" Tommy said. "Remember that vampire movie she was in? I heard each time they wrapped for the day, she'd strip down naked, stand there with her arms raised, and have them wash her down with Johnson's Baby Shampoo."

We let the image sink in.

"That'll work," I said.

"No argument from me."

"All the shit they put on us for gags," Kevin said, "it completely freaks out my skin."

"Exfoliation's the key," I said.

"Aztec clay masks," Tommy said.

"I have this homemade concoction for zits," Kevin told us. "Baking soda, lemon juice, honey. Stir it up, dab it on. Dries those fuckers out overnight."

The waitress brought over my Modelo. I grabbed a

bottle of lemon/lime salt called Twang from the basket of condiments on the table and added several dashes of it to the top of the beer, which was on the rocks—El Paso quirks I'd picked up.

Kevin watched me. "That is just wrong," he said.

"You talk," I said. "You're eating pork rinds with ketchup."

He shrugged and lit a cigarette. The one (really, the only) thing we loved about the Esperanza was that we could smoke indoors. California, where we all lived, had banned smoking in public buildings years ago. In El Paso, there was even a law that churches, hotels, stores, banks, and railroad depots had to provide spittoons for their patrons.

"You've been practicing your line?" Kevin asked me. "Let's hear it, man."

At the end of the climactic fight scene we'd be filming next week, it would be revealed that El Mano Silencioso was not a mute, after all. He'd utter one sentence, in English, just before he died. "I want it to be a surprise," I told them.

"Come on."

"How're you going to say it?" Tommy asked. "You going to pull out the old *I-rike-flied-lice* accent?"

I was still debating how to recite the line. I wanted to get it right. Because it was my sole line of dialogue in the movie, and because I'd had so much time to think about it, I had become obsessed with the possibilities of its delivery: the pitch, intonation, volume, speed, rhythm, tone, modulation, and, yes, pronunciation—what type of accent to use, and how thick to lay it on.

Over the months, the three of us had derided the various

dialects we'd had to affect during our careers: The "Mexican" accent for the cholos, migrants, thugs, farmworkers, coyotes, gardeners, and janitors that Tommy had had to play, when he was a third-generation Cuban American, born and raised in Miami. The "Oriental" accent for the dry cleaners, grocers, ninjas, Chinese waiters, Japanese salarymen, and computer geeks that I'd had to play, when I was from Hawai'i and primarily of mixed Korean and Okinawan descent. The "Black" accent for the drug-dealing pimps, Jhericurl athletes, ghetto brothers, deadbeat dads, crackheads, muggers, and gangbangers that Kevin had had to play, when he'd grown up on the Upper West Side of Manhattan with two corporate-attorney parents and had gone to the Dalton School and Middlebury College in Vermont.

"I want people to understand what I'm saying," I told Tommy.

"No one's going to understand what you're saying, no matter how you say it. That line makes no sense whatsoever. You understand it, Kev?"

"Too mystical for me."

I actually didn't understand the line myself.

"There's no logic to half the script," Tommy said to Kevin. "I still don't get why you can't screw the girl."

"You know why."

"You've done it before."

Kevin had once been in a Spike Lee film about interracial love, breaking the ultimate taboo (dark-skinned Black man/white woman), and had been the romantic lead in more than a dozen movies. He'd been named one of *People*'s 50 Most Beautiful People in 1994.

Alex Rudd was the only character in *Days of Scorn*

who didn't embody some sort of racist, sexist, homophobic, misogynistic, or xenophobic stereotype, no doubt
owing to the fact that Lucius Royal himself was African
American. Alex Rudd, before becoming a Navy SEAL and
Desert Storm veteran, had graduated from Princeton and
then attended Oxford as a Rhodes scholar. He was also a
wine connoisseur and played classical piano. Until he got
entangled in the present mess with the cartel and the triad,
he had been doing wetwork for the CIA (which was ironic
to me, since my father had been a career CIA case officer
and hadn't known a gun from a spatula).

However, Rudd would not be having sexual relations
with "the girl," EMMY PHILLIPS (who was being played by
the very white actress Carrie Potts), although there was
definitely an emotional connection there, an undeniable
romantic chemistry between them. Their interactions
would be confined to wisecracks, sighs, eyebrow raises,
silent whistles of appreciation, and occasional stares of
yearning, nothing more. The script didn't present any im-
pediments to their coupling, both characters single, het-
erosexual, and toothsome. In most of the scenes, Emmy
was running around in a black lace bra (for some reason,
she could never manage to find the time to button her
shirt), and Rudd had his own torso-baring exhibitions. Was
it because Lucius was afraid that crossing the color line
would hurt the movie's box-office performance? Because
he knew that for most of America it was still unsavory to
conceive of a Black man being with a white woman?

"Have you ever gotten to screw the girl, Al?" Tommy
asked me.

"I've never even gotten to kiss the girl."

"That's surprising. You're a handsome guy."

"Asian men aren't allowed to be sexual."

"Well, we all know why," Kevin said. "What happens if an Asian dude with an erection walks into a wall?" he asked. "Breaks his nose."

"What's long and black and smells like shit?" I asked. "The welfare line."

"How do you blindfold an Asian guy?" Tommy asked. "Put floss over his eyes."

"How do you fit a hundred Cubans into a shoebox?" I asked. "Tell them it's a raft."

Whatever Lucius's reasons for chastening Rudd and "the girl," it hadn't stopped him from sleeping with Carrie himself, as we'd deduced early in the shoot, which explained why she never joined us, her fellow cast members, for meals or drinks, always saying she was too tired and that she was simply going to order room service.

Or it could have been that she thought we were a bunch of dumb, juvenile, chauvinistic assholes who amused themselves with bad, off-color jokes, and that we should be avoided at all costs.

"Hey," Kevin said, "what do you call a redneck with a pig and a sheep?"

Case in point.

The next morning in the makeup trailer, amid the din of people working at six different stations, I said to Gaby, "You left some blood on me yesterday."

"Yeah?"

"Very negligent. I expect you to be much more careful from here on out."

"Do you now?" she said. "Well, you know what you can do with that attitude, pal."

Gaby was one of the special effects makeup artists responsible for blood and wounds, and she'd had to attend to me pretty much throughout the picture, because El Mano Silencioso seemed to get dinged up an extraordinary amount—punched, kicked, knifed, thrown against walls and through windows, hit by cars, and now shot. But he was extremely resilient. And relentless. The running joke in the movie was that characters—seeing El Mano get up from the ground once again, not giving up—would keep saying, "Who the fuck *is* that guy?" (a line that Lucius shamelessly ripped off from *Butch Cassidy and the Sundance Kid*).

I had watched Gaby create gashes, abrasions, bruises, and bullet holes on me with magical dexterity, yet she claimed this was all rather simple stuff. She much preferred the challenge of working on science fiction, fantasy, and horror movies, where she used molds, casts, and prosthetics to fashion aliens, monsters, werewolves, elves, and zombies. Really, the only difficulty with the SFX makeup in *Days of Scorn* had been the blood. First, its appearance and consistency. Lucius had insisted he didn't want blood that was obviously fake, resembling raspberry jam. He wanted dark, coagulating, realistic blood, and if the art department couldn't produce it, he'd have them buy pig's blood. Thankfully they hadn't had to resort to that. They'd found a formula to satisfy him: Karo corn syrup for some viscosity, a little opacifier so it wasn't completely see-through, liquid lecithin as an emulsifier, red food coloring mixed with a bit of blue and black for depth. This was the base. The color, texture, and thickness could be adjusted as needed, depending on the lighting and situation. Before shooting began, they'd prepared three fifty-five-gallon drums of it. They hadn't accounted for the possible ramifications of the sugary content.

In the trailer, sitting in Gaby's chair, I asked her, "What'd you guys come up with?" and scraped a fingertip across the blood on my neck.

"Hey," she said, "I'll have to redo that now."

I sampled the blood. "What's this made of? It doesn't taste sweet anymore."

"It took us all night to come up with the recipe. Sugar-free chocolate syrup, sugar-free Kool-Aid dark cherry, water, and a few chemicals you don't want to know about."

"You could've told me that before I tasted it."

"You could've asked before you made that smear." She fixed the blood on my neck with a sponge, syringe, and spatula, checking the photographs that she had taken of me yesterday for continuity.

"Am I going to see you tonight?" I asked, sotto voce.

"I don't know. Are you?"

We'd been sleeping together for the past few weeks, on and off. Ordinarily, below-the-line crew would stay at an Embassy Suites or Comfort Inn, but the Esperanza had over three hundred fifty rooms for cheap, so Gaby had ended up there, and we'd hooked up one night after running into each other in the basement laundry room.

She wasn't really my type. At that point in my life, I usually went for svelte, gorgeous, self-centered, shallow women with long hair and long legs (almost always white), because I was self-centered and shallow myself. Gaby was smart, funny, short, and a little chubby, with a beautiful face framed by an amazing pair of eyebrows—straight, thick, and elongated. She had black hair that was wavy and unruly, cut in a bob and parted on the side, which she often tucked behind her ears. She wore no makeup, not even mascara.

In addition to all the time we had spent with each other on set, several things drew us together. She was Asian, too, or half-Asian. Her full name was Gabriela Yim-Abaroa, her father Chinese, her mother Peruvian, which made Gaby a tusán, as half bloods were called in Peru. Gaby had been born in Lima, but the family had immigrated to Houston when she was a toddler. She lived in Austin now.

Another parallel was that she was an actor as well, and had faced her share of typecasting, alternately regarded as Asian or Latina, but never both, never neither. After playing prostitutes, maids, nannies, nail salon workers, fruit pickers, masseuses, and lab assistants, she'd made a vow not to take on any more roles that reinforced stereotypes, which meant that subsequently she hardly worked at all as an actress. After a bit part in a horror film, she trained to become an SFX makeup artist, and now, as a freelancer, she was offered more gigs than she could accept. It wasn't just films and TV shows. She also did SFX makeup for the stage, at theme parks, on cruise ships, for fashion shows, and at medical schools, police academies, and military training camps, doing moulage. She still went to auditions once in a while, invariably a fruitless exercise, and was bitter about her acting career, but she enjoyed the variety and finiteness of the SFX makeup jobs. She was rarely home, which suited her just fine. She got restless easily and disliked long-term commitments. This applied to romances as well, she made clear to me that first night.

I wasn't one to protest. My life was as peripatetic as hers, and I hadn't had a meaningful relationship in years. I'd started my career in musical theater, studying modern dance and tap and drama as an undergrad at Ohio State, after which I'd gone to New York, although more often than not I was on the road for regional theater or national tours. Even after moving to California, I never had a regular lifestyle, with day jobs as a line cook, a personal trainer, and then as a concierge at the Beverly Hills Hotel. (As a CIA brat, I'd picked up a smattering of different languages, principally French, Arabic, and Farsi. The latter made me popular with the Iranian Jews, or Persians, as they liked to be called, who were inundating Beverly Hills at the time.) Now, with sporadic roles in films and occasional guest spots on TV, I never knew what my schedule would be from day to day, and I was out of town quite a bit. Not at all conducive to a relationship. I'd never been married or had children. People outside the industry often suspected I was gay.

Yet it wasn't just our itineracy that stopped Gaby from considering anything more serious between us. Nor was it that we lived in different cities or that I was fourteen years older than she was. It was that actors were terrible relationship partners. We had gravitated to a profession in which we lied for a living, always pretending to be someone else. Most of us had some sort of psychological wound or defect that made us favor assuming other identities, fabricated identities, over residing in our own.

There was one additional factor. On location, it wasn't

uncommon for people to have affairs, and there was a tacit understanding that flings would not last beyond the wrap party. It was less common, however, for cast and crew to consort. Cast with cast, yes, crew with crew, yes, but cast (especially one of the leads) with crew, not so much. Gaby was paranoid that the revelation we were sleeping together would somehow hurt her future job prospects, so, like Lucius and Carrie, we were keeping it on the down-low, sneaking into each other's hotel rooms at night.

"Is nine good?" I asked. "Nine's good for me."

She gestured for me to get out of the chair, done with me. "We'll see," she told me, and then, as I was about to open the trailer door, she said, "Hang on." She sprayed sunscreen on me. "We wouldn't want you to get burned out there, would we?"

With the new blood, we were able to knock out the basin scene, then we quickly moved to town, to Segundo Barrio, to shoot:

EXT. CLINIC — DAY

One of the henchmen's monster trucks rumbles very slowly down an alleyway in the barrio, weaving back and forth, almost hitting a couple of dumpsters. Its passenger windows have been shot out, and the doors and panels are riddled with bullet holes.

The truck veers into the parking spaces in back of a clinic and abruptly stops. It is

still very early out, the clinic not open
yet, no one around. The driver's door of the
truck opens, and El Mano Silencioso slides
out of the seat and tumbles to the ground.

Holding his hand against his left waist,
which is bleeding badly (as is his head and
shoulder), he gets to his feet, takes a crowbar out of the truck, and stumbles to the
clinic's back door, which he pries open with
the crowbar.

Once inside the empty clinic, El Mano would revive
himself with stabs of EpiPens and whiffs of ammonia in-
halant, then sterilize the wounds with iodine, open them
up with a scalpel, pull out the slugs with a pair of forceps,
and close them with a surgical stapler—all without an
anesthetic.

But first we had to do the exterior scene. To make up
for the lost time yesterday, the second-unit director had
already shot the monster truck going down the alley and
parking behind the clinic with a stunt driver at the wheel,
but the rest of the scene, all fifteen seconds of it, with only
El Mano in frame, would still take hours. There were five
different setups, each of which would require Lucius block-
ing out the shot; the crew positioning the cameras, lights,
sound; another run-through; more tweaks; then four or
five takes. The alley would look deserted on screen, but it
was crammed with camera rigs, dollies, cables, lights, sound
and video equipment, monitors, tents, chairs, craft service
tables, trucks, and trailers. Over sixty people were scuttling

about, everyone from the DP to gaffers, grips, set decs, PAs, and genny ops. For me, it was a lot of hurry-up-and-wait, getting called to the set, rehearsing the scene or walking through specific marks, then going back to the trailer or sitting in a chair, waiting to be called again.

The difficulty with this particular scene was the lighting. It was midday, but the scene was supposed take place in the early a.m. I didn't understand why they weren't postponing it until a morning later in the week (it was rare in film for scenes to be shot in script sequence), but it wasn't my prerogative. I was there to fall, strain, stagger, and grunt.

We kept getting interrupted. A shadow, a reflection, a glare, a plane overhead, an ambulance.

We were set up for the shot where El Mano would laboriously rise from the asphalt. I lay down on the ground, which was hot, despite the reflective aluminum tarps a crew member had put on the spot to keep it cool. Costume, hair, and makeup (including Gaby) fiddled with me. The 1st AD said, "Picture is up. Quiet, everyone. Roll sound," and the sound mixer said, "Speed," and the 1st AD said, "Roll camera," and the 1st AC said, "Rolling," and then the 2nd AC said, "Scene 68F. Take 3," and the DP said, "Mark it," and the 2nd AC said, "Mark," and slapped the slate shut, and then some dogs started barking somewhere.

"Goddammit," Lucius said.

The dogs—a group of mangy strays down the alley— kept barking and yowling.

"Shut the fuck up!" Lucius said.

I stayed on the ground, trying not to move or sweat for the next take, and peered up at Lucius, who was wearing his usual garb: a wrinkled white linen shirt, cargo shorts, untied hiking boots, and a straw fedora.

He looked down at me. "Which restaurant you think those dogs will end up in tonight?" he asked. "Korean or Mexican?"

In retrospect, it was something Kevin might have said to Tommy and me—the old chestnut about foreigners eating dog—as part of our repartee, our boozy banter, when lampooning the racism we had faced. Except Lucius had never been privy to those exchanges. No one else had. The three of us were mindful not to let anyone else overhear the jokes, lest they get taken out of context and cause offense. So Lucius's quip, coming out of nowhere, was jarring. I didn't know quite how to take it. Neither did anyone else on the set. It was dead quiet for two, three beats. Even the dogs stopped barking. Then a few people chuckled awkwardly, several rolled their eyes.

"All right, let's try this again," the 1st AD said. "Lock it down. Picture's up!" And we resumed the shot.

I was willing to forget it, just let it go, but Gaby would not. She was incensed. In my room at the Esperanza that night, she said to me, "You have to do something."

"What?"

"Make him apologize to you and the entire crew."

"That's not going to happen," I said. "I'm not in a position to make Lucius do anything."

"Exactly," she said. "That's exactly why it was so unforgivable. He was mocking you, knowing he has every power over you."

Room service knocked on the door. I had ordered

dinner for us, and I rolled the cart to the window, set up two chairs, and took off the plate covers. "Come on, let's eat."

She sat opposite me. "Why aren't you more upset about this?"

"It was just a stupid joke."

"He managed to insult *both* my heritages."

"You're Chinese Peruvian, not Korean Mexican."

"To him, it's the same thing. Like, why couldn't he have found a Mexican or Chicano actor for Tommy and Sergi's roles? Or someone Chinese for yours?"

"Lucius is not a racist."

"Just because he's Black?" she said.

There were historical divisions, of course, between African Americans and Asian Americans and Latino Americans, but I'd always seen us as comrades in the same fight, and I wanted to think that Lucius did, too. Solidaridad. "All the leads in this film, except Carrie, are minorities," I said to Gaby. "Think about that."

"That term's passé. Use 'people of color.'"

"He could have written a white-savior story and gotten someone haole to play Alex Rudd, but he didn't. I'm sure the studio would have been happier if he had."

"This is the most racist project I've ever worked on," Gaby told me. "Everything about it is completely disgusting."

"I wouldn't go that far."

"No? You've said as much yourself. Every Mexican is either a cartel member or undocumented immigrant. 'Illegals.' Isn't that the phrase Lucius actually put in his screenplay? He doesn't know anything about the border, about Ciudad Juárez. He's reduced everything to narco violence.

There's not an ounce of morality in the entire film. It's just boys and their toys, glorifying gunfights, which is unconscionable after Columbine."

The high school shooting in Colorado, in which twelve students and one teacher had been murdered, had occurred three months earlier.

"El Mano Silencioso's no better," Gaby said. "He's a caricature."

"Maybe, but it's more screen time than I've ever had."

"You've got one line. That's not exactly a mark of career advancement."

"Now you're getting mean," I said. "It's a pretty decent role. Chow Yun-fat was lined up to do it at one point."

"Lucius humiliated you. Why aren't you taking this personally? Where's your self-respect?"

Internally I bristled. She didn't know me well enough to say such things, to question my pride. She didn't know what I'd been through.

"Your food's getting cold," I told her.

On a relative scale, Lucius's comment hadn't been that egregious. I had heard much worse over the course of my life and career. I'd been called a gook, a chink, zipperhead, dim sum. I'd been the butt of dumb wisecracks—"Hey, let's chop-chop"—and the object of dumb questions—"What are you?" "What's your nationality?" "Where are you from? . . . No, where are you *really* from?"—all assumptive that I was fresh off the boat, an immigrant, an alien, even though I spoke perfect English.

(When I told people I was from Hawai'i, I'd sometimes be asked, "Oh, when'd you move to the States?")

I'd always been regarded as someone who could not be a real American, the possibility precluded solely on the basis of my Asianness, and I had been denigrated and dismissed as an actor because of it, beginning in college and continuing in New York, where theatrical agents told me my look was too "specific" and they'd only be able to book me in certain roles, like in *The King and I* and *Miss Saigon*. Yet the leads in those shows usually went to white actors in yellowface.

For a while I was encouraged by what was happening off-Broadway, especially at the Public Theater, which advocated nontraditional casting. One of my proudest moments was playing the Third Citizen in *Richard III* with Denzel Washington in Central Park. But I found that if I wanted to get larger parts or do, say, Noël Coward, I had to go farther off-Broadway to companies like the Pan Asian Repertory Theatre.

The situation in Hollywood was even more depressing. I couldn't get in a room unless a part was written for an Asian or someone who was "ethnic." A character, it was apparent, could never just happen to be Asian American. I'd go on calls for commercials and TV shows, and the casting directors would ask me to do another reading, but this time be "more Asian"—in other words, do an immigrant accent. It was always obvious to me when an Asian actor stammering in broken English was actually a native English speaker. It sounded exactly like a bigot mimicking an Asian accent. I walked out of a lot of those auditions.

I went to Hong Kong for an action thriller after being told the film industry there was looking for more stars. I gave in to my agent's suggestion to change my name from

Alain Kweon to Alan Kwan to broaden my appeal. I was pretty sure I had a dollop of Chinese blood in me, and we exaggerated the proportion. I didn't know kung fu at the time, but I could follow the choreography since I'd trained as a dancer. In the territories, however, I was chided for being jook-sing because I didn't speak Cantonese. Jook-sing translated to bamboo pole, hollow on the inside yet partitioned with nodes so water couldn't flow through. The metaphor was for someone who looked Chinese but had grown up overseas and knew nothing about Chinese culture, someone with both ends cut off, not part of either world.

I returned to LA. To make ends meet, I started doing corporate videos on workplace safety and harassment, and documentary TV shows in which I was the pilot in a plane crash reenactment or an EMT in a true crime case. Ultimately, I capitulated and started doing auditions with an accent, whereupon I was hired to appear on *Law & Order, Nash Bridges, Chicago Hope,* and *Profiler.* Several times, the scripts in the shows called for characters to speak Korean, Chinese, or Vietnamese, which I didn't speak, and the directors would tell me to just speak gibberish, and I spoke gibberish, just like the actors did in *Miss Saigon.* Finally, I began learning kung fu and immediately got cast in a string of action movies.

Was I disappointed with the arc of my career? Was I frustrated I never got to act in anything with some profundity, some depth? Was I angry with the inequities and racism in the business? Was I ashamed I'd made compromises? Of course I was. But at least I'd been working steadily in recent years. At least I'd been able to make a living doing what I loved.

I also knew that my window was closing. I'd be turning forty soon. I was getting old for action movies. Already the stunts were taking a toll on me, my body aching after every gag. There was only so long I could keep doing this, and I wanted to squeeze as much out of it as possible.

It rained the next day. El Paso averaged three hundred days of sunshine a year, with only nine total inches of precipitation. Most of that rain, however, fell between July and September, when the prevailing wind direction switched from west to east, bringing in moisture from the Gulf of Mexico. Days might start out sunny, but then an isolated thunderstorm would roll in with torrential rain and there'd be flash floods. Wet streets and cloudy skies didn't fit the look Lucius wanted for the film—hot and punishingly dry, everything scalded by an unremitting, pitiless sun—and production had to be halted once again.

We used the dead time to rehearse the climactic fight scene, which would be unfurling in an abandoned cattle feed mill outside of town. Since arriving in El Paso, we'd been practicing pieces of the scene whenever there was a free hour or two, commandeering the ballroom in the Esperanza. There were mats on the floor, and banquet tables and stacked chairs and cardboard boxes had been arranged to stand in for the machinery and equipment in the feed mill. The stunt coordinator, Marcio Lovato—along with Lucius and the second-unit director—had blocked out every move and gunshot for the actors, stuntmen, and stunt doubles. We went through the paces, running from station to station, crouching for cover, pretending to fire our gun props and engaging in bursts of hand-to-hand combat.

Lucius had originally been a stunt coordinator himself and, in his quest for realism, had had us fire thousands of rounds of live ammo at a shooting range, coached by a former officer of the British Special Air Service. Lucius thought there were two cardinal sins committed in many action thrillers: 1) actors didn't line up gun sights with targets when shooting, meaning they weren't actually aiming at anything; and 2) characters would fire hundreds of shots without ever reloading. So the ex–SAS officer had had us shoot, reload, shoot, reload, with an emphasis on quick-draw and rapid-fire techniques, trying to make the handling of the weapons reflexive. We'd also trained in tactical three-gun, transitioning from rifle to pistol to shotgun. I had to learn to shoot a pistol with my left hand as well, since El Mano was a two-fisted gunslinger. After each day at the range, my hands were blistered and shaking.

Then there were the martial arts. We had to grapple, jab, stab, and kick in between fusillades of gunshots. Marcio had taught us moves that were a mix of Brazilian and Japanese jiu-jitsu, aikido, jeet kune do, Filipino Kali, wing chun, Krav Maga, Russian Sambo and Systema, and fu jow pai. In the ballroom, we went through the fight choreography for the feed mill scene, pretending to punch, head-butt, leg-sweep, and flip one another, and by the end of the day, after rehearsing for nine hours, all we wanted to do was get the hell out of the Esperanza.

Kevin had a driver. Both he and Tommy—per their contracts—had their own trailers, makeup and hair stylists, and personal assistants, and Kevin's agent had negotiated for him to have his own transportation, an A-list perk. We got into his SUV, and his driver took us down I-10 to a fast-food joint called Chico's Tacos, supposedly a local institution.

It was no longer raining out, but the air felt swampy. The restaurant sat between a cemetery and a park. Inside, the place was dingy yet crowded. We had to wait in line to order from the counter, and when it was our turn, we all chose the signature dish of tacos, along with large Cokes and crinkle-cut fries, then sat in a molded-plywood booth and waited for our number to be called.

"What'd Lucius say to you yesterday?" Tommy asked.

"You heard about it?"

"Rumblings. I want to hear it from you. What happened?"

I told them the story.

"What?" Tommy said.

"He really said that?" Kevin asked. "That is fucked, man."

"I might've clocked him if I'd been there," Tommy said.

I was surprised by their reactions. I hadn't thought they'd be all that perturbed. Now I felt embarrassed. I had dismissed Gaby as naive and presumptuous, but perhaps everyone else, too, was wondering why I hadn't been indignant with Lucius, why I hadn't responded to him— verbally or even physically. Did people think I was a wimp for doing nothing, a coward, personifying the stereotype of the spineless, deferential Asian male? Were Tommy and Kevin losing all respect for me?

"You know what?" Tommy said. "Fuck the *flied lice* accent. Fuck that line entirely."

El Mano Silencioso's sole line—after being taken down by an armor-piercing bullet that goes through his Kevlar vest—would be:

INT. CATTLE FEED MILL — DAY

Rudd and Emmy walk up to El Mano Silencio-
oso, who is lying on his back on the concrete floor, bleeding badly from the chest
and breathing with great difficulty.

Rudd kneels down, and El Mano smiles at him
weakly.

                    EL MANO
                (in a faint whisper)
    All river go to sea, but sea not full.

He closes his eyes. He stops breathing, and
his head slumps to the side.

The line seemed to be another one of those inscruta-
ble Oriental-like proverbs, but I had actually traced it to
the Bible—Ecclesiastes 1:7. "All the rivers run into the sea,
yet the sea is not full." I had been thinking that El Mano,
being from Hong Kong, would speak English with a Cantonese accent, which meant omitting *r*'s, pronouncing *a*'s
as *ah,* and vocalizing *er*'s as *ahhh,* so *producer* came out as
po-doo-sahh and *appreciate* sounded like *ah-pee-cee-ate.* There
were *l*'s in Cantonese, however, so really the only word
El Mano might mangle was "river." Yet I was sure Lucius
would want the full-on Asian accent for the line, as in "Arr
liver go to sea, but sea not furr." It was the rendition with
which I'd auditioned for the role.

Our number was called over the intercom, and we got our food, an order each of three tacos, which were stuffed with ground beef, rolled, and fried, then put in a paper boat and drowned in some sort of tomato sauce and smothered with bright yellow shredded cheese.

"Maybe I should use an upper-class BBC British accent," I said to Tommy and Kevin. "If Alex Rudd can come from a privileged background, why not El Mano Silencioso? That'd be an interesting character twist."

"Do it, man," Tommy told me. "It'd be nice if one goddamn thing in this movie wasn't a total cliché."

"If you could have your pick of deathbed speeches, what would it be?" Kevin asked.

"Hamlet," I said. " 'To grunt and sweat under a weary life, / But that the dread of something after death, / The undiscovered country from whose bourn / No traveller returns.' Although those weren't his dying words."

" 'The rest is silence,' " Tommy said.

"You got it."

The tacos were soggy and mushy. The tomato sauce was lukewarm and watery, virtually tasteless. The cheese seemed to be processed government cheese. Somehow the cumulative effect was delicious.

"I might have to get another one of these," Kevin told us. He had wolfed down his tacos and was now dipping the crinkle fries into the leftover sauce. "That'd be so funny if you recited Shakespeare instead of that stupid line. Lucius would shit a brick."

"We might all be shitting bricks after this meal," Tommy said.

★ ★ ★

Everyone—Rudd, Beltran, the drug lord, their henchmen, El Mano, and a band of corrupt DEA, FBI, and Border Patrol agents—converged in the cattle feed mill for the big fight to the end, each man armed with multiple weapons and munitions.

In theaters, the nearly seven-minute scene would flow harrowingly with no breaks, and most of it would be filmed right beside the actors with handheld cameras, the frame always moving, herky-jerky, the sequences feeling frenetic and spontaneous, as if the audience were right there in the middle of the firefights. Viewers would remark about the noise of the gunshots. Lucius had us shoot full-load blanks—cartridges with full charges of gunpowder—and the audio was recorded on set, not added later by foley artists, so the sounds the audience would hear were the sounds the weapons actually made, deafening, terrifying, and unrelenting (the crew wore huge ear-muff hearing protectors). But filming the scene was tedious and inter-minable, with untold starts and stops.

I'd fire a full mag from a Steyr TMP machine pistol—stop, wait in the trailer. I'd do an elbow strike and triangle choke—stop, wait in the trailer. I'd shoot a henchman with a double-tap to the head—stop, wait in the trailer. I'd do a joint lock and snap an arm—stop, wait in the trailer.

During a lunch break, Lucius came into my narrow trailer compartment (one of three in the wagon), holding a sheet of paper. I didn't know what he was doing there. We'd never talked privately before.

For days, I had been brooding over what to do, whether I should confront Lucius about his joke, whether I should insist that El Mano's last line be reconsidered, both its content and delivery. On the one hand, I didn't want to get a reputation in the industry as a troublemaker. On the other hand, if this ended up being one of my last jobs, at least I would have made a stand, fought for something, regained my honor.

Now, watching Lucius grab a bottle of water from the counter and take a drink, I wondered if he'd had his own misgivings. Did he know people were talking about him? Was he worried about word leaking out to the press or someone filing an EEOC complaint? Was he here to apologize to me?

"This is a new side we'll be distributing with tomorrow's call sheet," he told me, handing me the script page. "We're going to shoot an alternate ending, an extra scene. It'll still appear that El Mano dies, same as what we had originally, but this might be added later on."

```
EXT. CATTLE FEED MILL — DAY

Rudd and Emmy head toward his Dodge Chal-
lenger when suddenly TWO SHOTS sound in rapid
succession. Rudd whirls around, pointing his
SIG-Sauer.

Henchman #5 stands behind them, holding a
Colt Model 654 carbine. After a beat, he
drops to his knees and falls flat on his
face, dead.

El Mano Silencioso, still very much alive,
is behind the henchman, his two Beretta 92FS
```

pistols extended in his fists. He holsters
the guns and gives a subtle salute to Rudd
with two fingers, then limps away.

Rudd stares after him, incredulous.

                        RUDD
         Who the fuck _is_ that guy?

Lucius tilted his little straw fedora so it was cocked
on his head. "I've always thought of *Days of Scorn* as the
first installment in a trilogy," he told me. "After seeing the
dailies, the studio's almost guaranteeing a sequel. But you
know what? They're interested in El Mano Silencioso.
They're thinking maybe he should live. They have a hunch
he might be big with international markets. So we're going
to do two edits: one in which he dies, another in which he
lives. They'll do test screenings and figure out which ending audiences prefer. What do you think of that?"

I could get the same sort of deal Kevin and Tommy
were getting, I thought. Quote points. And perks. My own
trailer and assistant and stylists. I could name my price.

They were all on top of me, waiting for me to speak. I
was lying on the concrete floor in the feed mill, Kevin
kneeling beside me, Carrie Potts standing near my feet.
The camera was tilted down, close on my face, while Lucius, the DP, boom op, key grip, ADs, and ACs hovered
overhead. Behind them were Gaby and Tommy, waiting to
see what I'd do.

I had decided I would say the line essentially as it'd

been written, but even now, I had yet to decide how I would say it. If I played along, presumably El Mano Silencioso would get much more dialogue in the sequel and threequel, assuming there was one. Could I really live with myself, perpetuating a Chinaman accent for two more movies? Would that be my legacy?

If I said the line in unbroken English with a BBC accent or, say, a generic American no-accent, and refused to do a different reading, what would it prove? I'd save face, maybe. I could tell myself I was still the same guy who'd walked out of auditions years ago in protest. But I'd lose a plum role and a lot of money, and whichever way I said the line, it could be looped later in postproduction, even dubbed over by another actor. After all, no one had heard El Mano speak yet. His voice could be anyone's. But Lucius wouldn't even have to bother with that. He could just make a few simple edits—show Rudd and Emmy walking toward El Mano's body and then cut straight to his lifeless face, head slumped to the side, eliminating the line entirely.

As it turned out, the sequel would be greenlighted and go deep into preproduction but would never get made. The screenplay would have Alex Rudd trying to foil a plot by Middle Eastern terrorists to blow up the Empire State Building, and filming would be scheduled to begin in October 2001. Then 9/11 would happen, and the studio would postpone principal photography. The project would then be shelved forever. Nonetheless, the first installment of *Days of Scorn* would be a moderate hit, and El Mano Silencioso would become my most notable role, the one I'd be remembered by, if people remembered me at all. Years later, people would occasionally ask me, "Weren't you in that movie with Tommy Navarro? The silent assassin?"

Tommy would become the real star among us, working with Almodóvar and the Coen brothers and winning
an Oscar for supporting actor. Kevin's career would peak
soon after *Days,* and he'd be relegated to second and third
leads. Lucius would helm two more movies, both box-
office flops, then return to being a stunt coordinator. Carrie Potts would quit acting (no doubt sick of playing "the
girl") and become a director of dark TV mystery dramas.

I saw her once at an airport, MSP, about eight years
ago. We were both on the same connecting flight to LA.

"Hey, Carrie," I said to her at the gate.

She looked at me without recognition, and I had to
explain to her how we knew each other.

"Oh, that piece-of-shit movie," she said, laughing. "I
remember you and Tommy and Kevin holding court in
the bar, the three amigos. And Lucius was always hitting on
me. Didn't he spread a rumor I was sleeping with him? He
wanted everyone to think he was such a stud."

She boarded soon after that. She was in first class. It
was twenty minutes before my group was called, and when
I shuffled past her seat, she didn't look up.

I don't know what happened to Gaby. I don't see her
listed for anything on IMDb beyond 2005. A lot of SFX
makeup for film and TV has become obsolete since then,
replaced by CGI to save time. No more squibs, no more
full resets absent of blood.

As for me, lying on my back in the feed mill, I didn't
know that this would be my final film, that I'd leave the
business after *Days of Scorn II* got cancelled (which felt to me
like a reprieve) and go back to the theater—experimental

ensemble theater. I just knew, with the camera and crew and cast focused wholly on me, that this was my moment of truth.

The 1st AD said, "Picture's up. Roll sound," and the sound mixer said, "Speed." The 1st AD said, "Roll camera," and the 1st AC said, "Rolling." The 2nd AC said, "Scene 129N. Take 1," and the DP said, "Mark it." The 2nd AC said, "Mark," and snapped the clapper board shut.

I wish I'd said, "And shake the yoke of inauspicious stars / From this world-wearied flesh." I wish I'd said, "Here is my journey's end, here is my butt, / And very seamark of my utmost sail."

Instead, I opened my mouth and croaked out, *"Arr."* That was all that emerged. Something was caught in my throat.

Lucius said, "Cut. What? You've got one line, and you forgot it? Let's do it again."

We did it again, and I could only rasp, *"Arr."* It sounded like someone doing a bad pirate imitation.

"What the fuck?" Lucius said.

I couldn't seem to speak. I'd somehow lost the ability to talk. Nothing was coming out, as if I'd actually become a mute. I opened my mouth wide and exhaled as hard as I could. *"Arr!"* I cawed. *"Arr!"*

III

DAYS IN, DAYS OUT

• • • • • • • • • •

SHE LOOKED OLDER, OF COURSE. But so did I. It was May 2019, seven years since we'd last seen each other, seven years since Nikki had left San Francisco for New York, and she was now forty-eight to my fifty-nine. In the interim, we'd talked on the phone occasionally, we'd emailed, though mostly it'd concerned travel plans for her daughter, Beatrice—logistics. From time to time, Beatrice would post images of Nikki on social media or text photos of her directly to me, yet none of those things told the whole story. Nothing ever does.

"You look great," I said to her.

"You've always been a good liar, Alain," she said. "But thank you."

It was like that all day, little snippets and quips, exchanging a few lines, then getting shunted away by Beatrice or one of her friends or a relative, not being able to really converse. We were at Bryn Mawr College, just outside Philadelphia, for Beatrice's graduation. I had flown in from SFO the night before, and I was jet-lagged and a bit dazed throughout the brunch on campus, overwhelmed in particular with meeting Nikki's family again after all these years. I'd always loved the Chandras. Several of the

Kaneshiros—Beatrice's father's family—were there as well, and I kept hearing myself referred to as "Oh, yes, the actor" or "the movie star" or "Mr. Hollywood," although I hadn't appeared in a studio film since 2000, nineteen years ago now.

The one person I didn't see there was Rob, Nikki's partner. When I asked about his whereabouts, Nikki said, "Your guess is as good as mine."

This must have been a recent development. Beatrice usually told me everything.

We proceeded to the commencement ceremony, which was held on a lawn underneath a large white tent surrounded by Gothic buildings, and then there was an outdoor tea party in another quad, and then our group caravanned to Fishtown, a funky neighborhood northeast of Center City, for dinner at Murph's Bar.

Murph's seemed to be a fairly standard Irish pub, outfitted with shamrocks, leprechaun hats, Irish flags, Eagles pennants, and a bar countertop epoxied with copper pennies, but it had some eccentricities, like quite a bit of Elvis memorabilia—I counted no less than six busts plus a lamp in the King's likeness. Strangest of all was that in the back room of the pub was an unaffiliated, unadvertised, unnamed restaurant, reputedly offering some of the best Italian food in Philly. So with your pint of Guinness, you could order an insalata di polpo, tagliolini with black truffle, beef braciola with orecchiette, or strozzapreti with burrata.

Beatrice had reserved most of the room for us— thirteen iterations of Asian American ethnicities, gussied up in suits and dresses, eating Italian in an Irish pub—and with each bite we exclaimed in amazement at the quality of the food. "Who would've thunk, right?" Beatrice said to me.

After dinner, we walked down the block to a music club called Johnny Brenda's. Beatrice had arranged to play a set upstairs to celebrate the release of her band's first self-produced EP. Besides being an academic wunderkind (in August she would be starting med school at Harvard, the holy grail for model minorities), she was also a very capable singer-songwriter, albeit her genre of music—dream pop, electropop—wasn't really my kind of thing. But she was talented, and I took some pride in that. I had taught her how to sing and dance and play guitar in her youth.

Throughout her time at Bryn Mawr, she had sent me mp3s of every new song she composed, but I hadn't seen her perform live since her sophomore year in high school. It was a revelation. Her band, which she'd named Pearl Lady, was tight, executing precise synths and driving beats. Beatrice dominated the stage, singing in an ethereal keen, dancing and bouncing, issuing fuzz- and reverb-laden riffs from her Fender Jaguar that were grittier and far more interesting than any of the polished tinkles on the recorded versions of the songs. Her lyrics were about heartache and grief (e.g., *"When you lie down to die / You'll have it all"*), yet what struck me was the utter joy she projected up there. Gone was the emo/goth poseur of her teens ("What's the difference?" I'd asked her once, and she'd said, "Goth's when you hate the world. Emo's when the world hates you even more"). Here now was a confident young woman in her glory.

After the show, Nikki and I ended up sharing an Uber

back to Rittenhouse Square. It happened that she was at the Sofitel, and I was right across the street in the Palomar, a smaller boutique hotel. Everyone else was staying in a pair of hotels in Society Hill.

When we arrived at 17th and Sansom, I asked Nikki, "Want to get a nightcap?"

"I don't know. It's been a long day."

"Come on. For old time's sake?"

I took her to one of my favorite bars in the city, Good Dog, on 15th. A friend who belonged to the Pig Iron Theatre Group had taken me there once on a visit. I liked discovering hip dive bars. Like many people my age, I was drinking more than I used to.

The first floor of Good Dog was dark, with exposed ducting, a pressed-tin ceiling, and hundreds of framed black-and-white photos of dogs on the walls.

We sat at the long mahogany bar and ordered bourbons.

"You've become a hippie," Nikki said. "Your hair."

Hadn't she seen photos of me, via Beatrice? Hadn't she been curious? I'd grown my hair out as it'd grayed. I no longer had to worry about my appearance, how it might conflict with potential TV, film, or stage parts. Typically I tied it into a ponytail, but today I had it down, tucked behind my ears.

"I haven't had it this long since I was fourteen, maybe, when I was a skate punk."

"At least you don't wear it in a man bun."

I fidgeted.

"You don't, do you?"

I cringed.

She laughed. "You've been in California too long."

We talked about work. She had recently joined a private gynecological practice, and I had just opened my sixth boba tea shop in San Francisco.

"A little empire," she said. "Who would've ever imagined you'd be such an entrepreneur."

Not I. Going into the boba tea business had been a complete fluke. When I'd opened the first shop, I had intended it to be a one-off, a short-term diversion until I found something else better to do.

We talked about how happy Beatrice had seemed, what a terrific day it'd been, perfect May weather, a wonderful dinner, a rousing show.

"I feel like I hardly got to talk to her at all, though," I said.

"You'll have plenty of opportunity next week."

Beatrice would be visiting San Francisco over Memorial Day weekend. Every summer, she made a return trip to California, ostensibly to see her childhood best friend, Nadia, who'd remained in the Bay Area. But on these trips, Beatrice always chose to stay with me at my house.

"It's amazing to me you and Beatrice are still so close," Nikki said.

It was something I was unduly proud of.

Nikki and I had begun dating in 2009 when Beatrice was eleven. After four months, I put my row house in the Outer Parkside up for rent and moved into Nikki's place in Laurel Heights, living with her and Beatrice for three years. Unlike Nikki, I didn't have a regular job. I had servers and managers running the shops, and they usually only required my attention a few hours a day—phone calls and emails, mostly. So Beatrice and I spent an inordinate amount of time together. I made breakfast for her, assembled elaborate bento boxes for her lunches, escorted her to school and friends' houses and various appointments, took her shopping, taught her music and martial arts (a little wing chun, a little aikido, a little tai chi), made her dinner, helped with her homework.

We grew very attached to each other, which became a source of tension for Nikki, who was struggling to communicate with her daughter. As a preteen, rebellion blossoming, Beatrice directed any bouts of insubordination toward her mother, not me. "You have it so easy," Nikki would tell me. "You never have to say no to her, you never have to discipline her. You always just say, 'Ask Mom,' and then I become the bad guy."

Regardless, I thought we made for a terrific family. Those three years with them were the happiest of my life. My business was taking off, Beatrice was doing great in school, and I'd never been more in love with anyone than with Nikki. Then she was offered a job as the chief of gynecology at a hospital in Manhattan. A phenomenal job, one she couldn't really turn down. I didn't want her to take it. I didn't want her and Beatrice to go. I was willing to move with them. I proposed to Nikki. But the fact was, although the job had materialized out of nowhere (she hadn't applied for it, they'd approached her), she had gone to New York for a day of interviews and hadn't told me about it. She had wanted an out.

She was a leaver. She'd been in the process of leaving Beatrice's father, Billy Kaneshiro, a cancer researcher at Genentech, when he died in a motorcycle accident. She had left me, and now, apparently, she was leaving Rob.

"We've been fighting," Nikki said in the bar. "Beatrice and I."

"About what?" I asked.

"I'm not sure, exactly. She's been snapping at me, being sarcastic, condescending, like she used to in high school."

"Maybe she was stressed out about organizing everything for today."

"I organized most of it," Nikki said. "And footed the bill."

"Could it have something to do with Rob?"

"What about him?"

"You guys are breaking up, right? Maybe she's upset about it."

"She has zero feelings about it. It's ancient history. He moved out last fall."

"That long ago?" I couldn't believe Beatrice hadn't told me about it. "What happened?"

"It just ran its course," Nikki said.

"You're not seeing anyone new?"

"No," she told me, then asked, "What about you?"

It was apparent now that Beatrice could not be relied upon as a conduit at all. "No. I've been holding out for you," I said, but jokingly—a gutless gesture.

"Such a liar."

The truth was, I wasn't joking, I wasn't lying. I'd never let go of Nikki. The truth was, I had been thinking a lot about my life lately, mystified by the way things had turned out, bereft I'd never married or had children, terrified of the idea of dying alone.

We walked back to our hotels. Outside the Palomar, I said, "Do you want to come up and see my room?"

Nikki cocked her head at me and smirked. "Why would I want to come up and see your room?"

"The decor's kind of interesting. The view's nice."

She laughed. "I don't think so."

"How about if I come up to see your room, then?" I asked.

She kissed me on the cheek. "There's nothing there to see," she said, and walked across the intersection to her hotel.

In 2002, fed up with being cast as triad gangsters and communist spies and ninja, I'd quit Hollywood for good. (Not that anyone missed me. Toward the end I could support myself acting, but I was a C-list actor at best.) I moved to San Francisco to join an experimental theater ensemble called The Black Cube, which had a playhouse in the Presidio. We did everything from an interactive comedy on lucid dreaming, to a reworked *King Lear* set in space, to a heavy-metal cabaret emceed by George Wallace. I took a few parts in indie films, but gradually I withdrew from the entire movie industry, and my last role was a cameo in an indie feature called *Late in the Day,* with an all–Asian American cast, when I was fifty.

To make extra money, I started doing voiceovers and motion capture for a video-game company called Jiki Entertainment in the Mission. The founder, Marty Kitano, had opened the studio after working for Zynga and Sony Interactive because he'd wanted more creative freedom. Namely, he'd wanted to present multinational, multiracial characters without having to conform to formula, which I thought brave. I had recurring roles in several of his games

and their sequels, and was twice nominated for Best Performance by a Human Male at the Spike Video Game
Awards.

During breaks, Marty and I would often go next door
to a store called Pearl Lady, run by a young Japanese woman
named Hitomi Uchida. It was a tiny, kitschy place, filled
with snacks and toys that reminded us of our childhoods—
Marty's in Gardena, a Japanese American suburb in Southern California, and mine in Tokyo.

In Pearl Lady, there were plushies, Pocky boxes of every flavor, Ramune soda, erasers shaped like sushi and frogs
and ducks, pencil cases with pandas and alpacas, doll di-
oramas, Pokémon, and Hello Kitty galore, the prevailing
color pink. There was actually a name for this type of store.
They were called kawaii shops—"kawaii" being Japanese
for "cute"—and the cuteness quotient in Pearl Lady was
suffocating. Marty and I were not kawaii fans, but we were
devotees of two things in the store: Hitomi herself, whose
kawaii-ness and perky energy were straight out of an an-
ime; and her milk tea with boba, or pearls of tapioca, a.k.a.
boba tea on the West Coast, bubble tea on the East Coast.

A lot of stores and chains made milk tea by mixing
water with prebatched powdered tea, nondairy creamers
(Coffee-mate!), and artificial sweeteners and flavors that
contained high fructose corn syrup. They were unhealthy
drinks, full of empty calories.

But Hitomi used real tea and real milk. Her milk tea
was redolent of the royal milk tea I used to drink with
my mother in kissaten (coffee shops) in Harajuku. Japanese
milk was different from American milk. It was creamier,
smoother. It was hormone- and preservative-free, had a

higher fat content, and was pasteurized at a higher temperature with less oxidation.

Hitomi was getting her milk from a small organic
dairy farm in Tomales that produced a close approximation to Japanese milk. For each order, she scooped ice into
a cocktail shaker, poured in the milk and tea, sweetened
with cane sugar, shook the shaker to get the light, airy
texture and froth that had first inspired the name bubble
tea in Taiwan, where the drink had originated, then tipped
everything into a glass of ice with some boba (Taiwanese
slang for "big boobs") on the bottom, serving it with a fat
straw. Marty and I couldn't get enough of her boba tea.

In 2008, however, Hitomi's mother fell ill, and she went
back to Osaka to care for her—temporarily, she thought.
A week turned into two weeks, then three. Hitomi was
not only the sole proprietor of Pearl Lady; she was the
sole employee. The store had been shuttered, making no
revenue, all that time. She asked if I could open the store
occasionally for her most ardent customers—primarily little girls for the toys and snacks, office workers and hipsters
for the milk tea. I was fairly idle then. The Black Cube had
lost its lease to the playhouse, and there was some question
whether we'd resume somewhere else or simply disband. I
felt I could do this favor for Hitomi. We were not exactly
friends, but she'd always been so nice to me. I had retail
experience, and moreover, during my years as a starving
artist, I'd worked in coffeehouses and had been a bartender
and waiter. I'd produced plenty of lattes and cappuccinos
and espressos in my day, and I'd closely watched Hitomi
make her milk teas. Besides, I felt I owed it to her, because,
well, she'd let me sleep with her a couple of times.

So I operated Pearl Lady two or three hours a day, three or four days a week. It wasn't particularly stimulating, but it gave me something to do. As an actor, the biggest problem I'd always faced was finding something to occupy myself between gigs. There were only so many hours I could work out a day, going to the gym, running, kickboxing, practicing kung fu. Since moving to San Francisco, I'd gotten into biking, and I'd tried to learn how to kitesurf, though the water around the Peninsula was too cold and scary for my taste. Plus, I was afraid of great white sharks. I indulged in a lot of home improvement projects, and I tried picking up hobbies—painting, jazz guitar, blues harmonica. Nothing really stuck. I was often reduced to a persistent sport and pastime: seducing women. But of course, that began to peter out as I aged. As I neared fifty, I no longer flattered myself thinking that women might be looking twice at me, whereas when I was younger, I believed the only reason a woman *wasn't* looking twice at me was because I was Asian, not white.

A few weeks into my tenure at Pearl Lady, bored, I started fiddling with Hitomi's milk-tea recipe. I procured premium heirloom black tea in loose leaves and steeped it for a longer period, using young buds to start the brew. Instead of granulated cane sugar, I cooked up a natural, brown sugar–based syrup. I found better boba, made from cassava root, lending the pearls a bouncier, chewier consistency (they called the texture "QQ" in Taiwan). And I used wide-mouth Mason jars as shakers, in which I served the milk tea if it was going to be consumed in the store.

Marty was among my first tasters. "Man, this is primo," he said.

The Mission, like everywhere else in San Francisco, was becoming gentrified with the tech boom, and the area was gaining a reputation as a food hub. Some random foodie raved about my boba tea on his blog, several others Yelped me, word spread on social media, and all of a sudden, I had a line out the door of people willing to wait twenty minutes for my made-to-order milk tea.

Three months in, Hitomi emailed and confirmed what had already become evident: she would not be returning to the United States. She asked if I'd be willing to buy her out of Pearl Lady—take over the space and its assets. To this day, I don't know why I said yes. It was a crazy idea. I had no business plan, no real grasp of the retail food industry. Even crazier, Marty agreed to back me as a silent investor. And craziest of all, it somehow worked.

I had a fire sale to get rid of Hitomi's kawaii knick-knacks and snacks. Then I gutted the space and renovated it, installing a full glass storefront, black trim and railings, white subway tiles, shelves and counters in blond wood, antique brass fixtures, and Edison bulb pendant lights—a minimalist, modern aesthetic, nothing very special, but unusually stylish for a boba tea establishment at the time. I renamed the store Pure Boba, promoting it as artisanal, all-natural, ethically and locally sourced with the highest-quality ingredients that could be found.

Nikki, whom I met during Pure Boba's maiden year, believed I was onto something and pushed me to expand. After two years, I opened a second shop in the Inner Richmond, then a third in Potrero Hill after another year. At that point, Marty made me get professional help (for a silent investor, he was not exactly silent)—specifically in the form of a young, closeted total pain in the ass named Colin Tang, who had an MBA from Haas in Berkeley and who'd previously worked for Timbuk2 and Blue Bottle Coffee. Colin set up an office for Pure Boba in Jiki Entertainment's building, and as the company grew, he hired other MBA wonks to oversee marketing, logistics, facilities, sales, and analytics.

What was my role in all of this? I was still doing VOs and mo-cap for Jiki. Pure Boba subsided into a sideline. I was the public face of the organization, and if the media wanted to interview someone about our company or the boba tea trend, I was the one who went in front of the camera or mic. I was good at that. I had experience doing that. Otherwise, when I wasn't at Jiki, I would flit from shop to shop, checking in with the staff, and go to the office once in a while to sit in on a meeting. I let Colin and the team make most operational decisions, but I didn't let them forget that I was the founder and principal owner, the titular boss, and I wanted to be in on anything front-of-house that was important, like vetting additional tea choices and optional toppings and making sure all of our plastic was BPI-certified. As I got older, I cared more and more about what I put into my body and what was happening with the environment.

Which might explain why I took it upon myself one day to invite District 4 Supervisor Andrew Chau to our new Fillmore shop to announce his proposal to ban single-use plastic straws in San Francisco. I told the handful of gathered press members that Pure Boba would support the ban, that we saw this as an opportunity to show how companies could make sustainable business decisions. I did this without consulting anyone at Pure Boba.

"A disaster! A total fiasco!" Colin railed in the office the following week. "How could you be so rash?"

I thought I'd done my research. I thought I was ahead of the game. I thought I was being very clever. I had told a reporter from the *Chronicle* that I'd already found a supplier for the perfect replacement straw, one made of polylactic acid, or PLA, a bioplastic derived from cornstarch. But then the reporter had checked with the director of the Department of Environment, Bin Chen, and had learned that PLA straws would be out of ordinance.

"It's a PR debacle!" Colin said. "We're laughingstocks now!"

Pure Boba and I were apparently being mocked on the internet and social media, with the hashtags #pureboobs, #pureoops, #purebooboo, and #purebufoon.

"Calm down," I told him. "We've got plenty of time to find something else." The ban wouldn't be going into effect for over a year, not until July 1, 2019. I took full responsibility for the project.

But it turned out not to be so easy. We needed jumbo straws—straws that were eleven millimeters in diameter, compared to the usual five millimeters—to enable the slurping up of boba pearls. We needed straws that would remain firm while sitting in milk tea for up to thirty minutes, that wouldn't become brittle in storage, and that could be supplied to us in huge batches, to the tune of one and a half million straws a year. These straws were going to be expensive: instead of the usual one to three cents apiece for plastic straws, compostable straws would cost between six and twenty cents.

I spent months calling suppliers—many of whom

already had massive backlogs—and ordering samples. I
tested straws made out of paper, metal, rice, silicone, sea-
weed, glass, wheat, sugarcane, and pasta—over thirty types
of straws in total. I created a veritable science lab in our
office, outfitted with all sorts of beakers, clamps, scales,
and doohickeys to measure the structural integrity, tensile
strength, and internal friction of the straws, mindful of any
odd tastes or residue.

"You need to make a decision!" Colin would tell me.
"We need to get an order in! We literally cannot have a
boba tea business without straws!"

Finally in March, I settled on a biodegradable bamboo
fiber straw called the Colossus, manufactured by a company in Kansas. They could begin delivery of the straws in
early June. A tight schedule, not ideal, since we wouldn't
have much of an inventory on hand before the ban took
effect, but crisis averted. Or so I believed.

On Sunday, when I flew back to SFO from Beatrice's
graduation in Philadelphia, I switched on my cell phone
and saw that there was a voice mail for me from Colin.
Nearly half of the 75,000-square-foot straw factory in
Kansas had been destroyed by a fire. There was no way they
would be able to fulfill our initial order in time.

"We're dead," Colin said. "We're dead."

Beatrice arrived in San Francisco on Wednesday. "Everything okay?" she asked when I picked her up at the airport.
"You look more beat than I do, and I'm the one who took
a six-hour flight."

"Just something at Pure Boba—too stupid to even get
into," I said.

"Will you have to work this week?"

"No," I told her, "I'm all yours."

It'd taken me three days—three long, hellacious days—but I'd found some temporary straws. I knew it wasn't over, though. No one was happy, and Marty wanted to meet at the end of the week to talk things over.

I took Beatrice to one of our favorite sushi restaurants, Daigo on Clement Street, for dinner. A small corner neighborhood joint, Daigo was sort of a hole in the wall, with black vinyl-and-steel banquet chairs and Formica tables and counters, but the fish was fantastic, and they made their own shoyu. We sat at the sushi bar and both ordered the twelve-piece omakase.

"I wanted to ask you," I said to Beatrice, "why didn't you tell me your mom and Rob broke up?"

"I was up to my ears then," she said. "I was interviewing at HMS and studying for the MCAT. Then I sort of forgot—I guess because Rob's never been a big part of my life. During Thanksgiving and Christmas when I'd go up to visit, he'd always go up to the house in Nyack to see his kids. I barely ever saw him. They didn't live together that long. She kind of goes through them, you know—men."

"You mean before Rob? Or after?"

"I wouldn't know about after."

The hapa thing had always gotten Nikki a lot of attention. Beatrice, too. Nikki was half Indian, half Taiwanese. She had a narrow oval face and round hazel eyes, and her skin was lush, even now in her late forties. Beatrice, half Japanese on her father's side, looked much like Nikki, though she was shorter and her skin was whiter, her mouth smaller. Not all mixed-race kids turned out beautiful, but

Nikki and Beatrice had. They were often called exotic, which infuriated them. They were always suspicious of the motives of white men who approached them.

For a long time, I had dated only white women. As my politics changed, along with my relationship to my own ethnicity, I flipped to dating only Asian or hapa women. Sometimes I questioned whether this was reverse discrimination, whether I had developed my own form of Asian fetish.

"Don't you and your mom talk anymore?" I asked Beatrice.

"Not a lot."

"She told me you two haven't been getting along. What's up with that?"

"I've come not to like her perspective on life very much," she said.

"What's that mean?"

"I don't have a lot of respect for her values, for the decisions she's made—especially in regard to me, her expectations for me."

"You're being very cryptic."

"For one, I've never forgiven her for leaving you, for making me move with her to New York."

"Okay, well, yeah, I had problems with that particular decision, too."

"You know what she said to me? She said you were both dickless and a dick, that you were a womanizer, you could never commit to anyone, you could never stay in one place."

"Maybe a tad harsh." My womanizing days ended when I met Nikki. In the three years we were together, I never looked at another woman. Since she left, I'd become a loner, and largely celibate.

"All she cares about is money," Beatrice said. "She's a philistine. She's greedy and meretricious."

I'd never heard the word before and had to look it up later, but I caught her drift. "I wouldn't go that far," I told her, even though I had thought as much at times. Once, I'd said to Nikki, "Not everything's about money," and she'd said, "You are so naive. Of course it is. You have no practical sense whatsoever." In retrospect, probably the main reason I'd remained involved with Pure Boba was to prove her wrong.

"The way she pushed me about school, she was a total fascist," Beatrice said. "Nothing I did was ever good enough."

"I don't think that's true. She's always been very proud of you."

"Why are you defending her?"

I wasn't sure why. Beatrice was wearing a tank top, and I saw that she had gotten a new tattoo, another Japanese gothic manga character to add to the collection on her upper arms. She also had one of the baby mascot for Kewpie mayonnaise on her left shoulder (Japanese mayo, like Japanese milk, was different from American, made with egg yolks rather than whole eggs, with no sugar or water). Nikki hated Beatrice's tattoos, naturally. She thought Beatrice would regret getting them eventually, that they might jeopardize her professional future, but Beatrice said she didn't care. I did notice, however, that the tattoos seemed to be strategically placed so they wouldn't be visible even when wearing short-sleeved scrubs.

"I don't know if I want to go to med school," Beatrice said.

"What?"

"I'm thinking of not going."

"But . . . it's Harvard."

"It's never been my dream. It was hers."

"You always said you wanted to be a doctor. You always said you wanted to help people, save lives. Like your mother and father. You've worked so hard for this, Beatrice, for so many years."

"Yes, I know. *I* did it, *I* put in all the work, so I should be able to nullify it if I want to," she said. "It's my choice to make."

"Have you told your mother this?"

"God no. Are you fucking kidding me?"

We laughed.

"Seriously, though, what's prompting this?" I asked. "What's going on with you? Is it too much, going straight from Bryn Mawr to your summer job?"

"You mean the job Mom arranged for me?"

Beatrice was scheduled to start working at Jefferson Hospital in ten days, in a coveted paid research position, before going to Boston to begin her medical studies.

"You should ask for some time off this summer and do something fun," I said. "Travel for a week or two, maybe go to the Big Island or Kaua'i." Beatrice, Nikki, and I had gone to Hawai'i a few times together, always stopping by O'ahu to say hello to my father. They never got to meet my mother, who'd died at fifty-nine, my age now. "Use the money I gave you for graduation. Take Nadia with you. I'll pay for her flight."

"She'd never accept that, and you know it," Beatrice said. "She'd be insulted by the offer. Anyway, that's not it. I don't need a vacation."

"What is it, then?"

"I want to record a full-length album with Pearl Lady this summer, then go on tour with them in the fall."

For a moment, I was at a loss. "You want to drop out of Harvard Med School to become an indie musician?"

"I already am an indie musician. But now there's a label that wants to sign us."

"A major label?"

"Well, no," Beatrice said. "It's actually a vinyl shop in rural Maryland called Yellow K Records. But they have a surprisingly killer roster. And they've got full distribution."

"I don't know what to say," I told her. "This sounds— Frankly, it sounds crazy to me."

"Crazy? Really? I thought you'd be more supportive. You were in the arts."

"Can't you do this in your spare time? Record when you have free nights, do gigs on weekends?"

"It's not something you can do half-ass."

"Why not?" I said. "Thousands of musicians do it, with full-time jobs and families."

"I don't think you understand what med school in-volves," Beatrice said. "Anyway, I need to do this now, while we're jelling as a band, while we have the oppor-tunity. We stretch it out, people might disperse to other projects, other cities. It might die altogether."

"What about deferring?" I asked. "Maybe you could take a gap year."

"You can't defer at HMS."

"Well," I said, "I wouldn't want to be in your shoes, having to talk to your mom about this."

"I was hoping you'd help me break the news to her."

"Now I know you're truly insane."

The next day, Thursday, was sunny and warm, at least for the Bay Area, and we decided to drive an hour south to Rosarita Bay, a seaside town that was popular for day trips. We walked along Main Street, which was lined with restaurants and shops with shiplap siding, and then picked up sandwiches for lunch from Cuchi's Country Store and set off down Highway 1 again to Bidwell Marsh Preserve. We followed a path along a creek bordered by willows and cattails and bobbing yellow catkins. Eventually, the creek widened into an estuary, and we crested the sand dunes and trekked down to an area of rocky shale reefs and explored the tide pools. After we ate our sandwiches, we backtracked across the highway and hiked through a canyon into the hills, the ground covered with damp, spongy topsoil. We kept climbing until we were surrounded by groves of live oaks and old-growth redwoods, some of them towering three hundred feet above our heads.

"This is heavenly," Beatrice said.

It was a good day. She didn't revisit our conversation from the previous night at all. I was convinced now that she wouldn't give up her spot at Harvard Medical School, that she was simply feeling jittery thinking about the long, difficult road ahead of her as a med student, then as an intern, then as a resident. Eight years. Enough to give anyone a panic attack.

Her friend Nadia came over for dinner. I'd been marinating butterfish in sake, mirin, sugar, and miso for days in preparation for the occasion, and I was going to serve it with spinach ohitashi, chilled tofu, and simmered kabocha squash, very healthy, subdued dishes. But at the last minute— maybe thinking about Oʻahu the night before—I ditched the accompaniments in favor of some Hawaiian comfort food: Chinese chicken salad and fried rice. For the latter, I followed a recipe from the Side Street Inn, a kamaʻaina hangout on Hopaka Street that shared a parking lot with a strip club and was known for its generous portions of late-night stoner grub. The recipe called for three kinds of pork (bacon, char siu, and Portuguese sausage), peas, carrots, and day-old rice, dressed with oyster sauce and—this was the key—a hefty sprinkling of hondashi, Japanese instant soup granules. Thankfully neither Beatrice nor Nadia were vegetarians.

While I cooked, they sat at the kitchen island and drank wine and talked. They'd known each other since second grade, attending Peabody Elementary and Roosevelt Middle School together. From there, they'd diverged, Beatrice going to the Brearley School in Manhattan, Nadia going to Lowell High School, which was generally regarded as the best magnet school in San Francisco, although she'd been frustrated with how few other African Americans were enrolled there. She was now finishing her BA at Stanford and would be starting Berkeley Law in August—another outrageous overachiever. Ever since high school, she'd become involved in social justice advocacy, most recently as a volunteer for a community organization called Silicon Valley De-Bug.

Tonight, she told us about the controversy surrounding Assembly Bill 392, alternately known as the California Act to Save Lives and Stephon Clark's Law. The bill had been intended to toughen the standards for when police officers could use deadly force. But now, De-Bug and Black Lives Matter were dropping their support of the legislation.

"The language got completely watered down once the law enforcement lobby and unions got their hands on it," Nadia said. "They took out the definition of 'necessary,' removed the deescalation requirement, and gutted all the passages about criminal liability. Those were the three major provisions of the original bill! It's a total joke now."

Then she started talking about the concept of necropolitics, which she'd learned about in a course on the Black Radical Tradition. Necropolitics was the use of social and political power to dictate how some people may live and other people must die. "It's about how all the old systems of oppression and colonialism and slavery and inequality haven't receded one bit," Nadia said. "In fact, they've reconstituted themselves with a resurgence of racist, fascist, and nationalistic forces that are determined to exclude and kill us. Once again we're being targeted for erasure, for genocide."

In years past, I might have thought Nadia was being melodramatic, but not these days. I felt comfortable in the Bay Area, with the large number of Asian Americans here, with its progressive politics, but other than in California, Hawai'i, and Seattle, I didn't feel welcome in many parts of the country, I didn't feel safe. Ever since Cheeto Man had assumed office, I felt there were forces determined to shun me, even harm me and other people of color. I didn't think it could get any worse. I could only hope for a kinder world.

"Nowhere is that inequality more manifest than in San Francisco," Nadia said, "with all the fucking tech workers taking over, the white bro culture with their corporate buses and e-skateboards. I'm sorry, am I pontificating too much?"

"Maybe a skosh," Beatrice said.

"Alain, that smells delicious," Nadia said. "Tell me, when are you finally going to accept the inevitable and marry me?"

Nadia liked to provoke me. In junior high, she used to tease me by reciting a line—actually, the character's only line—spoken by El Mano Silencioso, the Hong Kong hit man I'd played in *Days of Scorn,* at every opportunity: "All river go to sea, but sea not full."

"The clerk at that store gave us that look today," Beatrice said.

"What store?" I asked. "What look?"

"The place we got the sandwiches, in Rosarita Bay. You know, that look. People look at me, then look at you, and they think, Wait, this does not equate, is that her father, or her sugar daddy?"

Beatrice and Nadia laughed, but I didn't find it funny at all, galled by the thought.

"You see," Nadia said, "there's a real problem having a quasi-stepdude who's still kind of hot and stylish in that boho-chic, outdoorsy, ponytail kind of way."

"Maybe the two of you will be having dinner somewhere else tonight," I said.

Other than Beatrice, Nadia was the most impressive young woman I'd ever met. I liked her enormously. But I knew that, underneath her teasing, there was a degree of disdain. And for good reason. San Francisco was indeed being ruined, and people like me were part of the problem. Nowhere was the gap between the rich and the poor more evident than in the Mission. The neighborhood was attractive to hipsters and yuppies because it was flat, sunny, with relatively little fog, and studded with renovated town houses and newly constructed luxury lofts that featured parking and modern amenities. The influx of white tech wealth was displacing longtime Latino residents with evictions and buyouts. The whole identity of the neighborhood was being lost. Bodegas, fruit stands, pupusas, and thrift stores were being replaced with trendy restaurants, slow-pour coffeehouses, French bakeries, and, yes, fancy boba tea shops.

Nikki had been the first person to point out to me that I was an interloper—the first time we met, actually. She had worked nearby at SF General and used to bring Beatrice to Pearl Lady. After I refashioned the store into Pure Boba, she popped in one day and said, "My daughter's going to be heartbroken. Where'd all the toys and treats go? What happened here?"

She watched me make a boba tea for her. "You know, I'm half Taiwanese," she said. "What are you? What's your name?"

"Alain Kweon," I said.

"Kwan. K-w-a-n?"

"No." I spelled it out for her.

"So, what, you're Korean?" she asked. "You're not making real milk tea. Nothing's remotely authentic about what you're doing."

"Maybe not, but wait till you taste it."

"You're making hipster, bougie boba. You're making boba for white people. There's nothing pure about it. This is all just slick packaging. You might be a pretty face, but you're exactly what's wrong with the Mission these days."

She tasted my milk tea. "All right, okay," she said, "maybe I was a little quick to judge."

On Friday, I met Marty for lunch at El Farolito, one of our favorite taquerias. He ordered an al pastor burrito, and I went adventurous and got the sesos—cow brains. We snagged a table and sat down to eat.

"You know," I said to Marty, "if Colin would just come out to his family, maybe he'd stop being such a fucking weenie. He's exactly the type of Asian who gives Asians a bad name."

"Come on, that's both homophobic and racist. He's not so bad."

Monday through Wednesday, I'd frantically phoned straw manufacturers, to no avail. Then I thought to contact other boba tea shops in the Bay Area to find out where they were getting their new straws. I talked to the owner of a chain called QQuick, who said they'd gotten a big order of hay straws several months ago. Only catch, the straws didn't come with pointed tips. QQuick used machines to seal flat tops over their cups, and they needed straws cut at a sharp angle to pierce through the cellophane. At first, the owner had had his workers snipping the tips of the straws by hand with scissors, but then he'd found another supplier that could provide him with precut straws. Now he had a bunch of jumbo hay straws he didn't need. He said he'd be happy to sell them to us—at a premium, of course. We took them. Hay didn't have a completely neutral flavor, but there were enough of the straws for us to get by until the factory in Kansas got back into production.

"Listen," Marty said, "Colin wants to open up a shop in the SGV."

"We're getting too big," I said. "We expand to SoCal, we won't be able to control the culture down there." Already, I thought we'd gone over the line. Pure Boba was now selling merchandise, and had added bastardized versions of horchata and aguas frescas to the menu. I hadn't liked the idea at all. It had felt akin to cultural appropriation, especially since we were based in the Mission.

"You know what Colin calls you?" Marty asked me. "The Herbie."

"What? As in the Love Bug?"

"Huh?"

"The Disney movie, the VW Beetle."

"What are you talking about? No, the Herbie's the term for a bottleneck in your organization, a process constraint, the thing that's holding up the business."

"And Colin thinks that's me," I said. "I got us emergency straws, didn't I? I fixed it. I found a solution."

"Everything about the straws has been a shitshow. This isn't just about the straws, though. Forget the straws for the moment," Marty said. "Pure Boba's no longer a startup. It's a full-fledged company, and structures and processes need to be in place. You had the vision to create this business, and you made it work. But as it's grown, you've sort of lost the plot. It's fine for you to continue to ideate, but the team shouldn't have to depend on you to make decisions."

"You want to push me out," I said.

"In a word, yes."

"I can't believe you, Marty. How long have we been friends?"

"We can still be friends," he said. "Your heart hasn't been in this for a long time. We both know that. What do you need this for? We scale up, this could really take off. Maybe someday we'll become Blue Bottle, and maybe someone like Nestlé will come along and pay us $500 million for a majority stake. You could just sit at home and count the money. You'd be on easy street, bro."

"What the fuck?" Beatrice said when I got home. "What'd you do to your hair?"

After leaving El Farolito, I'd headed up Folsom, and, fuming, I'd walked into a barbershop and had them cut off all my hair, a buzz cut with clippers, going down nearly to the scalp.

"You look like a Shaolin monk," Beatrice said. "Was this because of that crack Nadia made about your ponytail?"

"No, I was just sick of it," I said.

After the barbershop, I'd spent hours wandering through Golden Gate Park before driving back to the Outer Parkside. When I'd entered the house, Beatrice had been playing one of my acoustic guitars, singing a new composition: *"Where are you when I need you / Boy of mine / What do you want from me / Devotion by suicide?"* I hoped the song wasn't autobiographical. As close as we were, I didn't know much about Beatrice's love life. She never disclosed much. She'd told me once that she was bisexual and polyamorous. I hadn't probed any further.

I walked down to the kitchen and opened two bottles

of beer, then went to the living room and handed one to her. "When are you leaving?" I asked.

"Soon."

"What's on the docket tonight?"

"We're going to hang out at Nadia's for a while, then go to Mensho for ramen, then meet up with some friends and go dancing at a new EDM club in J-Town. You have any plans?"

"When you reach my age, you don't have plans on Friday night," I told her. "I'm just going to make something for dinner and watch something."

"You ought to go out more. Date."

"When you reach my age, you don't date."

"I worry about you sometimes."

"*You* worry about *me*?" I said.

"You still think I'm crazy."

"Beatrice, I know you're scared. I know you think you might not be able to cut it in med school. But you're going to do fine. More than fine. You are so smart, you are so together. You're going to shine over there."

"You don't think I'm good enough, do you? As a musician, I mean. You don't think my music is good enough to make it."

"I can't say. I don't know anything about today's music. I had to think twice what EDM is."

"You know enough," Beatrice said. "You have a feel for these sorts of things. What do you think, really? Do you think I have what it takes to make it?"

"No."

She was startled. I was, too. I hadn't meant to be so blunt, but there it was.

"Unequivocally no?" she asked.

"Even if you did, the chances of success—for any musician, not just you—are so low. It's a brutal industry."

"Like acting?" she said. "Maybe you're discouraging me because of what happened to you as an actor. You're bitter that you failed."

"I had my day. Then I decided to put it behind me."

"You didn't quit. It quit you. All you ever got to do was portray racist caricatures in schlock action movies and prance around in inane plays, and then even those dried up, and then what? You ended up becoming a fucking barista."

I nodded—hurt. "Actually, we prefer to call ourselves bobaristas."

After Beatrice left for the night, I made a stir-fry, plated it over rice, then watched a movie and drank more beer. Eventually I switched to the hard stuff. In my time living in LA, I'd chipped my share of coke, but now I drank, and I vaped. San Francisco had legalized cannabis in 2016. I was currently enamored with a high-potency sativa that had a nice woody, earthy taste that I got from a dispensary in the Castro. It helped me sleep, and I was convinced it was stabilizing my blood pressure, which was a little elevated a while back but had since stayed within parameters. It didn't stave off other ailments—high cholesterol, balky knees with no remaining cartridge, a pinched AC joint, arthritic knuckles, an occasionally spasmodic lower back, suspect hearing in my left ear, a low T count that sometimes required pharmaceutical assistance.

What did it add up to? I wondered as I lay in bed. I'd been searching all my life for my true self, my true place, where I could find my spiritual brethren and sistren, what Koreans called dongpo. I had hoped, at least, that I could subsist without having to compromise on the important things, but I didn't know what those things were anymore. What would be my legacy? Beatrice had been right in that it wouldn't be my acting career. And it wouldn't be boba tea, either. I had had this amorphous idea that my boba tea business would be a way to affirm and celebrate my—and other Asian Americans'—racial heritage. Yet boba tea wasn't Korean or Okinawan or anything else of mine ethnically. It'd simply been another appropriation, another commodification in the guise of cultural identity. What did it amount to? Had everything about my life been frivolous and inconsequential? Had it all been a lie?

I must have fallen asleep. The phone rang, and Nadia was on the other end.

"What time is it?" I asked.

"Almost three," she said. "Beatrice is in the ER."

She had gotten into a fight. A physical fight. Some guy had been hassling her all night at the EDM club, and then he followed her outside at closing time. He was trying to get Beatrice to go home with him, she said no, he kept insisting, she said no again, and then he called her a chink bitch and shoved her, and then Beatrice made, as Nadia put it, "some kind of Bruce Lee move on him." I would learn that she had grabbed his hand, rotated it in a pronating wristlock, torqued his arm behind him, and whipped him to the ground, grinding his face into the sidewalk—something I'd taught her how to do as a kid. I had wanted her to be able to protect herself. Especially against men.

Beatrice and Nadia had then jumped into their waiting Uber, but the guy picked up a velvet-rope stanchion and swung it against the backseat window of the Uber and shattered the glass, a piece of which flew into Beatrice's right eye. Nadia had the driver take them to Kaiser Permanente on Geary, and the ED doc phoned the on-call ophthalmologist, who recommended admitting her.

"I fucked up," Beatrice said when I saw her at the hospital. An aluminum shield was taped over her eye. "You always told me to lay 'em out so they can't get up and surprise me from behind. I should've knocked the motherfucker out."

"I also told you the first and best choice is always to walk away."

"I'm sorry I said those things to you. Please forgive me. Will you forgive me?"

"You don't need to ask me that."

The ophthalmologist came in at seven a.m. He examined her and said that she had a partial-thickness corneal laceration. He applied tissue glue and a bandage contact lens and said the injury would likely heal in four or five days. Luckily, it didn't look like she would have any residual scarring or decreased vision. He said she could be released later that day. But Nikki, already at the gate at JFK for her flight, talked to the ophthalmologist on the phone. She was concerned about infection, and she was enough of a noodge to convince the ophthalmologist to keep Beatrice at the hospital another night.

Midafternoon, Nikki landed at SFO and came straight to the hospital. "What in the hell," she said to me. "Why'd you shave your head?"

I hadn't slept. I went home to take a nap and eat something, then met Nikki later for a drink at Garibaldi's, a restaurant in our old neighborhood that we used to frequent. Nikki was staying down the block at the Laurel Inn, a newly renovated boutique hotel that was half a mile from Kaiser.

We sat at the bar. A few of the old staff were still there, but they didn't recognize us.

"Beatrice seemed surprised I'd fly out here," Nikki said. "What kind of a mother does she think I am?"

"I suppose because it didn't end up to be that dire."

"Thank God. When I got your call, I thought she might go blind in that eye. Did they find the asshole who broke the window?"

"No, not yet," I told her. "The cops came to interview Beatrice. The club gave them the security camera tapes. I'm sure they're worried about a lawsuit."

"As they should be. Where were the bouncers?"

I ordered another round of bourbons for us, and Nikki began to relax. Here we were again, I thought, having drinks, twice in less than a week, after not seeing each other for seven years.

I told her about what had happened yesterday, about Marty and Pure Boba, about my brief tiff with Beatrice, although I didn't get into her hesitations about med school. I still didn't think Beatrice was serious about dropping out, but if she was, it wasn't my place to intercede. She'd have to talk to her mother herself.

"The worst part was thinking she has no respect for me," I said.

"You know that's not true. She adores you. Billy died when she was five. You're the closest thing to a father she has."

"Which is both touching and sad. I only see her once a year."

"She knows you're there for her," Nikki said. "What are you going to do about Pure Boba?"

"I don't know."

"They want to buy you out?"

"No, I can keep my stake. They just want me to stay the fuck away," I said. "Isn't that hilarious? I'm that much of a liability? The thing is, I've come to hate the business. Just like I came to hate the entertainment industry. I don't know why I got into it in the first place. I feel like I've made all the wrong choices. I don't know what would have made me happy. What is it that gives one purpose?"

"You hate it so much, you should walk away," Nikki told me.

I hadn't expected her to say this. "You really think so?"

"Life is very short. I've only recently begun to realize that."

"Why? Something wrong?" I asked, fearing a diagnosis.

"Nothing physiological. Everything else, though, feels dubious lately. Getting older tends to do that."

"You don't have to tell me," I said. "If I bow out of Pure Boba, what would I do with myself?"

"Why don't you write another play, a full-length one. You always talked about wanting to do that. I loved the one you did."

Eight years ago, I wrote and performed in a one-act play about a father and son—a drama exploring what it means to be a man. It'd had a brief run at a repertory theater in Piedmont.

"When I was fourteen, fifteen," I said, "I could've never predicted this is where I'd find myself. I never would've thought my life would end up like this. Did you?"

"No."

"It's lonely, isn't it?"

"Yes," she said, "it is."

We watched the bartender make two servings of a cocktail, scooping ice into a shaker, using both hands to add alcohol and mixers, jiggling them until the shaker frosted, then straining the drinks into glasses and garnishing them with citrus peels and sip straws.

"Why did you leave, Nikki?" I asked. "Was it because you weren't over Billy?"

"No, that wasn't it," she said. "It was because— Maybe deep down I thought you were only with me to be with Beatrice, that you loved her more than you did me. I don't mean in an unnatural way. There's never been anything more natural than the relationship you two have with each other. I was always so jealous of that."

"One of the reasons I've stayed close to her all these years is to keep in touch with you," I said. "You know that, don't you?"

"I guess I did, but never let myself believe it."

We talked for another hour. Something dislodged, and we were able to be free with each other again, no wariness, no lingering resentments.

I walked Nikki back to her hotel. "The old neighborhood looks the same, pretty much," she said. "I'm surprised it hasn't changed more. I miss it."

We reached the Laurel Inn, and we stalled in front of the entrance to the hotel. "Do you want to come up to see my room?" Nikki asked me. "I have to warn you, the view's not what it used to be."

"I don't care about views," I told her. "But I bet it's heavenly."

Acknowledgments

Thanks to Jane Delury for her insights while reading every single word of these stories multiple times; to Rebecca Curtis for her editorial suggestions; to Paul Yoon, Laura van den Berg, and Jennifer Egan for their support; to Scott Buck, Sangita Chandra, Eric Byler, and Don Smith for their research help; to Cara Blue Adams, Paul Reyes and Allison Wright, Gerald Maa, David Lynn, Adam Ross and Eric Smith, and Patrick Ryan for publishing seven of these stories in their journals; and to Johnny Temple and everyone at Akashic Books for providing *The Partition* with such a perfect, lovely home.